City DREAMS

*Four Stories of Love
in the Metropolitan Heart*

Linda Lyle
Christine Lynxwiler
Tamela Hancock Murray
Kathleen Paul

BARB
PUBLISH
Uhrichs

D0006536

A World of Difference ©2001 by Tamela Hancock Murray
Beneath Heaven's Curtain ©2001 by Christine Lynxwiler
In the Heart of the Storm ©2001 by Linda Lyle
The Arrow ©2001 by Kathleen Paul

Cover design by Robyn Martins.

ISBN 1-58660-295-0

All Scripture quotations, unless otherwise noted, are taken from the King James Version of the Bible.

Published by Barbour Publishing, Inc., P.O. Box 719, Uhrichsville, Ohio 44683
http://www.barbourbooks.com

ecpa Member of the
Evangelical Christian
Publishers Association

Printed in the United States of America.

INTRODUCTION

A World of Difference by Tamela Hancock Murray
Sharon Delacourt and Rory Ford reunite a decade after meeting in Washington, D.C. Disillusioned with politics, Sharon is convinced her career will never make a difference for the Lord. Rory wants to expose how Sharon's devotion touches everyone around her. Through her denials, reignited love shines in her eyes, an ardor Rory wishes to win and hold forever. But will rumors of scandalous intrigue smash their City Dreams?

Beneath Heaven's Curtain by Christine Lynxwiler
Danielle Delacourt takes a job in an Atlanta nursing home and discovers neglect due to understaffing. When owner Nicholas Lancaster is confronted, he takes a job incognito at Danielle's nursing home to investigate. As they work side by side, Danielle and Nicholas grow closer, but a harrowing incident with a resident sends Nicholas back to his plush office. Will he face the truth or shatter Danielle's lofty dreams?

In the Heart of the Storm by Linda Lyle
Unable to escape God's tugging, Sabrina Delacourt finally accepts a short-term mission assignment in Hong Kong as an ESL teacher on a university campus. On her second day in the city, Sabrina is treated to a yacht cruise around the island along with several other missionaries, one of whom is Jason Wilkes. She is immediately attracted to him but pulls away after she realizes that he has already committed his life to full-time missions. What is God's true call for her life?

The Arrow by Kathleen Paul
Denise Delacourt's first teaching job is in inner city Houston. She's astonished when she discovers her tenth grade English class can't read on a fourth grade level. She follows her class to their hangout and discovers John Slann, a youth pastor, runs the "coffee house of the 50s" where her students are loved in spite of their backgrounds. Can she embrace that love too?

A WORLD OF DIFFERENCE

Tamela Hancock Murray

Keep yourselves in the love of God,
looking for the mercy of our Lord Jesus Christ unto eternal life.
And of some have compassion, making a difference.
JUDE 1:21-22

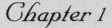

Chapter 1

S haron Delacourt felt the winter wind whip through her business suit, biting her skin with fury. Shivering, she wished she hadn't left her black wool coat draped over the back of her chair in her Capitol Hill office. Had she not been distraught about the way the Senate vote on her pet piece of legislation had gone, she wouldn't have been in such a hurry to leave. She would have been her usual composed, organized self. But she had fled, unable to face the disappointment she knew would be etched on everyone's faces as soon as they heard the news. Sharon especially wanted to avoid the new intern, Olivia. She couldn't endure her certain disappointment. The college student's optimism reminded Sharon of herself only a decade earlier, when she had first arrived in Washington, a place local radio disc jockeys boasted as the most important city in the world.

Today, the most important city in the world was draped in cheerless skies. Flickering storefront signs and lights from vehicles crawling through rush hour traffic barely penetrated the dusk falling over ashen roads and gritty sidewalks. Intermittent flakes of snow fluttered to Sharon's face, leaving pinpricks of cold where they landed before dissolving into water. The

Weather Channel had promised the snow would result in a light dusting.

For the first time since high school graduation, Sharon longed for a blizzard. The biggest blizzard of all time. One that would allow her to remain enveloped in the security and isolation of her two-room apartment, lollygagging without a worry about her appearance, bundled in the pink fleece bathrobe and fuzzy white slippers with bunny ears she had worn since high school. No news reports, no crises, no urgent briefings. No lobbyists to placate, no constituents to soothe, no dignitaries to impress. Just mindless comedies, game shows, and reruns on TV, savored until her mind went numb. She only wanted to be safe and secure, locked away in her apartment forever. Or until she had consumed the last bit of coffee in her cupboard.

As she passed a grocery store tucked into a row of retail businesses and offices, Sharon noticed several people inside, clamoring to buy bread and milk. In typical Washington style, city dwellers had panicked as soon as the first snowflake drifted from the sky, even though little accumulation was predicted. A miscalculation of three inches could be enough to paralyze the city.

Sharon would have chuckled at the irony had she not felt as dreary as the night.

Heavenly Father, she prayed silently, *if Washington is so significant, why do I feel so powerless? Didn't You send me here to take part in Your work, to use government to make this country a better place? Was I wrong, Lord? Did I misinterpret what You were telling me? Tell me, what do You want me to do?*

She waited, but no voice answered. Not a powerful thundering from a burning bush, not a reassurance from the clouds, not a murmur in her mind. Not even a feeling of peace. Casting her gaze downward, she hugged herself in an effort to ward off the chill.

"A pretty girl like you should be wearin' a coat."

Lifting her head, she spotted the familiar gray-bearded figure situated on his usual spot. Sharon was accustomed to the homeless man who made a comment to her each evening as she walked to the Metro. She wondered how he stayed warm, even with a constant stream of heated air floating from the sidewalk grate on which he wintered, swathed in a heap of newspapers. Though her carelessness had left her shivering, unlike the street people, she would soon find comfort thanks to central heating.

She stopped in front of him for their daily exchange. "You're the one who should be worried about staying warm, George."

"Don't need a coat. These here papers is good enough for me."

Sharon offered a suggestion, though she knew her words were pointless. "If it gets too cold, let the people from the shelter take care of you tonight."

A vehement shake of his head was her answer.

Sighing, she dug into her shoulder bag, retrieving the orange she packed for him that morning, as was her custom.

"God bless you." A smile, sans two front teeth, lit his face.

She smiled back at his usual good-bye. "God bless you too."

Approaching her Metro stop, Sharon suddenly wasn't in the mood to go home. She detoured from her customary route, intent on warming herself with a latte at a new coffee shop that was getting raves.

A restaurant emblem caught her attention. *An Exceptionally Rare Steak Indeed.* Seeing the sign revived a blizzard of memories.

11

She and Rory used to make fun of the long name, pronouncing it in the tone of faux aristocrats as they tilted their noses skyward. Yet all the while, they had relished seared slabs of beef that reminded them of their shared Midwestern roots. Never mind the cheap white plates and thin silverware. Good conversation, mainly the sharing of office travails interspersed with future dreams, was more important. She heard herself exhale and watched the resulting burst of breath turn to steam as it contacted frigid air.

Rory Ford. She hadn't thought of him in years.

Oh really? Don't kid yourself.

Suddenly she remembered a promise made long ago. Her heart began thumping when she realized the date.

Today. It was today. We were supposed to meet here.

Sharon shook her head. No way would Rory remember a date made ten years ago. Ten years. Had it been so long?

And hadn't Rory been joking when he suggested they reunite at their favorite spot? Of course he had been. It wasn't as though either expected anything of their relationship. Their attachment had been temporal at best, predictably ending along with their internships. She and Rory had simply been friends bonded by their common roots and uncertainty in their new environment.

There was no way he would want to spend his thirtieth birthday with her. Perhaps the thought had seemed appealing at the time, but not now. Certainly not after all these years.

They had just been friends. That's all. Love would not, could not, enter the picture.

Ten years ago, Sharon had been determined to finish school and jump on a fast-paced career track in Washington. Rory had been resolved to returning to the wheat fields of Kansas. Up front with both their agendas, Sharon and Rory developed an unspoken treaty to use their friendship as a safety net, a net that helped them bounce back when doses of new realities splattered in their faces. With the net swiped from under her, Sharon had been walking the tightrope alone. She prayed that after all this time, she wouldn't fall.

Unwilling to restrain her rambling thoughts, Sharon reminisced about the times she and Rory spent together. Wherever they went, Rory's Nordic blond looks and toned form attracted stares of admiration from women, changing either to envy or silent bravos for Sharon when they realized she was Rory's companion. Yet Rory never seemed to notice. His cobalt blue eyes remained riveted on her. With those handsome looks and his way of making a woman feel extraordinary, surely Rory was married with a pack of kids by now.

She hoped so. She hoped Rory's life had turned out the way he wanted. Fear clasping its fingers around her abdomen in a freezing vise, Sharon realized her fondest dream at that moment would be for Rory not to keep their date. How could she face him? How could she tell him the truth about her life?

She remembered his boasting. "Sure I want kids. Lots of 'em. Enough boys for my own football team. We'll give the home team a run for their money." A teasing grin would tickle Rory's mouth when he told Sharon his plans, but underneath, she knew he hadn't been far from serious.

Reading but not absorbing the menu posted on a glass-encased bulletin board beside the door, Sharon pictured Rory tossing a football to his oldest son. He looked robust, the type of blond once described as All-American. The others, all towheaded and blue-eyed, sat watching on the sidelines, waiting to grow up.

She remembered!

Rory's stomach jumped at the sight of the willowy figure. Blond hair had been transformed from the precision cut bob popular a few years back. Coifed into an easy flip, the style achieved the desired effect of lacking artifice. The black suit, envelope purse, and dress pumps with tiny heels popular in the past had been replaced with a black suit, shoulder bag, and dress pumps with stacked heels fashioned for the present.

Suddenly aware the object of his attention was without a coat, Rory experienced a shiver traveling like the touch of icy fingertips from the top of his hatted head to the tips of his booted feet. After shaking it off, he felt a grin cross his lips as he remembered his fond nickname for Sharon. Keying in on the theory that brilliant people can become so immersed in thinking that they forget life's details, Rory had dubbed her "Professor" after she walked into a meeting wearing one pump in navy blue and the other in black. Undaunted, Sharon gave an intricate presentation with more verve than Rory could have mustered under the same circumstances.

Rory was pleased to note that Sharon's posture exuded a sense of purpose and poise, even from a distance of a half block. No doubt, the form and substance of Sharon Delacourt was unmistakable.

She remembered!

Rory wondered how well she had fended for herself in the city. He had kept her in his prayers every night for the past ten years. As much as he wanted to protect her, Rory respected her desire for the independence he couldn't have offered her as Mrs. Rory Ford. At least, not the type of freedom she had wanted. The freedom she enjoyed today. Without him.

As he approached, he tried to gauge how she might respond to seeing him again. Nothing in her stance indicated she had one iota less confidence than she had possessed as an ambitious intern. She must have kept their date as a courtesy, so as not to hurt his feelings since she knew he was celebrating a birthday. Thirty years. Three decades. A hallmark. He let out a sigh. How pitiful he must seem to such a successful woman. If she had followed her dreams, which by all appearances she had, what use would she have for a man mired in scandal?

Maybe I should turn back now. Then I won't have to face her.

Swallowing from nervousness, he thought better of his momentary cowardice. Taking steps toward Sharon, Rory observed the curves of her feminine features. They were delicate in a way that defied the steely grit of her personality, a courage that had surely advanced her career. He had observed her daring in the professional arena. But Rory also perceived the tenderness underneath her determination. Caring always glistened in her teal green eyes, shaded by lustrous lashes.

Rory wanted to project a guise of self-assurance. Instead, a high-pitched voice chirped an inadequate, "Hi, Professor."

After giving a start, she turned to him, her eyes widening to reveal a mixture of awe and disbelief. Staring squarely into her face, he nearly lost his balance when he saw her beauty was more stunning than ever.

"Rory," she whispered. "Happy birthday."

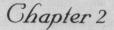

Chapter 2

Y ou remembered!" His boyish grin hadn't changed. His cologne was suddenly familiar. Its citrus scent freed a tide of memories. She caught her breath at the realization that her dream of meeting Rory again had become a reality.

Though he hesitated, Rory looked as though he wanted to wrap his arms around her in greeting.

Sharon froze in place, unsure as to why she suddenly felt reticent.

When she didn't respond by taking a step toward him, Rory stopped his motion. Sharon watched him rub his hands together as though the thick black gloves he wore failed to keep them warm. Ten years had passed. He looked the same, only better. She felt her heart beating in a way it hadn't in a long, long time.

"How could I forget?" she asked, her voice barely above a whisper.

Rory's blond eyebrows arched. He rubbed his left hand on his dimpled chin and rolled his blue eyes skyward as if in contemplation. "Could it be—you never wrote?"

Remembering three unanswered letters, Sharon clenched

her teeth. As a hot blush began at the base of her neck and traveled to her cheeks, she tried to shrug off her chagrin. "I'm sorry. I meant to write back, but I just got too wrapped up in work." Sharon cast her eyes downward toward Rory's black, wing-tipped shoes. She knew her excuse was lame.

"Your being here tonight makes up for every missed letter."

Relieved, she looked up at him. Lost to time was his baby-faced skin. Sharon used to wonder if Rory needed to shave more than once a week. Slightly chubby cheeks were now hollowed and bore evidence of a five o'clock shadow. Rory looked as though Michelangelo had sculpted him into the man he was today.

Oblivious to Sharon's close scrutiny, Rory flashed a smile that contradicted his wagging finger. "But I won't be so forgiving if you don't return my E-mails."

Sharon looked up at the darkening sky and let out a groan. "Do you have any idea how many E-mails I get in a day?"

"Hundreds, I'll bet."

She nodded.

"So you're still keeping up a frantic schedule. I'm not surprised. I'm just glad you weren't too tied up to see me." His eyes took on a sad light. "Unless, you're about to give me a reason why you need to leave before we can eat."

"No," she hastily reassured him. "Of course I can have dinner with you. I have all the time in the world." Then she remembered she was supposed to be attending a reception hosted by a group of insurance lobbyists within the hour.

"As do I." Extending his right arm, he opened the door.

One look at his face, glowing with pleasure, and Sharon decided she could clear her calendar. She paused for an instant, waiting for him to enter the restaurant first as would most professional men of her acquaintance. She was used to being treated as an equal but at a price. Small courtesies reminding women that they were special often disappeared in the business world.

Rory made a sweeping motion. "After you, Mademoiselle."

Unable to suppress a giggle, Sharon stepped into the restaurant, an act that seemed equivalent to entering a time machine taking her back a decade. The aroma of seared beef ignited hunger pangs and made her all the more eager for a hot meal. She'd barely noticed her lunch of cold salad that she'd eaten from a take-out carton as she prepared to brief the congressman on the latest brouhaha in the environmental camp.

Glancing at her present surroundings, Sharon noticed the Southwestern motif in shades of orange, brown, turquoise, and white. "This place hasn't changed a bit."

"And neither have you." Rory's smile was as warm as a summer day. "Except maybe for your hair."

"Got to look current, you know." Instinctively she placed a manicured hand on her shorn tresses. Though she anticipated spending the evening with her old friend, Sharon realized she'd be pricked by pangs of guilt all night if she didn't take action to insure her congressman was represented by someone at the banquet. "Um, they said there would be a fifteen-minute wait, right?"

His blue eyes widened as he nodded. "That isn't a problem, is it?"

"Oh, no. It's just that I need to make a quick call."

"Sure. I won't listen in." He winked.

Sharon grimaced. "I was in such a hurry when I left the office, I don't even have my cell phone with me." She remembered a phone booth in the foyer. Tilting her head in its direction, she said, "I'll use their phone."

"Don't do that." Rory reached for the inside pocket of his suit coat. Since he had shed his gloves, the gesture gave her a chance to notice his left ring finger was bare. "Use my cell phone."

"That's all right." Sharon hurried to the booth before he could insist. She didn't want him to know she hadn't told the complete truth about her evening plans.

She dug into her skirt pocket and was pleased to find some loose change from lunch. As people entered, bursts of cold air filled the foyer. She shivered. Glancing at her diamond watch, Sharon was relieved to see it was still early enough to catch someone at the office. One of the interns answered on the first ring.

"Are you sure you're all right, Sharon? You left the office in such a hurry."

"I'm fine, Olivia."

"Are you sure? I—I know the vote didn't go as we planned. Although I must admit, you do sound cheerful." She paused. "Um, you haven't been drinking, have you?"

"Drinking? Of course not." Sharon would have been offended had Olivia not sounded genuinely concerned. "Anyway, what difference do man's puny plans make? Everything's in God's hands." Without waiting for an answer, Sharon asked, "Is David still there?"

"No."

"How about Emily?"

"Sorry. It's just me and Maureen."

Sharon knew the receptionist, a mother of three who always hurried home at the stroke of six, had no interest in going to the event. She focused her attention on Olivia. "Say, how would you like to go to a banquet tonight?"

"Me?" Sharon heard an intake of breath. "I'd love to!"

"Good." She gave Olivia the details and added an admonition. "Now don't let them know you're an intern. Walk up and register like you're supposed to be there. Just say you're from the congressman's office. And remember, you represent us."

"I sure will!"

Sharon sighed as she returned the receiver to the cradle. Her quarter and dime clattered to their new home deep within the phone. Turning, she saw Rory motioning to her. She hurried to his side.

"Just in time. I didn't want to leave without you."

"Good. I'd never find you in this monstrous place," she whispered so the hostess couldn't hear.

He chuckled, his eyes scanning the tiny restaurant.

The hostess didn't bother to inquire if the cramped table near the kitchen door was suitable. A booth in the nonsmoking section, as they had requested, was the best they could hope for.

"I guess you're used to sitting ringside since you work on the hill," Rory speculated after they had taken off their coats and situated themselves on the cushy seats.

"Are you implying you're surprised I didn't use my influence to get us a better table?"

"No, you never were pretentious." His serious tone indicated he meant what he said. "But I'll bet you could have."

She shrugged. "I doubt it. Any congressman is a big deal back home, but unless they're very, very high profile, they're just one of hundreds here in Washington. And as for us Hill workers, I'm just one of thousands."

"You have a point." He paused. "So is everything all right?"

"Huh?"

"Your phone call. It seemed important. Is everything all right?"

"Now it is. Let's just say I made an intern's day. She'll be able to eat all the free food she wants tonight and hobnob with a few of the powers that be."

"Sending an intern to a bash, huh?"

"I admit it." Sharon felt her cheeks grow warm. "You caught me."

He chuckled. "I take it as a compliment that you cleared your schedule for me. Besides, I know you did your intern a favor. I remember when the prospect of a free meal was quite appealing, powers that be or no."

"So do I."

"But you're getting a free meal anyway," he teased.

"Not on your life. It's your birthday. My treat."

"Seems to me you've already given up enough by skipping out on your reception for me." He placed a hand over his heart. "I don't believe it. Could it be that Sharon Delacourt is no longer a workaholic?"

"Don't believe it. 'Workaholic' is part of the job description." Sharon unfolded a rough paper napkin. "I see this place still prides itself on its fabulous ambiance."

"Only the best," he quipped.

Even though his left ring finger bore no band, Sharon remembered her mother's admonition that men didn't always wear wedding rings. She had to know if Rory was married. "So your wife isn't livid about you meeting an old friend after all these years?" she ventured.

"My wife?" He waved his hand at her. "Oh, no. She's much too secure to be mad about an old friend, even one as beautiful as you." He cupped his hands around the back of his head, leaning back with a gesture of self-satisfaction. "Yep, she's already borne me eight sons. Linebackers, all."

"Oh!" Her stomach felt as though it was doing a flip before it dropped to her feet. She made a show of looking at the menu, concentrating on a photo of a steak and baked potato.

"Sharon." Cologne wafted Sharon's way as Rory leaned toward her. He placed a gentle hand on her wrist. "Have you really gotten as gloomy as all that?"

She looked up from the menu. "Gloomy?"

He nodded, taking his hand from her wrist. "So gloomy you can't even tell I'm teasing."

Sharon let out a sigh of relief she feared was audible. Determined to prove she could spar as well as he, she quipped, "Does that include the compliment you gave me?"

"That you're beautiful? Can't you answer that every time you look in the mirror?"

"You always were fond of answering a question with a question. You should have been a lawyer."

"Nope. Selling farm supplies is good enough for me."

"So you stayed in Kansas?"

"As I said I would." Stirring his glass of water with a straw, he watched the lemon wedge spin with the crushed ice. "But you're not the only popular one in town, you know. You do realize I'm also missing a fabulous banquet to be here tonight."

"Sorry," she said, covering her face with a look of mock sympathy.

"Not to mention a lecture on organic farming."

She laughed. "Sounds thrilling. Like standard convention fare."

"How did you guess?"

"So that's the real reason you're in town. And for a moment there, I thought you had flown all this way just to be with me."

"Who says I didn't?" Before she could answer, he became

the inquisitor. "So what about you? I was thinking you wouldn't show up at all. Or if you did, you'd tell me you had some great guy to rush home to."

"A great guy? Who has the time?"

A look of sadness crossed his face just before the waitress arrived with dinner.

Sharon wanted to ask Rory what was wrong, but something stopped her. Instead, she decided it best to dig into her baked potato.

Rory's hand touched hers. "Do you mind if I say a word of grace?"

"Of course not." Sharon felt her cheeks burn. She should have remembered Rory said a blessing before every meal. A spinning world of politics had succeeded in squelching the practice in her own life until it was as rare as the steaks before them.

Rory's voice was just above a whisper. "Heavenly Father, thank You for the food we are about to receive and for a friendship whose bonds have led us to be together once again. We pray in Christ's name, Amen."

———— ·•· ————

Rory observed the young woman across from him. Sharon was more beautiful than ever. Yet she wore an aura of sophistication that had replaced the naiveté he remembered. Perhaps this was a good thing. Perhaps it wasn't.

"Enjoying your meal?" he asked.

"Mm-hm." Nodding furiously, she managed to mumble in spite of the potato in her mouth.

He chuckled. "Good. Although I would have thought you'd be used to better food by now."

She swallowed. "Are you kidding? I'm lucky to grab a quick

lunch most days. And even if I go out to dinner, I'm usually required to listen to a political speech or a lobbyist. Sometimes both." She threw him a wry grin. "I barely taste the food."

"Work isn't as glamorous as we envisioned, is it?"

She averted her emerald eyes. "Oh, it has its moments."

"Then why are you so depressed?"

Her eyes shot up and looked at his squarely. "Depressed? Who says I'm depressed?"

"I do."

She shook her head. "No, I'm not. I'm happy." The shake changed to fast nods. "Very happy. Never been happier. Never been happier in my whole life." Her smile lacked sincerity.

Rory extended his hand, reaching for the delicate fingers, nails painted coral, that were wrapped around her glass of iced tea. To his delight, she didn't attempt to move them. "It's been a long time, but I still know you pretty well, Sharon. Maybe even better than you know yourself."

"I know I belong here. I have everything all planned out." Gently but firmly, she moved her glass of tea to the lips that were covered in a flattering shade that matched her manicured fingernails. After a somewhat exaggerated swallow, she said, "I stayed in Washington so I could be part of making laws. Good laws. Laws that would help people change their lives. And maybe even change their hearts and minds. I want to help people live godly lives, to pray and to rejoice in God whenever and wherever they like. I think our country should help them do that, not pass and enforce laws that stand in their way."

"Like what?"

As she leaned toward him, Rory saw the spark in her eyes he remembered from their days as interns. "I think the law should give families a break. And we should collect the amount of money we need in taxes to keep people from poverty and to maintain the best military in the world. But we shouldn't collect more than we need. We should encourage people to take pride in their work and accomplishments. We shouldn't cripple them under huge tax burdens. And though no one in America should be in poverty, our entitlement programs should be structured so they don't drain ambition and discourage marriage. The time to change these injustices is today."

"I can hear Kate Smith belting out 'God Bless America' now." Rory chuckled until he saw Sharon's eyes narrow and her mouth form a line so straight one could have used it as a short ruler. He brought his fist up to his mouth and cleared his throat. "Seriously, I agree with you. I can't imagine anyone arguing with that."

Leaning back into the booth, Sharon wrinkled her nose. "You'd be surprised." She sighed. "I've been a legislative assistant for almost a decade. And in all those years, it seems every time we try to take a step forward, someone trips us up. I don't see any difference in politics, or in the world, since I came here. If anything, things may have gotten worse." She folded her arms. "Maybe I don't belong here after all."

"Maybe not."

Sharon's eyes widened as she folded her arms even tighter, indicating she was disappointed he didn't argue with her speculation. "And He saith unto them, Follow me, and I will make you fishers of men," Sharon recited. She leaned one elbow on the table and looked into his eyes. "Ever since I interned on the hill, I felt led to go into government. The Lord's answers to my prayers seemed to confirm my idea." She sighed. "But maybe I misunderstood. Maybe I'm not supposed to work in government to fish for men after all."

"I wouldn't say that. But I think you might be biting off more than you can chew."

"How so?"

"Did Jesus tell you to clean the fish tank?"

"What does that mean?" She pushed her plate away and leaned on the table.

"You can bring people to Christ within the world we have today. But that doesn't mean you have to make the world itself a perfect place to live."

"Adam and Eve threw away that opportunity, huh?" A sardonic grin touched her lips.

"All the more reason to let everyone know that because of Jesus, all is not lost—even if the world does seem to be hostile to Christianity sometimes." He looked deeply into her eyes. "No one can expect to force everyone in the world to love the Lord. He wants us to come to Him willingly. He understands that there are some who will reject him."

"I guess you're right."

"I know I'm right." At that moment, Rory resolved to prove to Sharon just how right he was.

Chapter 3

"C areful! You don't want to get your nice shoes wet." Rory extended his hand to help Sharon avoid the muddy water that had collected in a shallow pothole.

D.C. had been wet that week, but not even cloudy skies could sour Rory and Sharon's mood. Over the past few days, they had made memories together. Now Rory's convention was over. Today was his last day in town.

Though she was already half off the curb, Sharon expertly grabbed his hand and allowed him to pull her forward. A slight jump was all she needed to avoid splattering sullied rainwater all over her black leather pumps and nude hose. "Thanks!"

"You're welcome. Maybe we should have changed clothes after church."

"That's all right." She shook her head in the negative. "What good are clothes you can't wear?"

Rory liked to think he wasn't given to egotism, but he couldn't resist wondering if Sharon had chosen to remain in her Sunday clothes to look nice for him. As far as he was concerned, she had succeeded. Underneath a mauve trench coat, her silky pink dress hinted at delicate curves. Sharon wore little makeup, letting her natural blond beauty shine.

He thought back to the lunch she had made for him at her apartment. He'd wanted to treat her to a restaurant meal on their last day together, but when she told him about her surprise luncheon, Rory's objections melted away. He knew his way around the kitchen well enough for a bachelor, but a home-cooked meal prepared with loving care was tops in his book. Sharon had been a pleasure to look at over Cornish game hen, twice-baked potatoes, green bean casserole, bread, and cherry pie.

Rory remembered the times they had shared together during the week. He had managed to slip away from all but the mandatory convention meetings, and he suspected Sharon had put off some of her work as well. For him, the missed meetings had been worth the price. Those hours gave him time to discover he felt more comfortable than ever with Sharon. He seemed to slip into her life and routine as though that was exactly where he belonged.

Rory suddenly realized Sharon had never let go of his hand. Not that he objected. He liked it just where it was. It felt so romantic to walk along the city streets, an impromptu tour one could take during a mild, if wet and messy, Mid-Atlantic winter.

How he wished he could stay.

But he couldn't. The best he had been able to manage was to delay his flight back to Kansas until seven that evening. In the meantime, he pushed aside unwelcome thoughts about his departure.

That morning, he'd attended worship with Sharon. She had joined Good Tidings Christian Fellowship in nearby Virginia. As he expected, the suburban church proved modern, massive, and mobbed. Rory couldn't say he enjoyed the contrast to his own place of worship. The tiny white frame building where he worshiped was nestled among huge oaks and surrounded by a gravel parking lot. Designated a historical landmark, Congregation of the Risen King served a small but vibrant congregation.

At the time, he had been driving around the church lot with Sharon sitting by his side in the rental car. "I can see we're not in Kansas any more," Rory joked, borrowing a line from *The Wizard of Oz* as he struggled to find an empty parking spot.

"Are you just now figuring that out?"

When Rory glanced at her face, he knew tolerating inconvenience to be near Sharon was worth the sacrifice.

After finding seats on the far side of the aisle, Rory and Sharon sang contemporary Christian songs with the rest of the congregants. The praise and worship melodies somehow managed to both soothe and energize him. Earlier frustrations about parking melted. Soon he became captivated by the sermon.

"So often you hear—erroneously, may I remind you—that our Lord was penniless," Pastor Thomas thundered. "Matthew 8:20 says, '*And Jesus saith unto him, The foxes have holes, and the birds of the air have nests; but the Son of man hath not where to lay his head.*'" He paused for effect. "Perhaps that sounds harsh to some of you. Maybe you think Jesus was impoverished. But was he?"

A series of negative responses filled the sanctuary.

"Perhaps in this day of homes with three-car garages—filled with three luxury vehicles, in most cases—college educations costing more than most people in the last century might have earned in their lifetimes, and so on, our Lord appears impoverished. But is a life in God's service a life of impoverishment? No. It is not." As the study of the passage continued, the pastor reminded his flock that to depend on the Lord for one's needs is a mark of true discipleship.

When the sermon came to a close with the promise that spiritual impoverishment would be discussed the following week, Rory was sorry he wouldn't be there to hear it. Sharon's choice of church was comforting. Surely she hadn't lost her way spiritually after all these years in the big city.

After lunch, they decided to spend their last afternoon together walking near her apartment, six blocks from the Dupont Circle Metro Station. To Rory, the scenery was inconsequential. Being with Sharon was the important thing.

Enjoying the warmth of her hand, Rory thought back to the day, a week ago, when they had met at the restaurant. He never would have guessed they would pick up right where they left off. When he was with her, the years seemed to vanish. He could almost imagine what it would be like to run for political office, as he had once promised Sharon he would do. All those years ago, he'd imagined that he'd start out on the town council, and next move up to the state house, then on to a position as a representative or senator in the nation's capitol.

Rory had vowed to himself that once he had attained that goal, he would return to Washington and tell Sharon how much he loved her. How much he had loved her all these years. How his love for her would never die.

But he had failed. His father had died unexpectedly of a heart attack, leaving behind an equally unanticipated financial mess. That summer Rory was transformed from a fun-loving college fraternity brother, his education financed by doting parents, to a young man in need of immediate employment.

Sometime during the week, in the middle of one of their long talks, Rory had told Sharon about his father's death. Even then, he'd left out the most painful details. If only he could omit the other bad turns his life had taken. Then he wouldn't have to explain the mess awaiting him at AgriBarn Farming Equipment and Supplies.

Just then, he felt Sharon give his hand a little squeeze. "A penny for your thoughts."

He hesitated. "My thoughts are worth at least a dollar."

"All right, then," she said. "A dollar for your thoughts."

Though her tone was light, the glimmer in her eyes and her unsmiling countenance told him she sensed something was bothering him. Clearly, she wanted to know the truth. He wasn't ready to give her that. Not yet.

"Oh," he mused aloud, "I was thinking about how I told you I'd run for office one day."

"Yes. And one day has never arrived."

To his surprise, he picked up no evidence of judgment in her words or tone. "You're not disappointed?"

"Of course not. Why would I be disappointed in you? I'd rather you be happy than carving out a career for yourself that makes you miserable." She looked him in the eyes. "You are doing something you want to do, aren't you?"

"I suppose it's good enough. It's a steady job. I guess that's something no one should take for granted nowadays." He gazed down at the sidewalk. "But selling cow manure is hardly setting the world on fire."

"Are you kidding? I'm sure you could take a pile of manure and start a pretty good fire with just one match." She chuckled.

He let out a laugh, which somehow made him feel better. "I suppose. But it's nothing as glamorous as politics."

"Politics and manure might have more in common than most people in Washington like to think."

"Touché."

Her pink lips curved into a self-congratulatory smile,

showing she appreciated his compliment of her wit. "Manure may not be glamorous, but fertilizer helps feed a lot of people. And when everything comes out in the wash, that's all most people really care about. Food and shelter."

"They don't care about love?"

Her eyes widened for an instant before she seemed to catch herself and transfer her gaze to the sidewalk. "Love is something you can live without. Shelter is difficult to live without. And food is impossible to live without."

Rory wondered how an electrifying woman like Sharon could live without love. The idea left his heart aching. He wanted to inquire, to explore her feelings further. But the silence that followed her observation did not invite itself to be filled.

In the meantime, Rory was only glad she didn't jerk her hand out of his reach. Wishing to be respectful about whatever she contemplated, Rory waited until the tension had eased before he spoke. Even then, he decided to change the subject. "So, do you miss Nebraska at all?"

She gave a start. Had Rory not held her hand, he was sure she would have come to a halt in the middle of the sidewalk. "How did you know I was thinking about home?"

"Because we're connected."

"Like you can read my mind?" A blond eyebrow arched in apparent doubt.

"Not exactly. I can just sense things, that's all."

"You sound like some psychic trying to get me to call a 900 number." Sharon threw back her head and laughed before she became serious. "I don't miss Nebraska itself as much as I miss my mom and dad."

"What about your sisters?"

She shook her head. "They're all living out of state now.

The youngest, Denise, is already in college, working on her teaching degree."

"A great profession. What level?"

"High school. And she even wants to try an urban school."

"What an opportunity. Good for her. They certainly need teachers willing to take on challenging schools."

"But do they have to take my baby sister?" Sharon stuck out her bottom lip in an exaggerated manner. Then her expression turned thoughtful. "I do admire her. I remember what high school was like. For every student who really wanted to learn, it seemed there were four who coasted along in boredom, one who stayed zoned out, and another whose life ambition was to make trouble."

"You and I must have gone to the same high school. Where were you when I needed a date for the prom?" Rory laughed.

Without letting go of his hand, she tapped him lightly in the ribs. "I can't imagine you needing a date. I'll bet the girls were all over you."

"It's more like I'm a legend in my own mind." He grinned and was pleased when she grinned back. In truth, Rory had always attracted his share of interest, first from his classmates and then from women at work and church. But no one except Sharon Delacourt had come close to touching his soul.

Rory observed the surrounding commotion. The wintry drizzle hadn't kept many people from venturing out. They constantly had to move aside for other pedestrians to pass. Bar hoppers, restaurant goers, coffee drinkers, book browsers, and music fans packed the retail establishments. On the street, all sorts of luxury vehicles passed them.

"Guess you can't get away with an old clunker around here, can you?" he asked Sharon.

"Why do you say that?"

"Look for yourself." He tilted his head to his left.

Sharon studied the scene as though it were a novelty. "I guess you're right. There don't seem to be too many old cars." She shrugged. "I take Metro most of the time. I figure I pay a premium to live in the city, so I might as well take advantage of the cleanest and safest subway system in America."

"Mayors of other cities might argue that point."

"That's why they're mayors of other cities."

Rory shook his head as he felt an indulgent grin touch his mouth. Sharon was always quick with a comeback. At that moment, he noticed a limo. "There really is a lot of wealth here."

As a fresh burst of wind bristled, blowing more rain in her face. Sharon pulled her hood more closely to her head. "There's wealth everywhere."

"I can argue with you on that. Have you been to some of the poorer pockets of the country lately?"

"If you're trying to make me feel guilty, don't. I do everything I can for the poor through legislation."

"I know you do. But when all you see are riches, even someone as sensitive as you can become immune." She shot him a look that suggested she was about to take issue with him. He hurried to make his next point. "No matter where we live, I think its important to have contact with all sorts of people so that we can appreciate the different types of challenges others face. Pretty soon, I'll be making a trip to the Ozark Mountains."

"If it's any warmer there than it is here, I'm tempted to say I'll join you."

"This idea of a winter day's walk hasn't turned out to be such a grand idea after all, huh?"

"Let's just say I'm glad we only have another two blocks to go before we get to my place."

He knew two blocks could still be a good hike. As the scenery suddenly changed from retail to residential, he kept one eye on the grand old town homes they passed and the other on Sharon.

She broke the silence. "You didn't tell me why."

"Why, what?"

"Why you're going to the Ozarks."

"Oh. I'm going with some members of my church to help build and repair houses for people."

"Wow! I'll bet that's a lot of work."

"You bet it is. But it's worth it." An idea occurred to him. "Speaking of work, I know how hard you hit the old grindstone."

"Most of the time. You wouldn't know it by the way I've been slacking off this week."

"If a full eight-hour day is what you call slacking off, I'd hate to see how long your day usually is."

"So do I. Believe me."

"Don't you have some vacation time built up?" he asked.

"I suppose."

"Then why don't you come with me? Get away from this unreal place of power, prestige, and politics. Visit the real America. What do you say, Sharon?"

Chapter 4

I f I decide to go, do I really have to work?" Sharon flashed Rory what she hoped was a mischievous smile.

She didn't want to admit that the prospect of putting in days of backbreaking labor held no appeal for her, even though Rory's cause was a good one. Facing mounds of letters from prickly constituents, demands from lobbyists cajoling her to grease the wheels of power, and incomplete work from interns who didn't always take their responsibilities seriously, sounded like comparative bliss. She hoped she could joke her way out of Rory's invitation without looking like either a snob or a slacker.

"Of course you'll have to work. That's part of the deal." He didn't look as though he was kidding. "Besides, since when are you afraid of work?"

Taking her eyes from his, Sharon busied herself by fumbling through her boxy black leather shoulder bag for her keys. They were approaching the ancient brick town house where she lived. The house had been divided into three apartment units. Sharon happily rented her two-room space for the ambiance of living in an old urban house, even though that meant ignoring booming rock music and zesty parties thrown by university students living next door.

She hurried up the five steps leading to the stoop, then threw open the oak exterior door without waiting for Rory to open it for her. Breezing through the foyer, Sharon tried not to look too eager to arrive at the red door at the top of the stairs that served as the entryway to her apartment, but the quick clacking of her heels on the wooden steps gave her away. Rory followed a couple steps behind.

"Home at last," she announced, turning the key. Without raindrops soaking her, Sharon already felt warmer.

The door opened into one large area that served as the living and dining room. Sharon had been told her apartment was a converted nursery. Walls had been added to create privacy in the bedroom, which led to a small bathroom. The minimalist kitchen appeared to be an afterthought, though the tiny room served the needs of a single woman living alone well enough. She realized what she paid to rent her apartment for one month would cover the mortgage of a three-bedroom home with an acre of land in the suburb of Topeka where Rory lived.

"Ready to warm up with some hot cocoa?" Sharon asked as she took his coat.

"Anything hot sounds good today." He lifted his forefinger, waving it once with flourish. "Especially if it involves chocolate."

"I have to agree with that. I'll be just a minute. If you don't mind, I'd like to hang our coats on the shower rack in the bathroom. I can set a towel down on the tile to catch the drips."

"Makes sense to me. I know you'd hate to get water all over these hardwood floors." His smile reassured her that he didn't mind.

"Good to see my odd habits make sense to you. Not everyone is so understanding."

After accomplishing her errand quickly, Sharon reentered

the living room, where Rory had made himself at home on the blue-and-white floral couch. She motioned for him to join her in the kitchen. She noticed him studying it, taking in every detail. "They call this a 'European' kitchen. I think that's just another name for 'old and small.' "

"Maybe so." He chuckled. "It's cute, though."

"Cute?" She stirred cocoa and sugar into simmering milk. "I know it's an insult when a man calls a room 'cute.' "

He rolled his eyes. "It's not so bad."

"My sister Sabrina was astounded when she came out here to see me a few years ago." Sharon shook her head at the memory. "She couldn't believe how tiny my place is. I could tell she felt sorry for me."

"Has she had to face economic reality yet?"

"She's a junior in college this year, so she's already seen how expensive textbooks and tuition are. And she's living off-campus in an apartment with three other girls this year, so she's had to deal with paying rent and utility bills. I think she can see some of what's coming, but Mom and Dad are covering her expenses. I'm not sure she's had a chance for everything to sink in yet."

"Does she know what she wants to do for her career yet?"

"She's majoring in languages and is fluent in more than one."

"Wow!"

"I'll say. She deserves a lot of credit. I barely got through two years of high school Spanish, myself. I told Sabrina I could get something for her at the State Department, but she doesn't seem too interested in the Diplomatic Corps." Sharon turned down the heat on the stove. "I have to admit I'm disappointed. She'd be excellent in that job."

Rory leaned against the refrigerator. "Maybe she just doesn't want her big sis to get her a job. Maybe she wants to succeed on her own."

"I thought of that." Sharon sighed. "If I had my way, I'd help all three of my sisters. But I doubt they'd let me."

"I feel the same way about my brothers. Guess we feel responsible for our siblings since we're both the oldest in our families."

"Yeah. We're the dependable ones. Sort of like faded jeans, old tennis shoes. . ."

"Station wagons, mini-vans. . ."

"Insurance agents, bankers. . ." Sharon made a show of yawning. "How exciting!"

A glint of merriment lit Rory's deep blue eyes. "One day, we ought to go sky diving at the South Pole or something, just to show everyone we can let loose."

"And give everyone we know heart failure? Not on your life!"

"There's responsibility, rearing its ugly head once again."

"Hmm." Sharon placed a cup of cocoa in Rory's waiting hands and motioned for him to join her at the table. "Oh, I almost forgot. Let me break out the cookies."

"Cookies? What are you trying to do, feed me so much they won't let me get on the plane home?" Rory's face held a wistful expression just for an instant, long enough for Sharon to realize he might like to stay.

"If only that were possible," she murmured, then realized she may have said too much. Desperate to escape, she skittered back into the kitchen for the cookies. The week had been fun, but she had to realize that this week was all they would ever have. Rory was settled at his job, and Sharon could never expect him to stay with her in Washington.

"Besides," she added as she arranged the cookies on a

CITY DREAMS

small, blue-and-white china platter, "I'm expecting Danielle to stop by on her way to Atlanta. If I had one of my friends here in town at the same time, wouldn't she be jealous?" Sharon chuckled. In fact, Danielle would be anything but jealous. She would want nothing more than Sharon's happiness.

"Uh, on her way to Atlanta?" Rory asked as Sharon approached the table, platter and dessert plates in hand. "That's a little roundabout if you're coming from Nebraska, isn't it?"

So her ploy to distract Rory had worked. "Yes, it is. Well out of her way. But I really think she needs me right now. She's just gone through a bad breakup with a longtime boyfriend. All of us in the family liked him, and we were sure they'd marry one day. Everyone feels awful that things didn't work out." Sharon's mouth twisted into a rueful expression. "I can't help but wonder if that's the real reason she's moving to Atlanta. To escape the pity. You know what it's like living in a small town where everyone knows your business."

"That I do."

She set the platter near Rory. "Even as close as the two of us are, I had to promise not to be too sympathetic before she'd agree to stop by for a visit before she moves in to her new place. I'm looking forward to seeing her."

"I'm sure you are."

Taking her seat across from him, Sharon nodded. "We've always been more like friends than sisters. Partly because we're the two oldest, and partly because we just click. I always told her she'd be maid of honor in my wedding."

Now why in the world did I say that? Sharon felt a rush of heat. She could only hope her whole face wasn't turning an unflattering shade of crimson.

If Rory realized she had made a verbal slip, he was either

sincerely unperturbed or an accomplished actor. "My brothers and I have an unspoken agreement that we'll stand up for each other." He took a swig of cocoa before choosing to sweep all five mint chocolate cookies from the platter.

"Hey!" she protested. "You took all my favorites!"

"I did?" He opened his mouth in mock surprise. "If they're your favorites, didn't you hold back a few for yourself?"

Sharon straightened her shoulders. "Of course not. That would be rude." She paused. "But on second thought, I was just as rude to say anything. I guess I was just surprised, that's all."

"Don't apologize. I shouldn't have taken them all." He placed two of the cookies on her plate. "Old habits die hard. In a family of three boys, if you don't snatch the food you want fast, it'll be gone." His lips twisted. "And brothers won't give it back either."

"Guess I'm used to girls." She returned the cookies to him. "Here, you eat them."

"Nope. I don't want them now." Wrinkling his nose, he said, "They have girl germs."

"But girl germs are cleaner than boy germs." She stuck out her tongue.

After good-natured laughter, they turned serious attention to the cookies and cocoa, and then whiled away the rest of the dreary afternoon in easy conversation. All too soon, five o'clock rolled around. Though he could have taken Metro, the trip would have involved a time-consuming switch from the red to the blue line at Metro Center. Instead, Rory opted to telephone a cab to take him to Reagan National Airport. Sharon suspected he wanted the extra time with her. Her heart beat with happiness.

After he hung up, Sharon asked Rory to join her in prayer.

"Heavenly Father, we ask in the name of Jesus Christ that You keep Flight 1782 in Your care. Be with the pilots as they fly the plane and the flight attendants as they see to the passengers' needs. Lord, we ask that you give Rory a safe trip on the ground as well, returning him safely to his home in Kansas. Be with him as he returns to his home and work."

"And while we are apart from each other," Rory added, "I ask that You walk with Sharon as well, Lord. Be with her each moment, and bless her efforts at work. Help her take time for relaxation, so her body, mind, and spirit can renew in Your love. In Jesus's holy name, Amen."

Sharon squeezed his hand. "Thank you."

Rory embraced her, resting his cheek against hers. All too soon he let go. His hands still upon each side of her waist, he looked deeply into her eyes. "You know, you never gave me an answer about going to the Ozarks."

She looked beyond him, as though a crystal art deco lamp she had bought at an antique store had become of the utmost interest. "I don't know. . ."

"Why not? There's nothing to be afraid of." After letting go of her waist, he beat his fists on his chest playfully. "I'll protect you."

Sharon laughed. "I'm sure you will. But to tell you the truth, I haven't done a lot of physical work since I don't know when."

"But you take step aerobics classes."

"I doubt one hour of stepping is the same as a whole day of putting shingles on a roof or digging a ditch."

"I'm sure you're in better shape than you think. I admit, you'll be sore and tired every night, but it will be a good kind of sore and tired. And the nights are free for fellowship. We always talk over the day as a group and hold a short devotional Bible study. Nothing too heavy." He grinned. "I know firsthand this trip will be good for you, body and soul."

Sharon had to acknowledge that the trip Rory described sounded good. Peering out of the living-room window, she noticed the sky hadn't become any lighter. If anything, the early dark of a winter night was beginning to descend. The massive oak beside the window blocked any light that could have shone through. Dense leaves offered pleasant shade from severe summer sun, but bare gnarled branches cast eerie shadows that weren't quite so comforting on gray winter days and black nights. Rain dripped off the boughs. A burst of warm sun would be greatly appreciated about now.

She turned her attention back to Rory. "What if I can't do the work? What if I really can't stand to be there the whole week?"

"People at different levels of fitness go on these trips. The jobs we do take more mental dedication than brute force. And we don't assign people to chores they know nothing about. For instance, one of our members is an electrician. He'll be in charge of any electrical work."

"Makes sense."

"If you want to know the truth, you'll probably be asked to do interior painting. It's usually the guys who do the carpentry work. I often end up roofing."

"Now that does sound like hard work."

He shrugged. "It's not so bad once you get used to it. Besides, the temperature isn't hot this time of the year. What's worse is being on a roof top all day when it's blistering hot in the middle of July. This trip won't be so bad. But trust me, we can find something for you to do."

"Promise you won't make fun of me?"

He placed three fingers in the air. "Scout's honor."

"All right. I'll go."

"Great! I'll e-mail you the details after I get home. You won't regret it."

The sound of a taxi horn signaled their time together had come to an end.

"Oh! I almost forgot!" Running to the kitchen, Sharon grabbed a paper lunch bag she had packed with a sandwich, cookies, and a soft drink. Hurrying back to Rory, she handed him the sack.

"What's this?" He peered into the bag.

"Dinner. I know they don't always feed you on planes these days."

"You even put in the chocolate mint cookies." A smile of pleasure seemed to cover his face.

"Of course."

"Thanks, Sharon. You're the greatest." Rory made the slightest move toward her, almost as though he wanted to kiss her. Seeming to think better of it, he turned and nearly ran out of the house, leaving Sharon to face the city alone once more.

———•———

Two weeks passed. Each day, Sharon awoke with an empty feeling. She didn't have to speculate on the cause. Rory's absence had created the emptiness, and only his presence would fill it again. She actually looked forward to working in the Ozarks the following week. In the meantime, E-mails and phone calls from Rory would have to do.

The day before the trip, Sharon tossed two oranges in her shoulder bag. One was for her midmorning snack. The other was for the man who lived on a grate she passed on her walk to work each day. Known to her only as George, the bearded man reminded her of the way Charlton Heston looked when he played Moses. Perhaps that's why she was drawn to him. Or perhaps it was just because he had made eye contact with her one day last winter, moving her heart.

That day she'd tossed him a dollar. Later that evening, she'd felt led to pray about the stranger. When the Lord guided her to offer him a portion of food each day, she, who had so much, couldn't refuse Him so little. The ritual had actually become a pleasure.

A glance at the kitchen clock indicated she had fifteen minutes to scan the headlines of the newspaper. She subscribed to the *Washington Times* so she wouldn't have to fight with the other staffers for the office copy. The office also subscribed to the *Washington Post*, along with the *New York Times*, the *Congressional Record*, and the top news magazines. So the staffers could keep up to date with news in Nebraska, the office carried the *Omaha World-Herald* and the *Lincoln Journal Star*. Each staffer's computer was bookmarked to key web sites as well. This reading was in addition to reports issued by congressional committees and subcommittees on which their representative served.

Reading the paper and visiting the Internet might have appeared leisurely to the casual observer, but these activities were part of their work. Staffers were expected to have a thorough grasp of news events that would affect the congressman's votes. Sharon had assigned each staffer one or two areas of interest, such as diplomacy, economics, and the environment, to name a few. She kept defense and family issues as her target areas.

As lead assistant, Sharon was expected to master everyone's areas well enough to brief the congressman with only a few minutes' notice. Sharon also needed to be well-versed on current news to field impromptu conversations with constituents, other congressmen and senators, and lobbyists. Though this part of the work was challenging, especially when events moved rapidly, Sharon prided herself on her knowledge.

Over the years, Sharon had learned how to make finishing her coffee and reaching the end of the paper coincide. She had taken her last sip when an item buried near the bottom of Section C stopped her cold:

AgriBarn up in Smoke

Topeka: Corporate Headquarters of AgriBarn, Inc., a Kansas farm supplies firm with branches in the Midwest, Ohio, and Virginia, burned to the ground last night. No injuries were reported.

Several AgriBarn executives are currently under investigation for fraud. Corporate offices in the four-story building were thought to house incriminating documents. Arson is suspected. Three of the primary suspects, CEO Woodrow Reed, VP of Marketing Frederick Nelson, and Lead Accountant Rory Ford, were not available for comment.

Sharon gasped. "Rory Ford?" She reread the item, hoping against hope she had misread the name. She hadn't.

"Rory. What in the world has happened?"

Chapter 5

Sharon felt Rory's eyes on her. She turned and saw him, hammer still in hand, admiring her handiwork. As a result of her efforts, a filthy wall had been cleaned and covered with a fresh coat of paint.

"See? I told you this type of work is the best there is." As on every day they'd been on the missions trip, Rory was flushed with heat despite the brisk mountain air that hovered around 45 degrees. Sweat had darkened his blond hair to a light brown. Dirt streaked his face and decorated his jeans and old shirt. Sharon found him more attractive than ever.

Knowing her looks were the worse for wear, Sharon didn't feel so vibrant. "I think you told me this would be good for me. But the best work there is?"

"So, maybe I exaggerate. Is there really any harm in that?"

"You tell me. Is there?" Sharon didn't like the icy tone of her own voice, yet she couldn't contain her feelings.

She didn't believe what she had read in the newspaper. At least, not word for word.

Yes, she believed something was going on at AgriBarn. And she believed Rory had somehow become a suspect. But accusations didn't make him guilty. Legally, the prosecutors had to prove the accused had committed the crime, rather than the accused having to prove his innocence. At least, that's how Sharon understood the law.

Regardless of where the burden of proof lay, she knew in her heart Rory was innocent of whatever they were saying he had done. Sharon was all too aware that, except for that one week, they hadn't seen each other for ten years. But the week had been an intense one, and she could see that over the past decade, Rory hadn't changed his values.

Then how did he manage to get himself tangled up in such a mess?

She wished she could answer that nagging question. If only Rory would provide her with an easy answer! They had been in this remote area of the Ozarks almost a whole week. Each night during free time, they had opportunities to chat alone. Not once did Rory come close to telling her anything about his work, in spite of Sharon's repeated attempts to throw him easy openings.

The fact that he didn't share his trouble was bothersome to Sharon. Shouldn't an innocent man be indignant upon finding his name splattered all over the papers as a suspected white-collar criminal?

A sudden thought occurred to her. *That's it. He doesn't read the Washington papers. He doesn't think I know.*

Her train of thought was broken as Rory took the paint brush out of her hand and placed it in the tray. "Come on. Let's break for lunch."

Eyeing his grime-splattered hand, she made a face. "Be sure to wash up first." Sharon doubted the well water, available out back via hand pump, was as sanitary as water treated by an urban facility, but it was better than nothing.

Extending both hands, Rory imitated her expression as he inspected them on both sides. "I think you're right, Miss Delacourt. It might be wise for me to wash up."

"I don't have a sister working in the medical profession for nothing," she teased.

Sharon waved to the three other women in her group, indicating she'd be deserting the painting project for a short time. No one minded. The first coat already covered the walls of the two-room house. Best to let the paint dry a little before applying more anyway.

To Sharon, the term "house" was polite. "Shanty" seemed to be more appropriate. She suspected that even after the church group had installed a new roof, rewired, and spruced up the place with paint and minor cosmetic repairs, the structure would still be little more than a shack. How could a young mother with four small children survive in a dwelling that made Sharon's modest apartment back in Washington seem grandiose? Yet to the young mother who had lost her husband to the coal mine, the house was home.

"The work you did today really shows," Rory noted as they exited.

"Whoever picked out that shade of ice blue has good taste."

He tipped an imaginary hat. "Thank you, Ma'am."

"It was you?"

"Why should you doubt it?"

"Never thought about it." She smiled. "I'm glad to see your artistic side."

With both thumbs, he pulled the fabric on the chest of the paint-splayed shirt he wore, demonstrating mock pride. "I have lots of talents and many sides."

"I'm sure." Sharon forced a smile as her stomach sank.

Comments that she would have never noticed before had taken on a sinister meaning since she had spotted the news item about the improprieties at Rory's company. Longing for the recent past that seemed so carefree, she wished she hadn't discovered that his firm's headquarters had been destroyed by an arsonist. At least Rory had been allowed to leave town for the missions trip. Maybe he wasn't a prime suspect any longer. Maybe he would be cleared of any wrongdoing. Convictions aren't made without convincing evidence. Sharon had no reason to believe Rory would be punished for a crime he didn't commit.

As they headed out the newly-installed front door, Sharon felt Ivy's dark eyes aiming spears at her back. A member of Rory's church, Ivy had taken every opportunity to flirt with the handsome blond all week. Rory, whom Sharon guessed was more oblivious than insensitive to Ivy's feelings, had made his friendship with Sharon a known fact among the church workers. Sharon regretted she had played a part in someone else's disappointment, however unintentionally. She comforted herself with the knowledge that she'd never seen Rory indicate to Ivy that her romantic interest was returned. Perhaps Sharon's presence on the trip would help Ivy discover she should set her sights on another man. A man who would find the attractive, cinnamon-haired woman enticing.

Every woman deserves someone who truly loves her.

She thought about her companion. Rory seemed to act like a man in love, or at least in intense like. They knew each other well, or so Sharon had believed before discovering his problems at work. Yet how could his feelings of love for her be genuine if he couldn't even find it in his heart to confide in her his troubles? By now he should have realized he could tell her anything. Especially if he was being falsely accused.

She sighed. How could anything about Rory be sincere if he hid from her who he really was? What if he really was a criminal instead of the Christian he claimed to be? Sharon hated even to consider the chilling possibilities.

"Come on," he said, breaking into her thoughts. "I know a clearing with a fabulous view. We can eat there."

She nodded weakly and acquiesced. Fifteen minutes later, they arrived at a flat rock large enough for them to spread out their food. Sharon saw that the hike up a steep dirt path, filled with treacherous tree roots protruding several inches on top of the ground, had been worth the effort. From their perch, they could see endless miles of sky and mountains. A small town was nestled in the valley a mile or so below. The picture reminded her of looking out an airplane window, only the view was even better because they were closer to the ground.

"Rory, this is gorgeous!"

"Makes you feel like you're on top of the world, doesn't it?" He inhaled, his chest expanding as clean mountain air filled his lungs to capacity. "So refreshing."

Following his lead, Sharon breathed in as well. "Quite different from Washington."

"A lot less pollution, that's a fact. Have your lungs gone into a state of shock?" He chuckled.

"Not yet."

He placed a hand on each hip and enjoyed the scene below them.

Placing her hands on her own slim, jean-clad hips, Sharon took in the details. A translucent pale blue sky suggested summer, but leafless timber told the truth. Nearby mountain tops were so close, Sharon could count the trees that covered them. Most of the trees showed gray branches and trunks, though a few thin white trees and green pines and scrub were interspersed, lending muted colors.

"I'll take a guess the clean air isn't the only difference between here and Washington," Rory said.

"There is a lot less pollution." Sharon folded one arm and, with the other, placed two fingers on her chin as though she were contemplating the fate of the world. "And there's a difference in temperature. The air here isn't as hot as it can get on the Hill sometimes."

"Good one." He chuckled.

After standing most of the day, Sharon was ready to take a seat, even one on an unforgiving stone. She dumped out the contents of the brown paper sack she had been given by the church that morning. "Looks like bologna on white bread." Unzipping the plastic sandwich bag, she inspected the condiments. "Oh, gross. They put yellow mustard on it."

"Wonder if all the lunches are the same?" Sitting beside her, Rory pulled the sandwich out of his own bag. "Yep. Looks like I got bologna with gross yellow mustard too. Although, I happen to like gross yellow mustard." He gave her a quizzical look. "What do you put on your bologna sandwiches? Ketchup? Mayo?"

Wrinkling her nose, Sharon grabbed her jean-clad stomach. "Eww!"

Rory laughed. "Plain, then. No wonder you manage to stay nice and thin."

"Thanks for the compliment, but going without condiments isn't my secret. For one, I don't eat bologna sandwiches. They're not only loaded with fat and preservatives, but bologna just is not my idea of an appealing slice of meat. But I do admit, before I became more health conscious, I used spicy brown mustard."

"Now that's gross." He inspected her strewn-out lunch. "Look at it this way. Once you eat the sandwich, you can reward yourself with the gorgeous red delicious apple." He picked up the large piece of fruit and held it up for her before relinquishing it in favor of a boxed drink. "Then you can sip red fruit punch. And it doesn't matter if it spills, since, unlike a white tablecloth or carpet, this rock won't stain."

She chuckled as he returned the drink to its place.

With his thumb and forefinger, he grabbed the bag of chips. "And who can resist America's favorite vegetable, potato chips!"

"Lovely." Sharon clapped her hands. "You're quite the salesman. I haven't gotten so excited about a lunch like this since kindergarten."

"Picky. Picky." He shook his head and shrugged. "If you don't want it, I'll be glad to eat it for you."

"Why am I not surprised by your generous offer?" She arched her eyebrows. "No, I guess I'd better eat this myself, even if I choke. I know nothing else is coming before dinner." She lifted the top slice of bread. With her forefinger, Sharon swished away the offending yellow mustard and wiped it on the white paper napkin included with her lunch. From the corner of her eye, she noticed Rory looking at her with an amused expression. She chose to ignore him. Biting into the bologna and bread, she discovered she was hungrier than she thought. Before she could count to ten, the whole sandwich was gone.

"Not so picky now, are we?"

"I guess not," she admitted. "I can see why people on those reality shows are willing to eat bugs."

"You actually watched those?"

"No way! But they run so many commercials, the highlights are hard to miss."

Folding his hands across bent knees, Rory stared into the sky. "Out here, I think it might be possible to miss commercials. And newspapers. And the Internet. And all the things that were supposed to make our lives better, but in many ways, seem to have made them worse." He sighed. "How would you like to live in the mountains, Sharon?" He tilted his head downward. "Like the people in that little town down there."

Thoughts of a quaint cottage, painted red with a black shingled roof, popped into her head. Smoke would be pouring out the chimney. She and Rory would be sitting by the fire, sipping cocoa, not a worry in the world about accumulating snow. The repast seemed pleasant until she recalled her fondness for high-tech gadgets. "I don't know. It's a bit remote. I sort of like civilization. But I wouldn't mind coming here for a couple of weeks every year. It's been really nice to get away from the feeling of being on stage all the time."

"On stage?"

"You said it. In Washington everything I say is subject to scrutiny. No matter where I go, I'm perceived as representing the congressman. If I hold an opinion that's a bit different from his, I don't dare let anyone know. All I'd need is for something like that to get in the paper." She spread her hands in a sweeping motion, as if reading the headline. "MUTINY? DISAGREEMENT BETWEEN CONGRESSMAN AND AIDE SUGGESTS TROUBLE IN THE RANKS."

His eyes widened. "It's really that bad?"

"If you say anything outside the party line to the wrong person, it is. Every representative has enemies. I guess everyone does." She gave him a knowing look.

"Especially those who live for Christ, whether they're in Congress or not."

A verse from the Gospel of John popped into Sharon's mind. She shared it with Rory: " 'I have given them thy word; and the world hath hated them, because they are not of the world, even as I am not of the world.' "

Rory didn't answer but seemed to be contemplating her words. For a moment, a heavy silence consumed the air.

"Rory, do you find it hard to live for Christ at your workplace?" she ventured.

He had just opened his mouth to answer when Ivy's shrill voice interrupted from behind.

"So here you are! Mind if I join you for lunch?"

Chapter 6

The next day came all too quickly, bringing with it the hour for Sharon and Rory to board separate flights to their respective homes. Determined to stay with Sharon as long as possible, Rory sat with her in the airport as she waited for her flight. He could see her off in plenty of time to board his plane an hour later.

As much as he had enjoyed the week with Sharon, Rory could feel her pulling away. He guessed she was worried about entering a long-distance relationship. He was aware that such an arrangement would be difficult to maintain under the best of circumstances. If brought to its logical conclusion, they would have to decide what to do about their careers.

Rory liked to keep up with politics, following every federal race in the Midwest and keeping an eye on the most significant political contests nationwide. The congressman for whom Sharon worked would be up for reelection next November, but he was much too popular to make the opposing party's list of vulnerable representatives. At most, they would put up their own candidate to achieve publicity and name recognition to strengthen that candidate's chances of gaining an office at the state or local level. Some token debates and a few ads would follow, but a landslide victory for the incumbent was inevitable. Sharon's job was secure.

Sighing, Rory found himself wishing Sharon's congressman would retire. Then perhaps she wouldn't think twice about leaving Washington. Or maybe he was just kidding himself.

Still, he hoped if matters came down to choosing him or her career, he would emerge as the winner. After all, he was the one with the steadier of their two jobs. Sharon could depend on steady work only as long as the congressman remained in office.

Not with Rory. No matter what the papers said about the new economy and the expectation that most people would enter more than one profession during their lifetimes, Rory wasn't worried. Tractor models and the additives in fertilizer were sure to change, but the market for agricultural supplies always had, and always would, exist.

Of course, there was the matter of the inferno that had annihilated company headquarters. Rory was disappointed when the fire department determined it had been set by an arsonist. Until their results were conclusive, he had refused to believe the rumors. He still wasn't willing to speculate on who might have set the blaze. Since the incident, Rory had tried to imagine who among his coworkers possessed the defiance and courage to commit such a bold act. No one came to mind. But he had a feeling the perpetrator was connected to the livestock care division. A few months ago, Rory had noticed an increase in their spending that didn't make sense. When he inquired informally, their accountants couldn't provide him with a satisfactory answer.

That turn of events had come as a shock. Before then, Rory had been certain the irregularity would prove to be an honest mistake that could be rooted out and remedied, ideally before the company's quarterly taxes were due. Instead, a sphinx had posed a riddle. Finding the solution required thrashing into muck certain to sully all it touched.

Sleepless nights of anguish and intense prayer followed. Thankfully, the Lord had told him to speak to the vice president about the inconsistencies. Rory had been in the process of beginning an internal audit when the building caught on fire. While distressed that destroyed files meant the financial mysteries would remain unsolved, Rory knew he had nothing to hide.

In the meantime, his office had been relocated to a trailer on the twenty-acre AgriBarn campus. Plans to rebuild corporate headquarters were in the works. Already he looked forward to returning to plush new quarters in a brand new building. Not a bad place to spend the next thirty-five years.

"What are you looking so self-satisfied about?" Sharon asked, approaching him from the side so that he hadn't spotted her. She handed him one of the cups of coffee she held.

He decided to ignore her query lest she think him too egotistical and contented with his life. "What's this? You said you were going to the ladies' room." He accepted the drink.

"I did. Only I made an extra stop. Besides, I have to play games. That's the only way you'll ever let me buy you anything." She took the seat beside his and held up four packets of raw sugar. "Care for any?"

"Depends." Rory lifted the paper cup. "What is this?"

"Café mocha. With an extra shot of espresso, just the way you like it." Grinning from ear to ear, Sharon looked pleased with herself.

"You remembered. In that case, I'll take two of those." He extended his hand to take the sugar. For an instant, his flesh met hers, sending a flash of excitement into his very being.

Seemingly embarrassed, Sharon sipped her coffee and

began looking through the morning's newspaper.

"I'm that boring, huh?" he teased.

"Never. But you know me. It's been so long since I've looked at a paper, I couldn't wait to get my hands on it." She shrugged and handed him the first section. "I'll bet you feel the same, even though you won't admit it."

"Oh, all right. I admit it. I'm a news junkie, too." He flipped through the pages, but nothing of special interest caught his eye. At least, nothing over which he was willing to sacrifice conversation with Sharon. Rory was just about to fold Section A and return it to her when a headline on the back page caught his eye: AGRIBARN HONCHOS FINGERED IN ARSON OF HEADQUARTERS.

Rory took in an audible breath. "Oh, no!"

"Oh, no, what?" Sharon peered at him. Unwilling to wait for an answer, she leaned over and adjusted the top of the page. Rory kept reading:

> The investigation of Midwest farm supplies firm AgriBarn is heating up in the wake of the fire that destroyed their corporate headquarters three weeks ago. Yesterday, marketing vice president Frederick "Freddie" Nelson told investigators that he had "no idea why anyone would want to destroy AgriBarn's records." Nelson did say that lead accountant Rory Ford "was aware of improprieties in the company's books."
>
> Ford will be out of town until next week and cannot be reached for comment.

"I don't believe it. I thought Freddie and I were on the best of terms. And now he's trying to make me the fall guy?" He slumped in his chair. "What's worse, I'm finding out about this in the newspaper. That's what I get for not taking the cell phone with me," he muttered as he turned to Sharon. He hesitated for an instant, knowing he couldn't conceal his distress. "I guess I'd better let you in on this." He sighed. "Where do I begin? Our headquarters burned down and—"

"I know." Her face was expressionless.

Rory's mouth dropped open. "You know?"

"I've known for the past two weeks."

Her confession only added to his confusion. "Then why didn't you say anything?"

"Why didn't you say anything?" Sharon folded her arms across her chest.

"I was going to tell you several times, but I wanted it to be private. Things are complicated enough without getting everyone at church talking about it."

"Makes sense."

"Remember when were eating lunch on the mountain? I was just about to tell you then when Ivy asked to join us."

"How well I remember."

"At that point, I just decided to let it go. I never thought anything big was going to come of it. I knew I had nothing to hide. Although you wouldn't know that from Freddie."

"According to what I've read in the papers, you've always been a suspect. Your name was listed right along with this Nelson guy, and the CEO—Woodrow Something, was it?"

Rory sat bolt upright in his chair. "Wait. You say I've always been a suspect?"

"That's what the report said the first day after the fire. Your name was in it." Her eyebrows shot up. "You mean, you had no idea?"

"Of course I knew there was trouble in the company, but I had no idea anyone thought I could have ever done such a despicable thing. Imagine, burning down the building where you've worked for almost a decade, then running off to do missions work. How hypocritical could you get? No way could I have acted so casual all week if I had known my name was in the paper in such a negative context."

"You really had no idea?"

He shook his head. "I don't understand it. There's no hint of anything like this at home."

"Then who do they think set the fire?"

"I don't know." His stomach took a sickening turn at another unpleasant thought. "You believe I'm innocent, don't you, Sharon?"

Her green eyes reminded him of lasers, piercing his pupils with their intense beams. She didn't relinquish her unrelenting gaze for a few moments. Finally she spoke. "Yes. Yes, I do believe you're innocent, Rory."

Her hesitation caused a fearsome feeling to rise in his chest. "It took you long enough to say it." His voice became louder. "You weren't always so sure, were you? When you first read the article, there was some doubt in your mind, wasn't there?"

Anguish filled her eyes. "I didn't really believe—"

"Even an iota, even a smidgen of doubt is too much." Rory felt anger growing, as if it could reach out from his chest and shake some sense into Sharon.

"But—"

He didn't want to hear any protests. No excuse for her betrayal was good enough. "How could you suspect me at all? Even for a second?"

"But I didn't suspect you, Rory. Not really."

"Flight 703, departing for Reagan National Airport," announced a female voice over the loudspeakers.

"That's your flight." Rory's voice held no warmth. "Guess this is it."

"Not for too long, I hope." Sharon's face held a quizzical expression.

At that moment, Rory wasn't sure how long it would be before he saw Sharon again. Why would he want to visit a woman who could question him? Not knowing what else to do, he took her soft hand in his. "Lord," he prayed, "please keep Sharon safe on her flight. Keep us in your care as we travel and beyond. In Christ's name I make this petition. Amen." As soon as the prayer was uttered, Rory let her hand go. He didn't allow his gaze to linger upon her exquisite face. To drink in her essence at that moment would have been too painful.

Her hand touched his shoulder. "Rory, I'm sorry. You're not mad at me, are you?"

His first instinct was to console Sharon, even if it meant not telling the whole truth. But the truth was, he wasn't sure what he felt. "This isn't the best time, Sharon. We'll talk later."

He turned away from the woman he loved. This was not how he had envisioned their good-bye. But Rory kept walking without looking back.

———•———

A week had passed since Sharon and Rory had parted. He had called once to let her know he was safely home and to make sure she was safe as well. Their conversation was brief and chilly. Once more, she begged his forgiveness. Her words had no more effect than a bucket of water poured into a volcano. He didn't discuss the next time he would be seeing her. Sharon's stomach had felt queasy after their talk.

Unwilling to face her feelings, Sharon resorted to the action she knew best. Working. Both taskmaster and friend, work would always be there. Work was happy to consume time, filling hours that would otherwise be spent wallowing in loneliness. Even better, work rewarded effort, paying back as much as its slaves were willing to give. Work never threw tantrums. Work never misunderstood simple communication. Work never looked for innuendoes and insults where they didn't exist. Work never doubted you or questioned your devotion.

Unlike unpredictable humans. Especially men.

Of late, Sharon had taken to going in to work early, before anyone else. Even an empty office was preferable to tossing and turning in bed, watching the bluish-green numbers on the digital clock turn from one agonizing minute to the next.

That morning, winter darkness still hovered over the city as she passed George, who was trying to capture the hot air coming up through the street grate. "Good morning, George." Smiling, she handed him an orange.

Reaching for the fruit, the gray-bearded man blinked, an indication he was still half asleep. "You've been passin' by before dawn every day for the past week, Blondie. What's your story?"

"Still catching up from that week I missed, George." Unable to tolerate the rank odor of his unshowered body any longer, Sharon stepped back to the edge of the sidewalk.

He nodded with big motions. "Ah. That week. Missed you. A funny time to be off on vacation. But you deserve it, workin' every day regular like you do. That's more than I can say. I never took too much to work myself." Throwing back his head, he cackled. "You're too pretty to be workin' so hard. Ain't some man wantin' to take care of you?"

An image of Rory popped into Sharon's head before she remembered how unsettled her relationship with him had recently become—if they even had a relationship. Her heart seemed to leap skyward, then dive into her stomach, landing with a splash into the orange juice, multivitamin, three calcium pills, and coffee that had served as breakfast.

"Not anymore, George." She realized the Lord had just handed her the perfect opening, the answer to the prodding she'd been feeling from Him concerning the man who lived on the grate. "I have Someone better than any man to take care of me."

"You do?"

"Yes." She paused, steadying her soul should he resort to ridicule. "His name is Jesus Christ."

"Jesus?" To Sharon's relief, George's face lit with a smile. "He takes care of me too. Don't you think He sent you, Blondie?"

She swallowed. "Maybe he did," she said in a voice barely above a whisper. Suddenly she remembered the book she had in her coat pocket. The purchase, along with a couple of music CDs, had been made at a Christian bookstore weeks ago, then forgotten until now. Sharon extended her hand, which held an inexpensive copy of the New Testament bound in imitation black leather. "This is for you. The words of Jesus are in red."

"That's mighty nice of you and all, Blondie, but I can't read." He shook his head.

"Oh!" Such an idea had never occurred to her. She cringed at the thought that she had embarrassed this strange man with whom she had nevertheless formed a bond.

"I've memorized everything I need to know anyway. And the King shall answer and say unto them, Verily I say unto you, Inasmuch as ye have done it unto one of the least of these my brethren, ye have done it unto me." The man gave her a quick nod. "Give the little Bible to someone else who can read and doesn't know no Bible verses. Tell 'em it's from their friend, George."

Sharon opened her mouth to protest, but something, or Someone, stopped her. She placed the book back in its snug hiding place. At that moment, a burst of wind whipped through her cloth coat, sending a chill throughout her body. She noticed George wore nothing but a flannel shirt over a T-shirt. His faded yellow blanket was so thin as to be nearly transparent. "This cold snap is predicted to last a few days, George. Promise me you'll go to an indoor shelter tonight."

"Don't you worry about me, Blondie. I'll be all right."

Chapter 7

On her way home Wednesday evening, Sharon looked for George. She was certain he'd be lying on his grate. The cold snap, a common occurrence during Februaries in Virginia, had passed, and more seasonable temperatures felt deceptively like spring. Not that temperatures in the midforties were idyllic, but Sharon knew from witnessing his habits that the brisk air wouldn't bother George as long as warm ventilation rose from the slots in the grate and he could snuggle in his yellow blanket. His absence over the past two days had comforted Sharon. George must have taken her advice and sought shelter indoors during the bitter cold.

As she approached his usual perch, she noticed someone was taking warmth under a thick comforter. This one was blue.

Good. He's finally gotten a better blanket.

"Hi, George," she called softly as soon as she was within earshot. Perhaps she was awakening the man, but it was just about six o'clock, and he had no reason to sleep this early in the evening. She waited for a moment, but the body didn't move. "George?" Her voice was louder this time.

A hand emerged from underneath the covers. "Huh? Wha. . . what's up?"

The voice definitely belonged to a male, but it didn't sound like George. Sharon remained frozen in place, curiosity and wonder not permitting her to move.

When he pulled the blanket from his face and sat up, Sharon saw the wrinkled, weatherbeaten face of a clean-shaven man. Like George, he had graying hair, but this man's was a mishmash of brown, gray, and black rather than the hoary white with gray streaks she remembered.

"Who are you, lady?" He blinked his eyes.

"Have you seen George?"

"George? The man who used to be here all the time?"

Sharon nodded.

"Oh, him." The stranger shrugged. "He's dead. This is my grate now."

"Dead?" Sharon wasn't sure which she found more shocking—the supposed death or the stranger's nonchalance. "But that can't be true. I just saw him a couple of days ago."

He pointed his index finger to the door of a nearby store. "If you don't believe me, go ask inside."

Sharon instinctively glanced up at the sign, even though she already knew it read "Liquor Land." So many advertisements for specials on beer, wine, and booze were posted on the tinted glass windows that she couldn't see inside. Sharon had never entered a liquor store. She wasn't sure what to expect, but fear wasn't about to stop her. Determined to find out the truth about George, Sharon sent up a silent prayer for protection and marched into the establishment.

"What can I get you today, Ma'am?" To her surprise, the middle-aged man behind the counter looked like a clerk in any other store and seemed nice enough.

"I wanted to ask about the man who used to live on the

grate outside." She tilted her head in that direction. "He had a long gray beard."

"He looked a little like Charlton Heston in *The Ten Commandments?*"

She nodded.

"I'm afraid he passed away. Froze to death Monday night." He cast his eyes down to the counter. "I tried to get him to go to the church up the street. They set up a temporary shelter every winter. But he refused."

The image of an independent George refusing to ask for help, then dying on the street, forced its way into her mind's eye. Sharon's face burned as she tried in vain to fight the tears. Her nose became stuffy, causing her to reach into her coat pocket for the clean tissue she kept handy. Embarrassed, she knew her face was turning crimson, and her nose and eyes were already becoming bloated. Movie stars might look glamorous when crying, but in real life, tears weren't so pretty. She wanted to run in the other direction so no one would see her cry, but it was too late.

"You're the lady who brought him an orange every day, aren't you?"

"Yes." She sniffled.

"He thought the world of you. He wouldn't want you to be so upset."

"How can I help it? He lived in such miserable circumstances."

The man's face softened, and his gray eyes lit with compassion. "He was happy. You and I wouldn't be happy on the street, but he lived the way he wanted to live. And in the end, isn't that all that matters?"

Remembering George's admission that he knew Christ,

Sharon nodded weakly. She almost said something about Jesus, when a customer interrupted. A quick exit seemed the best option at this point.

The new occupant of George's grate called out to her. "Did you find out I was right, Lady?"

"Yes." Tears streamed down her cheeks, but she ignored them.

Have you sent me someone new, Lord?

With a rapid motion, she withdrew the orange from her purse and offered it to the man.

He scowled. "I don't like fruit. Don't you have a few dollars so I can get some decent food?"

Sharon's eyes went to a brown paper bag lying near the man's side. From its shape, she guessed it contained a pint bottle of liquor. Probably a cheap brand.

You don't want to buy food. You'd rather use my money to buy a beverage.

"Not today," she said aloud. She fingered the New Testament that was still in her coat pocket. "Can you read?"

"Do I look stupid?"

She extended the hand that held the New Testament. "Then won't you take this? As a gift from your friend, George?"

His eyes narrowed. "I know what that is. I got no use for your religion. Always passing judgment on people. Trying to tell them what to do." His cheeks puffed as though he was about to spit in her direction.

Turning on her heel, Sharon headed in the opposite direction. She tried to ignore the curses and unflattering names that followed her.

Heavenly Father, please change that man's heart.

She slowed her pace only after she neared the coffee shop where she customarily stopped for a soothing cup of hot brew each afternoon. The store was a few blocks out of her way, but the walk gave her exercise and time to think and pray.

A tap on the shoulder interrupted her thoughts. Gasping in surprise, she turned and saw a tall man wearing an expensive overcoat. "Listen, my car broke down a few blocks away. I need to make a phone call and pay a cab. Could you spare ten dollars? I'll pay you back," he hastened to add. "Just write down your address, and I'll mail you the money."

Sharon doubted his story. Her tears, revealing she was upset and distracted, had made her a target. Sharon suspected he was either planning to keep the money or wanted her address so he could break into her home. "Not today." She started walking.

"But I promise!" Keeping up with her pace, he continued to plead until she managed to beat him across an intersection. Then she slipped into a small convenience store run by a Korean family. The wife nodded in recognition as she passed the counter. Sharon often stopped in for a quart of milk or other necessity in between big trips to a supermarket.

Sharon hurried to the back of the store, stopping behind a tall display of toilet paper. She waited until she heard the man's voice.

"Where did the girl go?"

Sharon's heart beat as a pause followed. *Lord, please protect me.*

The proprietor spoke. "What girl? I see no girl."

Sharon lifted her eyes heavenward. *Thank You, Lord.*

As soon as she heard the bells on the door tinkle, she knew he had left. She waited a few more minutes before she ventured past the counter. On her way out, she threw the Korean woman a grateful look.

I've got to change my route home.

A half hour later, the telephone was ringing as Sharon entered the safe haven of her apartment.

"Sharon?" The caller didn't need to identify himself.

His voice couldn't have sounded any sweeter to her if it had been the song of an angel's harp. "Rory! I'm so glad you called. What a day!" Upset and shaken by the evening's events, Sharon recounted them as though she and Rory routinely spoke each day.

"Sounds like you were safer in the liquor store," he remarked. "Maybe you should have stayed there."

"Very funny. I just don't understand why all these things had to happen in one day." She sighed.

"I know we parted on sour terms last time, Sharon. But I've spent a lot of time praying for and about you."

A lump formed in her throat. "I can't tell you how much that means to me. What did the Lord say?"

"I think He's trying to tell you something. Maybe instead of ministering to many people through government, He wants you to reach people one at a time."

"But I didn't reach anybody today."

"He never promised anyone would bat a thousand," Rory pointed out. "But look at how you touched the widow in the Ozarks."

Sharon remembered the brief talk she'd had with the woman. She was only thirty years old, but impoverishment had aged the widow beyond her years. Grateful for the improvements on her home, she told Sharon the fact that they were done in Jesus' name meant more to her than anything a government agency could have done to help.

"But I didn't do anything alone."

"You spoke with her alone and then carried what she said to the rest of us. Believe me, it kept us going."

"We were still a team, though."

"So? Jesus himself had twelve disciples. And Luke tells us He anointed seventy more to minister in His name during His time here on Earth," Rory reminded her. "Now it's your turn. There are plenty of people here in Kansas who could use you." Rory paused, as though he wanted the significance of his words to sink in. "Perhaps He's trying to tell you it's time to go home."

"Home? But this is my home. I can't let one or two events in a single day discourage me."

"True, but you told me you knew you'd be changing careers one day. So maybe you're destined for the Midwest."

"I have to admit, the thought has occurred to me."

"Keep thinking about it. Look, I've got to go, but I want to ask you one thing before I hang up. I'll be in town on business next week. Can we meet for dinner on Wednesday night? At the steak house at six?"

She swallowed. "Of course."

Rory didn't reveal more. Hanging up, Sharon wondered what he would have to say.

Chapter 8

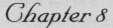

Rory was nervous as he headed toward Sharon's office. Rather than meeting her as they'd agreed, he was surprising her by showing up at her workplace unannounced. He hoped he wouldn't be disturbing her—at least not too much.

Passing a woman in the hall, Rory noticed her eyeing the dozen red roses he held. Ever since he'd bought the flowers, gazes from men and women alike followed him. He supposed the bouquet did make him look odd. Maybe buying flowers for Sharon was overdoing it. But what he had to say to her was important. Might as well pull out all the stops.

The office was unmistakable since it was labeled with the congressman's name. Immediately to the right of the doorway sat the receptionist's desk. Three other desks were located in the large, open room. Rory remembered his surprise when he first interned in Washington. He'd expected congressional staffers' offices to be plush. The typical open bay arrangement was hardly luxurious. Only the congressman enjoyed a lavish private office. Privacy wasn't considered a necessity for staffers, nor was vibrant color. The decor was a sea of beige dotted with heavy desks and filing cabinets. Rory found it hard to believe so much important work took place in such lifeless surroundings.

Sharon looked up from her paperwork, overriding the receptionist's efforts to greet him. "Rory! What are you doing here? Did I miss our date?" She stood and glanced at her watch. "Wait a minute. It's not six yet."

"I know. I just thought I should escort you to the restaurant." He flashed a smile. "Is that all right with you?"

"All right? Of course." Walking toward him, she swept her gaze downward at her maroon business suit. "But I'm still in my work clothes, as you can see."

"You look wonderful. In fact, these match your suit exactly." Taking his hands from behind his back, he presented her with the roses. From the corner of his eye, he noticed an approving look from the receptionist.

Sharon gasped. "They're beautiful!"

"Maybe we should take one and make a corsage for you since they're so close in color."

"And cut one of these stems? I wouldn't think of such a thing." Sharon turned to the receptionist. "If anyone calls, tell them I'll be in tomorrow."

"Sure will. Let me take those. I have a vase somewhere around here. They'll be waiting for you on your desk tomorrow."

"I hate to give them up," Sharon admitted, "but that's probably a good idea." She relinquished the blooms. "Thanks."

The brunette beamed at Rory. "I don't know what you've done to our workaholic, but I like it."

As Rory and Sharon exited the House Office Building, any residual anger he harbored melted away. All he wanted was to be with her. And from the look in her green eyes, she seemed to feel the same.

"I'm glad you let me know you're in town," she said. "After

you seemed so mad at the airport that time, I wasn't sure I'd ever see you again."

"Neither was I, if you want to know the truth."

A distressed look crossed her face, emphasized by the shadows cast by the street lights.

"The Lord and I had a talk, and He set me straight."

"He did some work on me too." She bowed her head, staring at the concrete just in front of her moving feet.

"Sharon, I need to apologize. For awhile there, I was almost convinced that I should give up our friendship."

"Why?"

"First, because I wrongly thought that you were a bad person for doubting me, and then because I started believing that I'm not good enough for you." It was his turn to bow his head. "Which is true."

"Oh, stop." She tapped him on the shoulder. "So is that what this is all about? You wanted to ask me to forgive you?"

They stopped at an intersection, waiting for the light to change from a flashing red hand to a clear hand, signaling they could cross in safety. "Yes, but I also wanted to let you know I no longer have the weight of the mess at work on my shoulders."

"That's great! What happened?"

"A whistle-blower came forward and spilled the whole story. She made it clear I had nothing to do with either the fire or the accounting improprieties."

Placing her hand on her chest, Sharon breathed an exaggerated but sincere sigh. "So now you can go back to work as though nothing happened." When he didn't answer right away, she asked, "Right?"

"Woodie asked me to stay, but I don't know. Gossip has already played its dirty little tricks. You know what it's like in a small town. And the perpetrators have a lot of powerful friends. I'm afraid my reputation might be marred forever, even though I'm innocent."

Sharon stopped dead. Ignoring passersby who cast curious looks their way, she spun to one side and grabbed him by the biceps. He could feel her grip through his coat, suit, and shirt. "You can't let gossips win, Rory. You have to go back and face them. If you let your life be ruined by slander, you won't be able to live with yourself. Ever."

The strength behind her words gave him courage. "I know you're right. But this isn't easy."

"Who ever said anything would be easy?"

———— • ————

Three hours later, Sharon and Rory were once again at Reagan National Airport. Only this time, Rory was headed for Kansas, and Sharon was just a cab ride away from her apartment. Realizing it was almost time for Rory to board his plane, they stood facing each other.

"I don't know whether my seeing you off is such a good idea," Sharon said. We don't seem to mix well at airports."

"I agree we should spend much less time in airports. Wonder how that can be arranged?" His voice was deliberately coy.

"Not easily, with our jobs located so far from each other." To Rory's dismay, Sharon's voice carried no clue of teasing.

"I know your career means a lot to you." He took her hands in his. "I want you to be happy. And if that means I can't love you—"

"Flight 765 for Kansas City, with continuing service to Topeka, now boarding rows four through nine," a voice announced over the public address system.

Sharon looked in the direction of the closest speaker. As

the announcement concluded, she turned her face back to his and shook her head. "That's you, isn't it? Isn't your seat 6D?" Her features were emotionless.

He nodded. "Did you hear anything I said?"

Keeping one eye on the waiting plane, she answered, "Something about my career."

"I said, I know you don't realize this, but I have always loved—"

"Flight 765, now boarding. Last call for Flight 765 for Kansas City and Topeka, rows four through nine."

Rory looked at the speaker. "Oh, shut up!"

The flight attendant who had been making the announcement shot him a dirty look. Rory hadn't intended for her to overhear him. He averted his eyes.

Sharon giggled. "You'd better get going before she decides to bump you from the flight."

"Worse things could happen." He spoke the truth. He wished he could remain forever with Sharon, the only woman he'd known who was as principled as she was beautiful.

Taking her by the shoulders, he pulled her closer and pressed his mouth gently against hers. His body flooded with a mix of pleasure and fear. He knew he should have warned Sharon before following his impulse. Not waiting for her to respond to his kiss, he pulled away. He glimpsed her face long enough to see her green eyes had widened, making them appear larger than ever. Pink lips were parted in apparent amazement. Without another word, he hurried to board the plane.

Sharon felt a skip in her step as she headed into the office the next morning. Rory's kiss had been a surprise, one she found herself wishing would happen again. His face, with its clean-cut features, popped into her mind more than ever. During her devotional time, for once her prayers focused on her relationship with a man, rather than her career. She could imagine seeing him, walking by his side for the rest of her life.

Lord, is this relationship what You want? Was Rory right? Are You really telling me it's time to go home?

She swept through the doorway prepared to tackle a stack of letters and to meet with a lobbyist at ten. Instead, she was greeted by an artfully hand-drawn banner: WE WON! CONGRATULATIONS, SHARON!

She stopped. "What do you mean, we won?"

Her office mates' expressions ranged from amusement to outright shock.

"Didn't you hear, Sharon?" Olivia asked. "There was a late-night vote. The tax bill finally went through. And the president has promised he'll sign it."

Olivia's words were greeted with a round of applause. Sharon had been working with the congressman on the bill for more than a year. Finally, in large part because of her efforts, working families would enjoy a well-deserved tax break without destroying the safety net for the poor.

Rounds of congratulatory hugs followed, then everyone dug into a plate of blueberry and chocolate chip muffins, along with cinnamon rolls and cherry tarts. A pitcher of orange juice and a pot of Sharon's favorite coffee, Swiss chocolate almond, were quickly consumed.

"You've made a world of difference, Sharon," David, another staffer, assured her. "The people of this country will be able to thank you every year at tax time when they can keep more of their money to save or spend as they see fit."

After Sharon muttered a polite response, her thoughts

turned inward. She had helped to make a difference in the lives of all Americans. On a personal level, she had made a difference in the life of a man she only knew as George, a man who spent much of his life living on a city grate. She had made a difference in the life of a widow in the Ozarks when she brought her the life-saving gospel. She had been where she was meant to be. She was sure of that now.

Suddenly, her reflections centered on Rory. He had said she could make a difference in Kansas. His kiss seemed to confirm his feelings. But did God want her in Kansas? She prayed she would soon find out.

———◆———

As pleased as Sharon was by the turn of events at work, she found herself constantly thinking and praying about Rory. If she had followed her own desires, she would have contacted him. When the urge became especially strong, her fingers seemed to lead themselves to the phone, eager to punch in his number. She always stopped midway and hung up. The Lord had told her to wait. Taking action would be disobedient. And so she waited.

Another Saturday arrived. Without worship services at church, volunteer work at the food closet, or chores at the office to keep her occupied, Sharon was itching to do something. Anything. Sitting by the telephone and checking E-mail every hour wasn't good for anybody. She needed to take some sort of action. One that didn't defy the Lord.

How much longer, Lord? Or is Rory's silence Your answer?

Discouraged, she decided to throw on a pair of shorts and a T-shirt. A workout at the gym would be therapeutic for her body. Maybe even for her spirit. Thirty minutes of running on the treadmill and then a few minutes of light weight training were sure to clear her head. She could decide later how to while away the rest of the day.

As soon as she was finished tying her shoes, Sharon heard a knock on the door. She was surprised by the identity of her visitor. The tall and handsome, jean-clad blond was the answer to her prayers.

"Rory!" Her heart seemed to skip a beat.

"Looks like I interrupted a workout."

"I was just about to go to the gym. Glad you caught me now, or else you would have been waiting over an hour." Moving to the side, she tried to act casual. "Have you had breakfast? I can make coffee, and I have a cinnamon raisin bagel left."

He shook his head. "I had pigs in a blanket on the plane. Besides, I didn't fly all this way to eat. I want to talk to you."

Her stomach lurched in anticipation. "You're not in town on business?"

"Not this time. I know I should have called first. But I decided to take a chance you'd be here." He gave her a wry grin. "If you weren't here, I was going to try the office next."

"I won't say I've never spent a Saturday morning at work. But not today." She took a seat on the blue sofa, motioning for him to follow her lead. "The bill I was working on night and day finally passed the House. It came out of conference committee on Thursday. The president is expected to sign it into law."

"That's great." His voice was flat, his handsome features without expression. "That's what you came here to do. To change the world."

"I can't change the world. Only God can do that." Noticing the room was dim, Sharon flicked the switch on the lamp. The soft light made his face look even more appealing. "That's better."

"Yes, it is. I can see you now." Though his eyes were alight, Rory's voice took on a businesslike tone. "Flush from success. You must be thrilled."

She looked down at her hands, now folded in her lap. "Not as thrilled as I thought I'd be. I love the idea of helping people, and my work has resulted in legislation that has tried to do that. But lately I sense I've done my part here. When I pray, the Lord seems to confirm my feelings." She looked up at her visitor. "I hope I'm not misreading Him."

For the first time since he'd arrived, Rory's face took on an expression of hope. "I don't think you are." He took her hands in his. Deep blue eyes stared into hers. "I guess you wondered why it took me so long to contact you."

"I thought maybe you'd had a sudden attack of shyness," she said only half-jokingly.

He rolled his eyes and his mouth twisted. "Embarrassment is more like it. I'm sorry if you felt I took advantage of you at the airport."

"No. I didn't feel that way. Far from it." She didn't dare tell him how her mind had lingered over his kiss, replaying it over and over. "But," she said, "I appreciate you considering my feelings enough to apologize. Although I hope you didn't fly out all this way just to tell me that."

"Maybe I should have, but I didn't. What I have to say is more important. Sharon, I've been praying to the Lord about you too. I want you to be happy. That's why I never tried to contact you after I left Washington all those years ago. Believe me, it took all my willpower not to reach for the phone. You have no idea how happy I was when my thirtieth birthday arrived. Our appointment gave me an excuse to see you. To see if you remembered."

"Of course I remembered. I never forgot."

"But obedience to the Lord comes first. And if you believe He wants you to stay here, I'll leave you alone again. Even if that means I have to live without you forever."

Sharon felt her heart's rapid beating. "What are you saying, Rory?"

"I'm saying you can make a difference no matter where you are, as long as you're where God wants you to be."

"I think so too."

"So you've been praying about this?"

She nodded.

"So have I," he confessed. "What do you think the Lord is telling you? Do you think this is where God wants you to be?"

"I used to think so. But lately I've thought about moving back home to Nebraska and starting over. With my experience, I can get a job in state government." She shook her head. "But every time I consider the idea, I feel it's just plain wrong."

He hesitated. "I–I, don't suppose you've considered Kansas?"

His implication was clear. Sharon's stomach seemed to leap to her throat with anticipation. "What is there for me in Kansas?"

"A chance to make a difference in my life. By being my wife."

Rory had said the words. The words that she knew were God's answer. Unable to contain her joy, she threw her arms around his neck. "Oh, Rory, I know now this is what the Lord wants for us. And to be your wife is what I want too. More than anything else in the world."

This time, his kiss came as no surprise.

TAMELA HANCOCK MURRAY

Like her character, Sharon Delacourt, Tamela was a Congressional intern during her college years. She has authored several successful Christian books, both fiction and nonfiction, for children as well as adults. *Picture of Love,* her debut contemporary, was released in 1997. *Destinations,* set in Regency England, was released in 2000. Tamela's novella, "A Man of Distinction," appeared in Barbour's *Rescue* anthology.

Tamela has also written Bible trivia books for Barbour. *FUN! Bible Trivia Volumes I and II,* and *Great Bible Trivia* are for children. Adults can test their knowledge with *What Do You Know?* or *Bible Survival.*

In addition to her books, Tamela has written for magazines such as *The Clergy Journal, Pockets, Decision, DevoZine, Virginia Country,* the electronic magazine *Folksonline,* and newspapers such as *The Washington Times.*

Tamela graduated from Lynchburg College in Virginia with honors in Journalism. When she's not writing, Tamela takes an active role in church and her daughters' school. Tamela and her husband, John, enjoy attending Bible studies together. They also teach Sunday school as a team. Tamela's hobbies are reading, music, and embroidery.

BENEATH HEAVEN'S CURTAIN

Christine Lynxwiler

To my wonderful husband, Kevin,
whose loving patience and constant encouragement
made it possible for this story to be written.

I owe a huge debt of gratitude to
Tracey V. Bateman and Tamela Hancock Murray
for help above and beyond the call of duty
and to my other crit buddies, as well.
Thanks to my family and friends,
whose support has been phenomenal.
A special thanks to Sherry G. of the
Atlanta Humane Society for her helpful information
about the No Ball at All.

It is he that sitteth upon the circle of the earth,
and the inhabitants thereof are as grasshoppers;
that stretcheth out the heavens as a curtain,
and spreadeth them out as a tent to dwell in:
That bringeth the princes to nothing;
he maketh the judges of the earth as vanity.
ISAIAH 40:22-23

Chapter 1

Danielle Delacourt ventured one more peek at the shimmering Atlanta skyline. Putting her hand to her stomach, she turned her back to the glass wall of the elevator and met the amused green eyes of her fellow passenger.

The well-dressed man scanned her face and raised one eyebrow. "You do know there's an elevator inside the building, don't you?"

Glancing behind her again at the breathtaking view, Danielle nodded. "Yes. But I'm new in town, so I thought I ought to try this way at least once."

"Riding to the top of Plaza Towers will probably be one of the least painful experiences you have here."

The unexpected roughness of his tone sent fingers of apprehension up Danielle's spine. Surely a glass elevator, here in the better part of the city in broad daylight, would be safe. She reevaluated the clean-shaven man in the expensive suit and paisley tie. With blond hair cropped short, ending far above the collar of his starched sea-foam green shirt, he epitomized the up-and-coming young executive.

Still, her mom had taught her not to talk to strangers. Clamping her lips together, Danielle stared at the oak-paneled doors.

The elevator stopped, and when the doors slid open, she

exited quickly, not looking back at the man. She spotted a sign indicating the ladies' restroom and hurried down a carpeted hallway. After applying a light coat of lipstick, she ran a brush through her unruly curls.

She left the safe haven of the restroom with a prayer on her lips and retraced her steps past the elevator until she found the right door. She pushed it open and approached the receptionist.

"Hello. I'm Danielle Delacourt, here to see Mr. Lancaster."

"Hmm. . ." The woman, impeccably groomed, with neatly trimmed gray hair and wearing a tailored suit, scanned the appointment book on the desk in front of her. A long pale fingernail followed the names written there. Looking back up, her eyes scrutinized Danielle as if trying to see through her. "I don't see your name, Ms. Delacourt. Are you sure your appointment was today?"

"Actually, I don't have an appointment." She felt heat creep up her face. "I need to talk to him about an important business matter regarding his nursing homes."

The woman's eyes grew frosty as she tapped the sign on her desk. NO SOLICITING.

Danielle shook her head. "Oh, no, Ma'am. I'm not a sales rep. I'm an employee of Lancaster Manor."

The woman considered her for a moment as Danielle stood, unmoving. Abruptly, the receptionist stood and indicated a small but well-decorated waiting area. "Have a seat here, and I'll check and see if he's in."

Danielle shrugged out of her tweed coat and sank into the plush maroon chair as the receptionist disappeared down a long hallway. Five minutes later, she returned, motioning for Danielle to follow her. When they reached a massive oak door, the gray-haired woman turned and hurried back to her workstation.

Danielle aimed another silent plea heavenward and stepped into the room.

Her heels clicked on the hardwood floors as she approached the huge mahogany desk. Bright sunshine glared through floor-to-ceiling windows, reducing the figure behind the desk to a silhouette. When her eyes adjusted enough to focus, she recognized the enigmatic man from the elevator.

Struggling to contain her surprise, she thrust out her hand. "Hi, Mr. Lancaster. I'm Danielle Delacourt, the physical therapist at Lancaster Manor—the West Paces Ferry Branch."

He stood and shook her hand, then indicated the chair across from him. When she was seated, he sat back down and said nothing.

In the uncomfortable silence, Danielle resisted the urge to fidget. "I needed to talk to you," she offered finally.

"Oh, you did, did you?" He raised his brow in a gesture she was becoming familiar with. "Enough to brave your fear of heights to do it, huh?"

"Actually, I enjoyed the ride."

"Could've fooled me." He grinned and sat back in his chair, fingertips steepling together on the desk in front of him. "You said you were new in town. Where are you from?" He grinned and sat back in his chair, fingertips steepling together on the desk in front of him.

"Nebraska."

"I guess y'all don't have many glass elevators in Nebraska, huh?" His smile grew broader.

"No, Sir. Well, maybe in Omaha or a bigger city, but not in Titusville." Small talk was supposed to help her relax, she was sure, but her nerves grew more taut each moment she delayed the inevitable confrontation. For all the pleasantries, he wouldn't like the reason she'd come to see him.

"No wonder you were scared."

"I wasn't scared." Her pride insisted she protest, even if he was the boss. "We have water towers. Great big shiny silver spiders perched on mile-long legs. I climbed one once." A smile sprang unbidden to her lips as she remembered Denise's dare and her subsequent rescue. "Well, I climbed halfway up anyway, then my little sister had to rescue me."

"Why do I get the feeling that your impetuousness has put you in many situations where you needed rescuing?" he asked, wry amusement evident in his voice.

The phone on his desk buzzed. He held up a finger to excuse himself and picked up the black receiver. "Yes?" A frown crossed his brow. "Put her through."

"Alexis, it's nice to hear from you." He swivelled his chair toward the windows and lowered his voice. Danielle considered stepping out of the room until he finished his obviously private conversation. Before she could rise, he spun back around. "All right, then, have a good trip. Bye." He hung up the phone and flashed Danielle a grin.

She sat up straight and tall and cleared her throat. "Mr. Lancaster, as I mentioned, I recently began to work in a nursing home you own." She couldn't believe how quickly her anger had drained in the face of his friendly banter and disarming smile. A shrewd businessman like Nicholas Lancaster knew instinctively how to diffuse a disgruntled employee.

"I thought you might like to know. . .the residents there are suffering because of a shortage of staff." She clasped her hands together in her lap. "They deserve better care, and it's up to you to see that they get it."

He had moved little as she spoke, and his grin remained

fixed, but his eyes regarded her coldly. "What happened?" he asked, sarcasm edging his voice. "Did the volunteer in charge of Bingo call in sick and leave the residents in an uproar?"

Temper flaring, Danielle shot to her feet. She placed her palms on the desk and leaned closer, meeting his surprised gaze head on. "This is not a matter to be taken lightly, Mr. Lancaster. Numerous things have happened. If you want to know what was the straw that broke the camel's back, I'll tell you."

She fought to keep the tears at bay. Crying when she was angry had always been her downfall. The waterworks made her seem weak and childish, but the tears always came when her temper flared. "A resident lay in a wet bed for at least an hour today, maybe longer. If I hadn't happened by, there's no telling how long she might have remained there, suffering."

Taking a deep breath, she forced her words to come out in a soft, even tone. "It wasn't because she couldn't get to the button. She pushed it. When I spoke to the nursing assistant on duty, she told me she knew about the problem, but there had been a life-threatening situation. There weren't enough hands to help, so Mrs. Wheeler had to wait. I don't know about you, but to me that's a little more serious than a missed Bingo game."

"Are you done?"

"Yes."

"Good." He rose, shuffling papers on his desk as he stood, as if he was already moving on to more important matters. Turning his attention from the papers back to her, he pinned her with another piercing gaze. "I'll tell you what, Ms. Delacourt. You do your job, and I'll do mine."

"I am doing mine. Why don't you do yours and take care of the precious elderly people you're responsible for?" Blinking against the hated tears, she spun and walked to the door, but as she touched the smooth, cool doorknob, his deep voice stopped her.

"Oh, one more thing. . ."

Not sure she wanted to hear his "one more thing," she whirled around to face him with a clenched jaw.

"The nursing assistant could have been telling the truth about a life-threatening crisis that kept her from responding to the woman you spoke of," he said, his tone as smooth as honey, "or then again, she could have been doing her nails instead of her job. You're not in small town USA anymore, where everyone tells the truth. This is the big city. Here, people say whatever's necessary to protect themselves and their jobs." His green eyes burned into hers with an intensity that left her breathless. "Think about that the next time you're ready to fling accusations."

Abruptly he turned to face the window, effectively dismissing her.

Danielle stood rooted to the spot and stared at the back of the most infuriating man she'd ever met. When he made no movement and uttered no sound, she turned toward the door, but anger at his dismissive attitude propelled her around again. She stomped back over to the desk and spoke to his back. "Mr. Lancaster, I don't really care how dishonest you think people from the big city are. But since I'm an uncorrupted small-town girl, believe me when I say, I've seen first hand how dedicated your pitifully underpaid and overworked staff is."

She drew in a small shuddering breath of courage. "Few even take the time for breaks, and lunch is eaten between duty calls. I seriously doubt any of them worry about doing their nails while the patients lie in cold, wet beds."

Throughout her tirade, he hadn't moved a muscle, but at this last assurance, he turned slowly around. She bore the brunt of his glare and recognized the look's meaning, loud and clear. "You'd better stop right now if you value your job," it screamed. But her righteous anger hadn't abated.

Matching him scowl for scowl, she took another deep breath and blurted out the crux of the matter. "If you had ever taken the time to leave your precious leather chair and actually drive down there, you'd have seen this for yourself."

A muscle twitched in his jaw, and she had the distinct feeling he was fighting not to throw her bodily from his office. "Tell me, Miss. . .Delacourt, was it?"

"Yes."

"Do you like your job?"

Danielle nodded, her stomach churning at the unemployment she could see coming. "I love my job." Rather than wait for the inevitable, she forged ahead. "Enough to want the nursing home to stay open so I can keep it."

His brow shot up, his eyes hard and challenging. "Are you threatening me?"

Aghast that he would construe her warning as a threat, she shook her head vehemently. "Of course not. I'm just asking you to consider how you'd feel if your parents were in a care facility that was understaffed to the point of being neglectful."

"Come now, aren't you being just a little overdramatic?"

Danielle raised an eyebrow of her own and met his cold eyes head-on. "Would I have braved that elevator, not to mention downtown traffic, to discuss this with you if I was just being overdramatic?"

"Oh, I don't know." His stiff stance belied his slow lazy drawl. "Small-town girl wants to make a splash in the big city?"

"Spare me, please. I don't care about making a splash. All I care about is giving those residents the attention they have every right to expect. People are complaining. I just thought you'd like to know." When he didn't respond, she added, "And I had hoped maybe you were decent enough to actually care." Leaving him to ponder her words, she spun quickly on her heel and exited the room before he could complete his attempt to fire her.

Alone in the hallway, she slumped against the wall for a second, exhausted from the fruitless battle of wills. Suddenly his words about small towns being where "everyone told the truth" echoed in her brain. Someone should have reminded Jared of that before he lied to her that last time, she thought with a short laugh. Shaking her head at Mr. Lancaster's faulty reasoning, she nodded to the startled receptionist and followed the signs to the indoor elevator.

———•———

Nicholas pushed aside the unpleasant thoughts swirling through his mind for a moment and squinted down at the tiny figure of the woman below as she approached the busy street. Even though traffic stopped, she leaned her head forward, dark curls bouncing on her shoulders, and looked both ways before stepping onto the white-lined crosswalk.

She definitely hadn't been in the city long. The smell of sunshine seemed to follow her into the room. When he'd looked at her freshly scrubbed face, a line of freckles parading across her pert little nose, he'd been fascinated. He'd thought years of knowing city beauties, perfectly made up and coifed, had calloused him to a woman's natural allure, but when her blue star-burst eyes filled with tears, Nicholas realized he'd been wrong.

He shook his head. Why did people like that come to the city? Why had he? He'd had a heart full of dreams when he'd arrived here eight years ago. Where had they gone?

Chapter 2

D anielle, hurry. Mrs. Martin's afraid you're going to
cause her to miss Andy Griffith." Susie smiled and
rolled her eyes as she sat in her chair behind the nurses'
desk, but Danielle picked up her pace anyway. She knew how
much Mrs. Martin enjoyed her favorite television program.

When she entered the room, she fought to keep from
wrinkling her nose. An unpleasant odor wafted through the
room. A sweeping glance revealed an overflowing trash can in
the corner.

Not wanting to make Mrs. Martin uncomfortable about
something beyond her control, Danielle smiled. "Hey there.
How are you doing today?"

"Pretty good. It's almost time for Andy, though. Think
we'll get done in time?" The old woman's eyes twinkled, and a
smile creased her wrinkled face.

Danielle nodded. "I'll try, Mrs. M., but first I have to get
you in the chair." She reached over and pushed a button.

Susie's hurried voice answered, "Yes?"

"Susie, while I move Mrs. Martin into a chair, can you call
housekeeping to bring a fresh trash bag to her room?"

"Sure. This is your lucky day. We've got a new housekeeping

attendant. I'll call him."

"Great." Danielle took a step toward the bed and cringed as her feet encountered a sticky substance. Pushing the button again, she added, "If you don't mind, have him bring the mop and bucket too."

The elderly woman smiled apologetically. "I spilled my milk last night." She held up her blue-veined hands. "These old things don't work as well as they used to."

"We'll work on your hands today too," Danielle said as she moved the woman to the shiny black chair with practiced ease. "You're really improving, you know. Before long, you'll be back down in the TV room watching Andy with your friends."

"You are praying for me like I asked you to, aren't you, Honey?" The woman clutched Danielle's hand.

"Yes, Ma'am, I sure am. That's why I know you're going to be better soon." Leaving her left hand ensconced in the elderly lady's, Danielle patted the papery skin of the woman's hand with her right.

"Will you pray with me now?"

"Well, actually. . ." Danielle looked over her shoulder toward the door. She knew that the nurses and nurse's assistants weren't allowed to pray or discuss religion with the residents. As a physical therapist, she probably had a little more leeway, but she was sure it would still be frowned upon. Looking back at the woman's earnest face, and trusting eyes, she nodded. "Yes."

Clasping Mrs. Martin's hands with both of hers, she bowed her head and began to pray. "Dear heavenly Father, thank You for giving us another day to live for You. Please, Lord, guide me today and keep my hands sure and strong, and help Mrs. Martin so that her leg will respond well to the therapy. Be with her, Lord, so she won't be lonely, and help her to remember how much You love her. In Jesus' name, Amen." With one last pat, she released the woman's hands.

The clatter of a mop bucket behind her alerted Danielle to the fact that the attendant had entered the room during her prayer. What timing. She'd spent all morning worrying that Nicholas Lancaster had sent word for her to be fired, and now she had been caught doing something questionable.

Not turning to meet the attendant's eyes, she forced her voice to be cheerful but firm. "The trash can needs a new bag, and the floor beside the bed needs mopping. While you're doing that, I'll wash my hands and prepare to start." She glanced at him, but apparently shy, he kept his eyes to the ground and nodded. Staring at the top of his head, she grinned. He didn't seem to be the type who would cause trouble, she thought as she headed to the sink.

When she came back into the fresh-smelling room, Mrs. Martin sat in the shiny black chair, and the timid attendant was gone.

"He certainly left in a hurry, didn't he?" she mused almost to herself.

"Yes, he did. He was very kind, though. . .asked me if I enjoyed you praying with me. I told him I begged you to." The woman's eyes twinkled.

Danielle grinned. "Thanks for trying to keep me out of trouble," she said as she knelt on the floor and began to slowly work Mrs. Martin's leg. Both bones in the older woman's lower leg had been broken in a fall nine weeks earlier. Before the accident, she had been one of Lancaster Manor's most active residents.

She will be again if I have anything to do with it.

Three hours later as she headed toward the time clock and shrugged out of her blue jacket, Danielle realized she'd made it through the day without getting fired in spite of her earlier confrontation with the owner. The hallway was empty except for the new attendant walking ahead of her. Speeding up a little, she moved toward him. She'd like a chance to explain to him about the prayer. When she'd narrowed the distance between them to a mere ten feet, she spoke, "Excuse me. . ."

To her dismay, he cast a startled glance over his shoulder and broke into a rapid walk. Before she could say another word, he turned the corner.

She reached the corner and stared down the empty corridor. Where did he go? How had he just disappeared, and for that matter, why did he want to? He must be shy. Tomorrow, she'd make an effort to reach him.

———•———

Nicholas collapsed on the sofa in his penthouse apartment. He'd forgotten what it felt like to have muscles that ached and feet that hurt. His fatigue at the end of the day was usually a mental one, not this physical exhaustion that permeated his very being.

He'd tried to do the work of three people today, desperately hoping to prove his theory that the problem didn't lie in Samuel not providing enough staff, but in the staff not being willing to work, preferring instead to socialize and loaf.

Regardless of his theory, reality had slapped him in the face at every corner. All the staff pulled their weight and more but still couldn't get the job done.

He slid out full length on the couch, moaning as his aching muscles protested the movement. His mouth stretched into a wide yawn, and he closed his eyes. Danielle's image flickered behind his eyelids just before he succumbed to the cotton haze in his brain.

When he woke, the morning sun was barely peeking between the tall buildings outside his floor-to-ceiling window. He jumped up and winced, pressing one hand to his sore back. After a quick shower, he dressed in one of the white uniforms he'd been given the day before, shrugged on his oldest jacket, and hurried down to his rental car, a beat-up Volkswagen Bug he'd searched the city to find.

He'd called his friend and business manager after Danielle had left his office two days ago. Samuel had basically told him what Nicholas had told Danielle: "You do your job and I'll do mine." Nicholas had hung up the phone and decided to investigate before he antagonized Samuel further.

He'd instructed his closest staff members to clear his calendar for the next thirty days. His assistant had panicked, but Nicholas had convinced him that if they worked together on the phone and through E-mail, they could pull it off short term. A month should be long enough to tell what the real situation was at the facility.

The administrator of the nursing home where Danielle worked, a silver-haired woman with sympathetic eyes, had reluctantly agreed to go along with his plan. He'd had to work hard to convince her he wasn't investigating that nursing home in particular but rather the possible staffing problems in his whole network of facilities. She had looked particularly puzzled when he'd insisted she not tell a soul, not even Samuel, but she had obligingly written his name down as Nick Davis.

Now here he was, about to begin his second day of mopping floors, emptying trash, and doing whatever no one else wanted to do.

He pulled into the employee parking lot and frowned. The night staff should still be here clocking out, along with the day shift clocking in. The half-empty parking area lent credence to Danielle's accusations.

His heart sank. In order to give Samuel a fair assessment, Nicholas had determined to wait the whole month to make a decision as long as he didn't believe patient safety was being jeopardized. But it was looking more and more like Danielle was right.

He pulled his sunglasses from his pocket and put them on just in case he ran into her again. She'd probably been scared to death by his bizarre behavior yesterday afternoon when she'd hailed him in the hallway. If she saw him, more than likely she would be the one to run this time. Why did that thought send a twinge of disappointment through his heart?

When he had walked into a resident's room yesterday and overheard Danielle's heartfelt prayer, he'd been shocked. Didn't she know religion had no place in a facility like this? He remembered when he'd bought his first nursing home, he'd wanted to provide a chaplain or someone to counsel the patients spiritually. Samuel had quickly pointed out that with so many different beliefs, a businessman would be leaving himself liable to all kinds of problems.

Samuel had also insisted on cutting the staff down to the bare minimum the government would allow. Could he have been wrong on both counts? Nicholas recalled the sparkle in Mrs. Martin's eyes when she had told him how much she appreciated Danielle's prayer. It was something to think about.

As he walked down the hallway, he glanced with distaste at the crinkled mauve paint on the wall and the fading gray tiles on the floor. Surely Samuel could squeeze out a little more for the decorating budget.

The perky nurse behind the desk looked up with a smile.

"Nick, glad you're here. There's a spill in the cafeteria. Can you get on that right away?"

"Sure."

"Hey, Nick?"

"Yeah?" He kept his voice casual. Had he blown his cover already? Maybe she'd recognized him from a newspaper article or something.

"The sun's really not very bright in here. I'd lose the shades if I were you."

He nodded, yanked them off, and shoved them in his pocket. As Susie smiled her approval, he hurried to the supply closet, grabbed the cleaning cart, and rolled it toward the cafeteria.

He pushed open the swinging doors and cringed. Danielle Delacourt stood with two other women near a mess on the floor. Ducking his head, he sauntered over to the spill. He placed the cart between himself and the ladies and began to clean up the broken plate and its contents. When he was mopping for the final time, he heard the women's voices move away, accompanied by the clicking of heels. At the swish of the swinging doors opening and closing, he breathed a sigh of relief.

His relief died a quick death when a pair of white shoes and white pants entered his range of vision. A slight lifting of his eyes confirmed his worst fear as he saw the hem of a mid-thigh blue jacket.

"Hi. I'd have cleaned that up. Theresa turned around into Judy and dumped her tray. I told them I'd go get a broom and mop, but they insisted on calling for someone else to do it."

He grunted and kept mopping. Maybe she'd go away.

But no, the woman who had driven to downtown Atlanta and braved her fear of heights to confront him would not be put off that easily.

"Listen. . .about yesterday in Mrs. Martin's room. I'm sure you probably realize it's a little unorthodox for the staff to pray with the patients, but she specifically asked me to. . ."

She had edged closer to him, and he could feel her gaze searching his face. Involuntarily, he looked up to meet the scrutiny. He quickly ducked his head again, but not before he saw her bright blue eyes widen.

"What are you doing here?" she hissed.

Chapter 3

Danielle couldn't believe her eyes. Urbane Nicholas Lancaster mopping the floor? Glancing at his tag, she read *Nick Davis*. "Nick?"

"Shh. Come with me. We can't discuss this here."

She allowed him to guide her out of the cafeteria and down the hallway. Neither spoke until Nicholas unlocked a door with his key, yanked it open, and shoved the cart inside. Danielle stood silently waiting, but when he stepped in and motioned for her to follow, she balked. "Excuse me? You don't seriously think I'm going in there?"

"Hurry." His commanding tone hadn't changed a bit from the boardroom to the janitorial closet. "You're going to blow the whole thing." He grabbed her hand and pulled her inside, shutting the door behind her before she could protest further.

With her hands on her hips, she demanded, "What's going on?"

"I decided to check out what you said in the office. This seemed like the most logical way."

"Oh, other than believing me, you mean?" She stared at the green eyes boring into her as a faint bleach smell tickled her nose.

"Miss Delacourt—"

"Don't you think our surroundings warrant you calling me Danielle?"

"Only if you'll call me Nick."

"Okay, Nick, so why are you still here? Surely you've seen enough."

Regret flashed across his face, and the look in his eyes was pensive. "Nothing's ever as simple as it seems."

"What do you mean?"

"Look, we can't discuss it here either. Are you busy tonight?"

"Yes."

"Yes?" His mouth turned down in grim frustration. "This is really important. Is it something you can't change?"

Her shoulders stiffened at his casual dismissal of her plans. "Yes, it is. Kristin, my roommate, wants to show me the 'coolest place to eat.' It's called the Varsity."

"The Varsity," Nick repeated, wonder in his voice. "I haven't eaten there in years. Mind if I tag along? We really need to talk."

"Yes, I mean no," she stammered. The butterflies in her stomach began to flutter in earnest. She looked over at an old-fashioned radio sitting next to a stack of paper towels on the shelf—anything to avoid his gorgeous emerald eyes. "Is there more to tell?"

"Definitely. It's important to me that you understand why I'm here." His whispered voice sent chills down her spine. "Besides, I want to hear more about your impressions of the staffing situation. I'll pick you both up at seven if that's okay."

She considered arguing, but the thought of getting to know him better, coupled with her desire to help the nursing home residents, made her reconsider. "Okay," she said and rattled off directions to the house she shared with her old college roommate.

"Danielle?" He caught her gaze, and she was reminded of how she had felt as a child in her uncle's welding shop when the beautiful sparks were flying—aware of the danger, but unable to look away.

"Yes?" The husky note in her voice dismayed her, and she cleared her throat. "What is it?"

"I owe you an apology for how I acted when you were in the office. I was upset by your accusations, and I'm afraid I took it out on you. I'm sorry."

"That's okay, Mr. Lancaster." As he shook his head with a smile, she corrected herself, "Nick. I understand, really."

She grabbed the smooth knob behind her back and twisted it, stepping out into the brightly lit hallway. Not waiting to see whether he followed, she turned and hurried to her office.

Danielle stood up from her position at Mrs. Martin's feet. "You're definitely doing better, Mrs. M."

The elderly woman beamed. "Thank you, Danielle. That nice attendant was here earlier, and he said the same thing. You know, the new one. . . Nick?"

Danielle nodded, her heart in her throat as she thought of that nice attendant.

"I asked him to pray with me, and he did, but it was really short. I think he's a little rusty." The woman's wise eyes met Danielle's. "He could use some encouragement. It'd probably be better coming from a pretty young woman like you rather than a crusty old thing like me."

Forcing a light tone, Danielle laughed. "Now, you know better than that. Who was elected Miss Lancaster Manor last year? Not me."

The woman twittered, and her face blushed a becoming pink. "And I'm starting to believe you really will have me on my feet again in time for me to crown my successor. You're a wonder, Danielle."

"So are you, Mrs. M., but right now I've got to go down and check on Mr. Johnson's shoulder."

"That old codger? There isn't anything wrong with his shoulder that laying off the horseshoes wouldn't fix." Her eyes softened when she spoke of the widower, belying her harsh words. "But since you have to have a job, you fix him up good, okay?"

"Yes, Ma'am, I'll do what I can with God's help." She waved good-bye and let herself into the hallway. Was Mrs. Martin trying to fix her up with Nick? She chuckled at the elderly woman's machinations until she remembered her plans for the evening. A shiver of anticipation ran down her spine. Even though Kristin would be with them, Danielle knew this was no laughing matter.

Flustered by the insistent ringing of the telephone, Danielle fumbled with the lock on the front door of the small house she shared with Kristin. Despite the fact that the other girl's car was in the driveway, the phone continued to ring. As Danielle crossed the living room to retrieve the jangling instrument, a glimpse in her friend's bedroom revealed Kristin sitting cross-legged on the bed, headphones nestled in her bright red curls.

She was deeply engrossed in a thick textbook. The bass beat emanating from the tiny foam-covered speakers caused Danielle to shake her head. Danielle liked to listen to music; Kristin insisted on experiencing it. Running the last few steps, she grabbed the phone and offered a breathless "Hello."

Her older sister's familiar voice filled the phone with excitement. "You'll never guess what, Danielle." Sharon paused only a second. Apparently unable to contain herself, she burst out with her news. "Rory and I are engaged."

"You're kidding! I knew you were seeing each other, but I had no idea it was that serious." Danielle's mind swirled. "Besides, I thought he lived in Kansas. Is he moving to D.C.?"

"No. I'm moving there."

Danielle's mouth dropped open in shock. She couldn't imagine her big sister giving up the political career she had spent so many years building. "Rory must be special."

"Believe me, he is."

"Sounds like you know what you're doing." Danielle grinned at her own words. If anyone knew what she was doing, it was Sharon. Now if only Sharon's little sister could be so wise. "I'm happy for you, Shar."

"I knew you would be. But I have another reason for calling." Sharon's voice grew softer. "I want you to be my maid of honor."

"Me?" Danielle fought back sudden tears, honored that her sister had remembered their childhood promise. "Oh, I'd love to!"

"Wonderful! I've got everything all planned. The wedding will be this Christmas Eve. You'll wear dark green velvet with a white sash and carry a bouquet of red-and-white roses. Denise and Sabrina will wear red sashes and carry red roses. My bouquet will be all white roses."

"Sounds beautiful."

"It will be. Listen, I hate to run, but Denise and Sabrina will kill me if I don't let them know ASAP. I've already told Mom and Dad. Look, send me an E-mail so I can catch up with you, okay?"

"Sure, Sis. Love you."

"You too."

Danielle hung up the phone, imagining her beautiful sister walking down the aisle to meet the man of her dreams. "Dum, dum, de dum," she hummed as she walked in to share the news with Kristin. Danielle had dated Jared for years, yet his face had never popped into her mind when she thought of weddings. So why had Nicholas Lancaster dominated her mind's eye view ever since Sharon's announcement?

She knocked on her roommate's open door. At the movement, Kristin looked up and motioned her in. Sliding the headphones off her shoulders and pushing the power button on the CD player, the graduate student grimaced. "Why, you might ask, am I studying frantically when I was supposed to do that after we got back from the Varsity?"

Danielle resisted the urge to laugh at the dramatic girl, but curiosity won. "I'll bite. Why are you studying now?"

A frown hovered around the edges of Kristin's expressive mouth. "Because they called me in to work tonight." She held her heavy textbook up in front of her face and shrunk back from Danielle. "Please don't hit me. Jim was sick, and there was no one else to fill in."

"I'm not going to hit you, Silly." Danielle laughed at Kristin's exaggerated sigh of relief. "But, it's your loss. I had us a date for tonight."

Kristin's eyes grew big as Danielle told her the day's events. "Oh, man, wouldn't you know it?" Offering her roommate a cheeky grin, she commented, "Guess I don't have to ask whether you'll go without me, huh? You'd have to be a goofball to pass up an opportunity like that."

"Well, actually, we're just going to discuss the nursing home situation. I was joking when I called it a date."

Ignoring Kristin's muttered, "Yeah, right," Danielle told her friend Sharon's big news.

"Wow," Kristin said, looking envious. "It must be nice to be that sure of someone."

"That's exactly what I thought." Danielle started toward the door and then turned back. "Don't worry, Snow White, someday our princes will come."

"Ha! Easy for you to say, Sleeping Beauty," Kristin countered with a wry grin, "but if you'll remember, Snow White had to eat a poisoned apple first."

Laughing, Danielle hurried back to her room to get ready.

Thirty minutes later, Kristin stuck her head in Danielle's doorway. "I'm about to go. Have fun tonight."

Danielle looked up from painting her nails. "I will, but it really isn't a date. Like I told you, we're just going to talk business."

"Still, it's good to see you out and about again. After that rat, Jared, and his inane—"

"Kristin, we agreed that if I moved in with you, you wouldn't mention that. Remember, I came to Atlanta to get away from what felt like a whole state full of pity in Nebraska." She grimaced as she remembered how her mom and dad had acted like there had been a death in the family. Sharon had even offered to host her escape from their hometown by letting her move to Washington, D.C., with her, but the sympathy in her voice had prompted Danielle to call Kristin instead. They'd remained close friends, even after Kristin had moved to Atlanta to attend graduate school.

Danielle closed the lid on the bottle of pale pink fingernail polish and placed it on her dresser. Extending her fingers out on each side of her, she faced her red-headed roommate who had a temper to match. "Besides, you know I was lucky to find out about Jared when I did. He and I were together out of habit, and his habit of picking up that girl after our dates was the last straw, but my heart wasn't broken."

"Yeah, I know, but still. . .it's good to see you get out. Especially with one of Atlanta's most eligible bachelors." Kristin crossed the room to the window. "What's that noise?"

Danielle walked over beside her, peered out the window, and smiled. "Looks like my 'most eligible bachelor' is here."

Kristin stared at the dirty white Volkswagen Bug that apparently had no muffler. When a man in jeans and a denim jacket emerged and started up the sidewalk, she turned to Danielle. "That's Nicholas Lancaster?"

"Actually," Danielle replied, laughter bubbling in her throat at her friend's incredulous tone, "I think that's Nick Davis."

Chapter 4

Blowing on her fingernails one more time, Danielle hurried down the hall. When she reached the front door, she glanced over her shoulder to find Kristin right behind her. Glaring at her roommate's huge grin, she whispered, "Let's not overwhelm him, okay?"

Kristin laughed softly. "A little touchy, aren't we, for someone who's just going out with him for the sake of the nursing home?" But she turned and walked toward the kitchen. Pausing at the entryway, she whispered, "Could it be that your prince is already here, and you didn't tell me?"

Danielle shooed her away with her hands. When the bell rang, she took a deep breath and glanced in the foyer mirror. She'd tried on three outfits before settling for blue jeans and her favorite red sweater. Oversized, it came halfway to her knees, but what it lacked in shape it more than made up for in softness. Jared had hated it. She always suspected he disliked that it hid her trim figure.

Shaking off thoughts of the prince-turned-toad, she opened the door. As soon as he saw her, Nick's handsome face broke into a knee-weakening grin. Tempted to slam the door and run back to the safety of her bedroom, Danielle instead countered with what she hoped was a gracious smile of her own. "Come in and let me get my coat. Kristin can't go tonight, after all. She has to work."

He stepped inside. "Oh, that's too bad." He rubbed his hands together. "Whew, it's nice and warm in here. Just when I thought spring was here to stay, we have another cold snap."

"Well, I've already learned what they say about the weather around here. If you don't like it, just stick around until tomorrow, and it'll be different." She gathered her tweed coat from a hook on the wall and almost bumped into him when she turned around.

"Let me help you with that." She allowed his big hands to take the coat from her and stood like a child as he wrapped it around her. "It's a shame to cover that sweater. Red looks great on you."

A nervous tingle buzzed through her mind. He kept saying all the right things. His gentle manner and kind words didn't match the image she had of the hard-nosed businessman, lining his pockets at the expense of the elderly.

She spun around as Kristin cleared her throat and spoke from the doorway. "I'm leaving now."

Danielle bit back a grin at the forced introduction. "Kristin, I'd like you to meet Nicholas Lancaster."

Before Danielle could finish, Kristin strode over to Nick and stuck out her hand. "I'm Kristin Sampson. It's nice to meet you. I've heard a lot about you."

Nick chuckled. "I bet you have. Hopefully, I'll get a chance to change your mind about me. . .or at least your roommate's mind."

His green eyes were teasing as they flickered over Danielle's face, and she felt the heat creep up her cheeks. She turned toward the door, and he followed her lead. "Bye, Kristin. It was nice meeting you too."

"Have a good night at work," Danielle called over her shoulder, ignoring the thumbs-up the redhead flashed her behind Nick's back.

The cold air soothed her hot face, and by the time she climbed into the Volkswagen, Danielle had determined not to let herself be so affected by this man. His interest in her, she was sure, was purely business. She'd do well to keep hers the same.

Nick placed the key in the ignition, but instead of starting the car, he turned toward Danielle. "Let's make a deal." His eyes sought hers and held her gaze.

"What kind of deal?" She tried to keep the wariness from her voice.

"Let's start over. I know this is blunt, but something about you makes me want to tell it like it is."

Her heartbeat accelerated as his voice rang with sincerity.

"Danielle, I feel a connection with you I've never felt with anyone else. Could we explore that and see what happens?"

The hopeful note in his voice touched her. In spite of her misgivings, she answered softly, "I'm not sure what you mean by explore. . ." She took a trembling breath, and with a silent prayer for the right words, placed one hand on the door handle. "But I need to tell you right up front I'm a Christian and, at the risk of sounding corny, I take that very seriously."

She watched in amazement as his face flamed bright red.

"Oh, no." He groaned. "I don't know what you thought I meant, but let me assure you, I didn't." Rolling his eyes in self-disgust, he said, "I know you're a Christian." He laid his head back against his seat and looked up at the ceiling. "Unfortunately, it seems I don't live it enough for you to recognize that I am too."

An awkward silence filled the car, and Nick realized he'd been right about Danielle. She had integrity. She didn't say a word to refute his statement. Any other girl would have stammered and denied not knowing he was a Christian, but Danielle just looked at him as if assessing his sincerity, then slowly relaxed her death grip on the door handle.

He took that as a signal that it was okay for him to start the car. The loud putt-putt of the motor obliterated the silence. He shifted gears as the little vehicle gained speed, being careful not to bump her knee. She'd probably jump from the moving car if he did.

When he saw the famous red-and-white sign, he eased off the interstate and pulled into the Varsity parking lot. He ventured a small grin at Danielle as he killed the motor. Her answering smile gave him enough courage to jump out and open her car door for her. She didn't protest when he attached a proprietary hand to her elbow as they made their way across the brightly-lit parking lot.

Reluctantly, he released her arm to open the door. When they stepped inside, the overpowering smell of French fries coupled with the fact that he had worked through lunch caused his stomach to growl loudly.

Danielle's eyes twinkled, and she pressed a hand to her mouth, obviously smothering a giggle.

"I wouldn't laugh if I were you."

"Oh, you wouldn't? Why not?" she teased.

"Because," he said, then bared his teeth, "I'm the big bad wolf, remember? I might decide to just eat you up."

"Wait a minute. I never said you were the big bad wolf."

"Hmm. Maybe not, but you thought it, didn't you?" He

laughed at the conflicted expression on her face as she struggled for an appropriate answer.

"Well, I might have thought you were the big, misguided wolf," she said with a guilty grin.

They moved near the crowded counter, behind which red-garbed employees buzzed around like a hive of bees. Loud calls of "What'll you have? What'll you have?" drowned out any possible conversation.

He looked over at Danielle to gauge her first impression of this local icon. She stood, mouth open and eyes sparkling, as first one customer then another called out their order. Cries for a naked dog, Mary Brown steaks, and strings filled the air and were rewarded with food at an astonishing speed. When an obvious tourist would ask for a cheeseburger and French fries, the man behind the counter would translate the order.

Taking pity on Danielle, Nick leaned down to speak in her ear. "What do you want to eat?"

"Um, a cheeseburger and a bag of chips would be fine." She shook her head as if in disbelief of the whole bustling scene.

Nick took a deep breath and stepped up to the counter.

"What'll you have? What'll you have?" a clean-cut African-American man bellowed.

"Two glorified steaks and two bags of rags."

When two cheeseburgers and their bags of chips appeared, Nick sighed with relief that his memory had been reliable. His relief was short-lived when the man queried, "Drinks?"

Hoping Danielle was easy to please, he hurriedly answered, "Two Varsity Oranges."

He turned with the food on a tray to see her grinning at him. "What?" he demanded in a mock gruff tone.

"I'm just glad you were here."

Danielle couldn't believe how well she and Nick had gotten along during the meal. They'd talked of everything under the sun but hadn't gotten around to the supposed reason for the dinner. She hated to bring up the nursing home situation, but as Nick pulled the car into her driveway, her conscience wouldn't allow her to remain quiet. Maybe she could ease into it without being obvious. "Caring for the elderly must be very important to you. How did you end up in this business?"

He raised an eyebrow at her stiff-sounding question. She thought he would call her on it, but when he answered, his voice was sincere. "When I first came to the city, I was an administrator for a nursing home in Cobb County. After I'd been there a year, the owner put it up for sale. I pulled some strings and gathered the financial support necessary to buy it. It was my dream."

Danielle looked at his face and could see the excitement he must have felt when he was able to buy that first facility. "And?"

"And my biggest supporter—a man I couldn't have made it without—was Samuel Bryant. He signed for me at the bank and worked for the first year as my business advisor with no pay. Of course, he's well-paid for his services now." Nick sighed. "For the last year, I've realized he's phasing me out of the hands-on business of the nursing homes."

"Why would you let him do that?"

He shrugged. "Gratitude, I suppose."

"So you really didn't know Lancaster Manor was understaffed?"

"No, I really didn't know," he mimicked with a rueful grin. The smile disappeared. "But I've suspected, among other things, that he wasn't conducting business like I would. Your unexpected visit was the clincher."

"So why didn't you just talk to him and tell him to add more staff?"

"I did talk to him, Danielle. He exploded." Pain filled Nick's eyes as he recalled the obviously unpleasant confrontation with his mentor. "After I hung up the phone, I decided to go undercover for a month. I promised myself that unless I saw evidence the residents were in jeopardy, I'd give it the full month before I made my decision."

Samuel Bryant was obviously very important to Nick. Danielle just hoped he didn't regret putting the man's feelings above the residents' safety. "I see."

"I don't know how you could. I'm not even sure I do. But thanks for trying." He leaned over toward her, and the moonlight glinted in his eyes. "I had a great time tonight, Danielle. Thank you for letting me take you."

Danielle ordered her runaway heart to be still. "What do you mean, thank me? Thank you. No tellin' what I might have ended up with to eat if you hadn't been there." She opened her door and gasped as the frigid air sluiced into the little car. Grabbing her belongings, she glanced back at Nick. "I had a great time." She jumped out and wiggled into her coat, then started with surprise when Nick appeared beside her.

"A gentleman always sees a lady to her door," he said and smiled down at her.

He put his arm around her shoulder, and even through the heavy tweed, she could feel the warmth and security in his embrace. Or at least she thought she could.

They walked silently up the porch steps and grinned at each other as the second step squeaked loudly. "Some father from long ago probably put that there on purpose," she said.

Nick chuckled and motioned to the porch swing hanging

in the shadows. "Thankfully there's no overprotective parent waiting there now."

"Know why there's not?"

"Why?"

Danielle pulled the key from her pocket and unlocked the door of the dark house before she answered. "Because I'm old enough to take care of myself." She leaned up and kissed him quickly on the cheek. "Night, Nick. Thanks again," she said as she slipped into the house and closed the door behind her, softly turning the lock.

She peeked out the blinds and watched him stand for a second with his hand on his cheek, then turn and walk slowly down the sidewalk.

At least I hope I'm old enough, she thought, her traitorous heart thudding in her ears.

Chapter 5

N aomi, Honey, please take me home."

Danielle stood by the elderly gentleman's bed, choking back tears of compassion. She patted his leathery hand, wondering what he might have been like as a young husband and father.

Suddenly, he grabbed her wrist with a strength belied by his frail appearance. "Please, Naomi. . ."

"Naomi's not here." She spoke, her calm tone at odds with her pounding heart. "Remember, Mr. Spinelli, I'm Danielle, your physical therapist."

His cloudy blue eyes cleared, and he stared as though seeing her for the first time.

Danielle smiled. "It'll be lunchtime, soon. Are you hungry?" She despised the false cheerfulness in her voice but knew he needed to get his mind off his late wife and a home that no longer existed.

He dropped his lids closed and heaved a sigh. "No, not hungry. . .just tired."

She stayed beside the bed until she felt his grip relax and heard light snoring, then gingerly slid her hand from his. Mr. Spinelli's erratic behavior had worried her during their early morning session, so she'd popped in to check on him during her break.

She'd mentioned his confusion to a nurse, but the busy woman had just muttered, "Alzheimer's," before rushing on to answer a patient's call.

Danielle's training had taught her not to become too emotionally involved with the patients. Brushing away a tear as she exited Mr. Spinelli's room, she realized she should have listened better.

With a quick glance at her watch, she headed to the cafeteria. If she hurried, there would be just enough time to guzzle a cup of coffee before her break ended. The sight of the handsome blond man sitting at a corner table caused her to consider giving up caffeine and going back to work immediately. That would probably be safer all around.

She tried to ignore the way his eyes lit up when he saw her, but when he waved her over, she took her cup of coffee to his table and sat down.

His gaze traveled tenderly over her face. "Danielle, what's wrong?"

Biting her lip, she shook her head. "Nothing, really." She mustered up a big smile. "Why do you ask?"

Nick leaned forward and lowered his voice. "Well, my sister used to call it 'sad movie syndrome,' but when I was about twelve, I dubbed it 'raccoon eyes' just to irritate her."

Danielle grinned at the impish glitter in his green eyes. It was so much easier to imagine Nick Davis as a mischievous boy than it was the cold businessman, Nicholas Lancaster. "Ahh. . .my runny mascara gave me away."

"Yep. So 'fess up."

"I had an unsettling encounter with a patient. He thought

I was his wife."

"His wife must be beautiful."

Flustered by his admiring words, Danielle joked, "Yeah, either that or she has 'raccoon eyes.' " She took a sip of her coffee, and her smile faded as she remembered Mr. Spinelli's desperation. "Actually, she's dead. He has Alzheimer's."

"I'm sorry."

"It's okay. This sort of thing comes with the job."

"Your compassion makes you a wonderful physical therapist, Danielle." His husky voice did little to relieve her warm face.

"Thanks, Nick. Speaking of my job, I'd better fix my face and get back to work if I want to remain employed." She stood and pushed her chair up to the table.

"I don't think you're in any danger of losing your job. I'm pretty sure your boss thinks you're great."

She leaned down and dropped her voice to a mock whisper. "You'd better hush if you don't want to blow your cover," she said, then turned and hurried out the door.

Nick tied a knot in the corner of the industrial-strength trash bag and carefully fitted it over the lip of the black garbage can. He'd become quite proficient at garbage duty. He straightened and automatically put a hand to his aching back. When this was over, his chiropractor would never understand how Nicholas Lancaster had gotten into such bad shape.

He'd spent the weekend sleeping and trying to recover. Now halfway through a new week, he found himself longing for another two-day break. Actually, he hadn't slept every minute during his time off. Part of the time, he'd been fighting the impulse to call Danielle. Every nuance of their conversations told him he'd scare her if he didn't take it slow, but his heart wanted to rush in.

Deftly sliding the clean trash can back in its place, he decided he'd been patient long enough. He'd thought they'd get to know each other naturally working in the same facility. But he had only caught glimpses of the back of her blue jacket since their conversation in the cafeteria a few days ago. She was definitely avoiding him.

He checked his watch. Break time. Time to find the missing physical therapist. After checking the usual places, he followed a hunch and pushed open the door leading to a tiny enclosed garden, rarely used until summer. There she sat, cradling a cup of steaming coffee in her hands.

He cleared his throat so his presence wouldn't startle her and cause her to slosh the hot liquid.

She turned with a smile. "You finally caught me, didn't you?"

"You forgot to tell me we were playing hide-and-seek. That hardly seems fair." He grinned and slid onto the faded wooden bench beside her.

"You know what they say about fair, don't you?" Her voice was soft and melodious.

"You mean 'all's fair in love and war?' So which is this, Danielle? Love or war?" He watched as lovely color highlighted the freckles on her cheeks.

She opened her mouth, then closed it again, appearing to be suddenly fascinated by the small statue in the corner of the garden.

Nick started to pursue the question, but wisdom overcame impulsiveness and he dropped the subject. "So, do you have a big Easter weekend planned? You going home?"

"No, I haven't been here long enough to warrant a trip back to Nebraska." Danielle's smile grew a little self-conscious.

"I do have plans, though."

Nick realized he should have known. A gorgeous woman, inside and out, she wouldn't be unattached long. His heart sank at the thought. Striving for a light tone, he asked, "Hot date?"

Danielle laughed. "I guess that depends on the temperature. I was hoping for at least warm, but if it keeps this up, it'll be a rather cold date. I'm volunteering for the big egg hunt here Saturday." She nudged him with a playful jab. "How about you? Will you be playing Easter Bunny's helper too?"

"Sure. I'll be here." With an inward groan, Nick realized he really was besotted. He'd seen the posters asking for help but had never considered volunteering. Surely, no one who labored here all week would willingly come on a holiday weekend.

Saturday morning dawned warm and sunny. When Nick approached the group who'd gathered an hour ahead to hide eggs, he had to rethink the conclusion he'd jumped to earlier. Sprinkled amidst the expected grandmotherly volunteers were many faces he recognized from the weekday shift at the nursing home.

He spotted Danielle immediately. She'd traded in her standard blue and white for a bright yellow pantsuit. Her brunette curls were pulled up in a bouncy ponytail, and when she turned to greet Nick, her eyes sparkled even more than usual.

"So, tell me," he grumbled, "do we give y'all a big fat bonus for showing up on your day off?"

Something akin to frustration clouded her beautiful face. She opened her mouth, then shut it again and turned her head back toward the woman who was explaining the rules of egg hiding.

"Well?" He knew she was irritated with him, but he had to ferret out the explanation behind the unexpected appearance of so many employees.

"We do it for a reason you apparently wouldn't understand," she muttered, then moved away from him to gather a basket of colored eggs from the hundred dozen in boxes.

"Try me. Is this the shift supervisor's pet project?"

The cold look she gave him left no doubt he'd offended her. He picked up a basket and quickly began to drop eggs into it before she could fill hers and get away. "Danielle, I don't mean you. I'm sure your presence here is nothing but altruistic, but what about the others? Surely you can't think they're all motivated by goodwill toward men?"

She met his gaze head on, her eyes as cold as a winter frost. "You're going to break those eggs. Some things are more fragile than you realize."

He watched her stride away, then slowly finished filling his basket. When he was done, he ambled over to a small grassy area, dotted with trees. He began to place the eggs in the grass as he'd seen a couple of people in the adjoining area do.

"Hey, Buddy." A bulky, half-bald man sporting a goatee sidled close to Nick and gestured toward the brightly colored eggs laying on top of the green grass.

Recognizing the man as a cafeteria worker, Nick inclined his head. "What can I do for you?"

"I'm not trying to tell you your business, but these kids will find them eggs lickety-split." Nodding at a hand-lettered sign, he explained, "This section's for kids seven through nine." His snaggle-toothed grin was kind. "They need more of a challenge, otherwise it's no fun for them or our folks." He motioned to the long concrete patio where elderly people were already ensconced in lawn chairs and wheelchairs, waiting for the arrival of the children.

"Thanks." Nick offered an embarrassed grin to his egg-hiding mentor. "Guess I just wasn't thinking about ages."

"Aw, that's okay." The large man stuck out his massive hand. "Name's Bob."

"Nice to meet you." Nick returned the firm handshake. "I'm Nick."

"This your first time?" Bob's kind grin set Nick at ease.

"Yeah. Yours?"

"No way. I've been doing this for three years. Ever since I started working here. This time, my wife's gonna bring our boys out to hunt." Bob lowered his voice and leaned toward Nick. "She'd rather go to yard sales, but when I explained to her how much it means to our folks, she gave in."

"You have family here?" Nick asked.

Puzzlement flashed across the man's face, followed swiftly by understanding. "Oh, you mean cause I call them 'our folks?' Nah, that's just how I think of them. You get attached after awhile, you know?"

"Yeah, I guess you do." Nick replied softly as he hid his last egg. He remembered the cynical comments he'd made to Danielle, and the heat that crept up his face had nothing to do with the warm sun.

Chapter 6

Danielle bit back a laugh at the shell-shocked look on Nick's face. Children of all ages swarmed the grounds. But even worse were the parents and grandparents, each determined that their own little Jill or John would get either the most eggs or the prize egg. Nick stayed close to the elderly spectators, and Danielle didn't blame him.

A heavily made-up older woman passed by with her shirttail full of eggs. Beside her a little girl, about seven years old, carried a full basket of eggs and whined, "Hurry, Memaw. You have to find the prize egg."

Stepping forward, Danielle spoke. "Ma'am."

The woman's head whipped around, and her cold eyes dared Danielle to say anything. "Are you talking to me?"

"Yes, Ma'am. I'm sorry, but it's against the rules for grown-ups to hunt the eggs."

Drawing herself up to an intimidating height, the woman towered over Danielle. "My granddaughter isn't old enough to hunt by herself. I'm just helping."

Danielle studied the hard face and prayed for the right words. "I'm sorry. But we announced the rules at the beginning of the hunt. You'll have to put those back." She nodded at the shirttail load.

Just as the woman opened her mouth to argue, Danielle felt the pressure of a hand at her waist.

"Is there a problem here?" The smooth voice left no doubt as to the identity of her rescuer. Neither did the star-struck look on the older woman's face.

"No, not at all," the gray-haired egg thief hastened to say, casting one more hard look at Danielle. "I was just returning these eggs to their hiding places." She surreptitiously stuck two eggs under a clump of grass and shoved two more in the base of the tree behind her. Batting her eyelashes at Nick, she asked, "Wanna help?"

"Sure," he replied, relieving her of half the eggs she held. "Why don't you let your granddaughter go on and hunt while we find a place for these? Time will be up soon."

The older woman practically shoved the little girl away and turned her full attention to Nick. Danielle choked back a giggle at the pained expression on Nick's handsome face. Served him right for his caustic comments earlier. Giving him her most grateful smile, she left them to their egg-hiding and wandered over to check on the residents.

Many were confined to their beds and couldn't come out, but most of the residents were able to enjoy the warm day in wheelchairs, and some were even ambulatory. She nodded to Mrs. Martin, then walked down to where Mr. Johnson and Mr. Spinelli leaned against the wall. "Mr. Johnson, how's your shoulder?"

"Much better." The elderly man flexed his arm and smiled. "Thanks to you."

"Glad I could help." Danielle turned to Mr. Spinelli. "How are you feeling today?"

"Right as rain, young lady. These kids sure are having fun, aren't they?" His grin broadened, but she recognized the confused look that never totally left his eyes. He lowered his voice and leaned toward her. "Which ones are my grandkids?"

"Your grandkids couldn't be here today, Mr. Spinelli. Remember? They live in Florida." He stared at her in disbelief. Pity welled inside her. "Your son did say they might be here this summer, though."

"Oh, yeah." He turned and looked again at the activity on the lawn.

"See you later," Danielle said, spying another resident she wanted to speak to. She took about three steps when Mr. Spinelli's voice stopped her.

"Naomi?"

Danielle turned around. Mr. Spinelli was staring at her as if he'd seen a ghost. Feeling helpless, Danielle walked back over to him.

"Will you dance with me, Naomi?"

Startled by the request, Danielle scrambled to find a good answer. "Remember, Mr. Spinelli, I'm Danielle, your physical therapist." At his crestfallen look, she continued, "I'd be honored to dance with you sometime, though."

He sank down in a chair and stared wistfully out at the scampering children. Danielle stayed near to be sure he wasn't going to say anything else. When he remained silent, she moved on, but her heart ached for the bewildered old man.

"You okay?" Nick appeared from behind her and wrapped an arm loosely around her shoulders.

She leaned gratefully against him. "Yeah, I'm okay. It's just tough sometimes." She blinked back the tears and lowered her voice. "Patients like Mr. Spinelli are the hardest. Sometimes they seem very sensible. . ."

"And then the next thing you know they're calling you by someone else's name, right?" Nick's eyes lit with compassion as he finished her thought.

"Right."

"Come on, Sport. Let's go see who got the prize eggs."

"Well, thanks to you, it won't be a certain grandma."

"That's right, and I hope you appreciate my sacrifice." He shook his head in mock despair, amusement creeping across his features.

Danielle hurried down the corridor, lost in thought. The week and a half since the egg hunt had been wonderful. She and Nick had spent every break together, a scheduling perk she was sure he'd arranged. It had been great. . .until this morning when she'd looked at the calendar and realized that his month-long investigation was three-fourths over. Soon he'd go back to being sophisticated businessman Nicholas Lancaster, and she'd be that broken-hearted little gal from Nebraska.

"Dani?"

Danielle's head spun around at the familiar use of her nickname.

Nick smiled, "Ah, so you do answer to Dani. Somehow I thought you might." Catching up with her, he gave her ponytail a little tug. "It suits you." He matched her stride, frowning when she didn't slow down. "Where are you off to in such a hurry?"

"It's time for Mr. Spinelli's PT appointment." She tossed him a smile but kept walking.

"Oh, well, that explains it. . .Mr. Spinelli. You're getting pretty attached, aren't you?"

She stopped and faced him. "A good therapist cares for her

patients." She tapped her foot. "So what?"

"I don't know. I just wondered something. Seems like you've been avoiding me today." He grinned. "Is Mr. Spinelli my rival now?"

"Jealous?" she shot back.

He shrugged, his grin growing wider. "I might be. What's that guy got that I don't have?"

Her eyes widened at his cheekiness, then quickly narrowed, "A bum arm and a late therapist." Without another word, she hurried down the hallway, leaving Nick staring after her.

"Nick Davis—Mop to room 117." The loud page jarred him from his reverie. He retrieved the mop and bucket from the closet and hurried down to room 117. This job had given him new respect and admiration for people who worked in care facilities. Particularly those in his facilities. Danielle had been right. He'd never find a more dedicated staff.

When he finished the clean-up job, Nick headed to Mr. Spinelli's room. He breathed a prayer of thanksgiving when Danielle slipped out of the room just as he got there.

"Got a minute now?"

She smiled up at him. "Sure. Sorry I was in such a hurry awhile ago."

"That's okay. Was Mr. Spinelli upset that you were a few seconds late?"

Her brows drew together. "Actually, he wasn't in his room when I first got there. I had to go looking for him."

"Playing hooky, huh? He must not like you as much as you think." He grinned.

Capturing her lower lip between her teeth, she drew a deep breath. "I'm not really sure where he was. He wasn't in any of the break areas. But when I checked back in his room, there he was." She rubbed her arms as if chilled, and her blue eyes grew solemn. "He said he'd been dancing with Naomi."

Seeing the worried look in Danielle's eyes made Nick feel like a heel for joking around. He'd grown very attached to the elderly man himself. "Did he seem okay after you started the therapy?"

"Yeah, he didn't mention it again." Shaking her head as if to throw off the troubling thoughts, she shook her finger at Nick and scolded, "And before you say another word, I have not been avoiding you today." Nick marveled again at the warmth in her eyes. As if she realized how she affected him, she broke the connection and focused her attention on some point past his head. "I've been busy."

"The reason I was trying to find you, in case you're wondering. . ." He was rewarded with her gaze turning back to meet his. "I have a charity function Saturday night that I can't miss, and I was hoping you might go with me."

"What charity?"

The question was so unexpected that Nick almost laughed. "The Atlanta Humane Society. Is that acceptable?"

She chewed her bottom lip while she considered his invitation, a habit he found endearing. Amazement filled his mind when he realized how his focus had shifted. This Nebraska girl had turned his world upside down. He dreaded the day it righted and he became hard-nosed businessman Nicholas Lancaster again.

"Okay, I'll go."

He grinned. "That was too easy. I had a speech prepared to convince you of the worthiness of Atlanta's animals."

"Actually, I'm a softy when it comes to animals. My parents have two golden retrievers and an assortment of cats." She smiled. "My little sister, Sabrina, even has a guinea pig."

"How long have you been here?"

"Just a few months."

"Homesick?"

"Sure, I miss it—especially my family—but Atlanta is so. . . invigorating. Don't you think?" Her eyes sought understanding.

"I guess. Sometimes maybe a little too much. They don't call it a rat race for nothing." He chuckled to take the edge off his cynicism. "Oh, yeah, I remember. . . I'm the biggest rat of all, right?"

She put her hands on her hips. "If you don't quit trying to make me feel bad for telling you the truth about your nursing homes. . ."

"You'll what?" He drew himself up with a grin, towering over the petite brunette who had squared off against him.

"I'll sneak up to the microphone Saturday night and announce that you keep goldfish in pop bottles and a Great Dane locked in your closet."

The stubborn look on her face combined with her ridiculous but ready answer caused him to throw back his head and laugh. Suddenly, he looked forward to this year's No Ball At All more than any party he'd ever attended.

Chapter 7

S haron, please, you have to help me!" Danielle looked at the pile of dresses on her rumpled bed and emitted a groan. "He said cocktail dress, but you know I don't drink. I don't have a clue what to wear. And Kristin is even more clueless than I am." She held the phone away from her ear but could still hear her older sister's loud laughter.

Her determination to be good-natured died a quick death when she heard whispers and realized Sharon was passing along news of her sister's social ineptness to her fiancé, Rory.

"Sharon! I'm serious!" She gripped the cordless phone harder. "What does cocktail dress mean?"

"I'm sorry, Honey, it's just not like you to panic so easily. This guy must be really something, huh?" Sharon's voice softened to the soothing tones that had helped her succeed in the political world for so many years.

"Yeah. . .I mean no. . ." She ran one hand through her unruly curls and sank down on the end of the dress-strewn bed, fighting tears. "I don't know what I mean."

"Danielle, please don't cry. I'm really sorry," Sharon said, sincerity and worry clouding her voice.

Danielle shook her head, then laughed through her tears as

she remembered her sister couldn't see her. "I'm okay. Just tell me what to wear."

"You remember that cute little black dress with the jacket you wore to that reception when you were visiting me?"

"Yeah." Danielle jumped up and began rummaging through the pile until she located the dress in question. "Think it'll do?" she asked, praying this was the right choice.

"Definitely, Hon. You'll knock his socks off."

Danielle began to stammer a protest until she heard Sharon laughing again.

"Danielle, I'm just teasing. Lighten up a little."

"Easy for you to say. You go to these fancy parties all the time."

"You'll do fine. Just be yourself."

Danielle glanced at the clock and gasped. "Oops. I have to go, Shar. Time for me to make myself glamorous. . .er. . .I mean, be myself." She giggled. "Thanks for the advice. I'll let you know how it goes."

"You do that. Love you."

"You too." Danielle hung up the phone with a smile and hugged the black dress to herself as she looked at her reflection in the wall mirror. She'd better get busy if she was going to transform from country mouse to city mouse in one short afternoon.

———◆———

Nick maneuvered the black Jaguar through Danielle's neighborhood and pondered his presence there. When he was in college he used to pray God would allow him to find a wife who would share his faith and commitment to his creator. She'd never materialized, and he'd long ago given up on that prayer, preferring to find his feminine companionship in someone who promised no emotional attachment and expected none in return.

Samuel's daughter, Alexis, had filled that bill well. She was as cold as if she'd been carved from a block of ice, but her presence served the purpose of keeping him from attending functions like this alone. He assumed his did the same for her. But that was before Danielle spun into his life like a tornado, destroying his perceptions of women.

Nick spotted Danielle's house and whipped the sports car into the driveway. As he approached the door, he grinned when his foot hit the squeaky second step. He and Danielle had gotten much closer since that first night on the porch, but his heart still hammered against his chest when she was near. Tonight he felt like a teenager on his first date.

He rang the bell, and his mouth went dry when Danielle opened the door. Her shiny brunette hair was done up in a French twist with a mass of bouncy curls cascading down to her delicate neck.

His gaze caressed her glowing face, stopping on her bow-shaped mouth, and then flickering up to meet her confused eyes. Their deep blue background with white star-bursts seemed reminiscent of the fireworks going off in his heart as he stared, speechless, at the stranger in front of him.

"Nick?" Her voice was husky, and she stepped back to allow him to enter.

Shaking himself from his paralysis, he moved into the foyer. "Dani. . .you're beautiful." He knew he sounded like a blithering idiot, but his tongue seemed too thick for his mouth, and his palms were clammy.

He'd been so sure. So sure it was the novelty that had attracted him to Danielle. After all, she was a simple country girl, different from all the other women he knew. For the past few weeks, he'd been telling himself this novelty was the basis of his fascination. He found himself trembling at the ramifications of her effect on him tonight.

"Thanks. . .I think." She hooked her arm in his. "Do you want to sit down?"

"No." He cleared his throat. "No, I'm ready to go if you are." He picked up the small black jacket lying on the back of the sofa and held it out.

When Danielle slipped into it, he caught a faint whiff of something delicious. He leaned his mouth close to her ear and whispered, "Did you intend to knock my socks off, or is this an accident?"

She spun around, and a becoming blush suffused her face. Without answering, she just shook her head and opened the door.

Danielle stared out the window of the Jaguar at the impressive houses that lined the shady lane. The trip had been quiet. She could only suppose that Nick was as shaken as she was by the attraction that had leaped between them like an electric charge.

The street seemed particularly crowded with cars parked all along the curb, so she guessed they were nearing the party. Confirming her suspicions, Nick eased the car in behind a Mercedes and killed the engine. Danielle looked at her black heels and then at the long, uphill driveways of the huge houses. Maybe she should have brought along some tennis shoes.

Nick swiftly made his way around the car and opened Danielle's door, a courtesy she was becoming accustomed to. Accepting his hand, she stepped out into the cool night air.

"So, tell me something," she said.

His green eyes met hers, and he seemed to be mentally girding himself for her question. "What?"

"Am I going to be the only woman there in heels? Does everyone else wear tennis shoes for the hike?" She motioned toward the steep driveways.

He laughed. "Actually, that isn't necessary." He nodded at the headlights coming down the street toward them. "Here's the shuttle now."

A white minivan painted with silhouettes of running dogs and cats pulled up beside them, and Nick and Danielle swiftly boarded. Nick paused to thank the driver, a gray-headed man wearing khaki pants and a golf shirt that proudly proclaimed he was an Atlanta Humane Society volunteer. The man nodded and smiled, then turned his attention to the crackling walkie-talkie. A disembodied voice announced a party of two waiting down the street.

As Nick and Danielle settled into their seats, a chorus of "hellos" greeted Nick, and he returned the salutations warmly. He introduced Danielle to the other two couples, and they looked at her with interest. Nick placed his arm loosely across the back of her seat, and she fought against the fish-out-of-water feeling. She choked back a giggle.

"Something funny?" Nick asked in a low voice, his warm breath tickling her ear.

She smiled at him. "I was just thinking I'm a fish out of water. Then I realized I'd better be careful." She leaned toward him and whispered, "Considering that this is a Humane Society meeting, someone's liable to pick me up and throw me back in."

His answering grin made her feel like things were back on a more even keel, and by the time the shuttle stopped at the top of the driveway, she was much more relaxed.

Her mouth fell open in awe as she absorbed the wonder of the lovely antebellum home. Two large white columns graced the house on either side of long stone steps. Suddenly, she felt like Cinderella making her grand entrance at the ball. Kristin would be surprised that Danielle wasn't Sleeping Beauty anymore.

"It's stunning," she breathed, as they began the ascent to the porch.

"You're stunning," he murmured against her ear, his warm breath sending a shiver up her spine.

"So, tell me, Prince Charming," she said, suddenly feeling daring and carefree, "does the Jag turn into a pumpkin at midnight?"

Nick's eyes widened in surprise, then slowly his gaze sought hers in a way that made her breath catch in her throat. "This is no fairy tale, Dani." His voice was husky. "What's happening between us is real, isn't it?"

There was no time to answer, not that she could have spoken anyway, as they were swept through the double doors and into the most beautiful home she'd ever seen. She had to force herself not to gawk at the ornate crystal chandelier twinkling above the expansive foyer.

When they entered the ballroom, she could almost picture the elaborate parties that must have been held in that very room 150 years before. Long windows lined the opposite wall, covered in Scarlett O'Hara green velvet drapes that brushed the floor in scalloped folds. A sleek, black, baby grand piano sat in one corner of the room, graced with a brass candelabra.

"Pretty, isn't it?" Nick asked, obviously aware of her awe.

"Yes, if you're in the mood for understatement." She grinned up at him.

Nick chuckled. "Know what I love best about these parties?"

There was so much she couldn't even begin to guess. She shook her head.

"The food."

Danielle giggled as he led her to the long, elegantly decorated tables adorned with equally elegant food.

As Danielle filled her plate with many different delicacies, her eyes lit on a glistening black mound. Tossing a mischievous look at Nick, who was sipping his water, she whispered, "Oops, guess they're not as nice to fish as I thought they were." At his puzzled glance, she pointed at the caviar and mouthed, "Fish eggs."

When he choked with laughter, she innocently patted his back. "You okay? Did something go down the wrong way?"

"You're dangerous, did anybody ever tell you that?" he murmured.

"Not since I was about nine and went through that stage of experimenting with Super Glue. I thought my big sister would be glad not to have to keep locking her diary." She smiled innocently. "Oh, it also seemed like it would be better if my mom's knickknacks couldn't get knocked off the shelf."

"Remind me to keep you away from Super Glue."

She nodded, "Yep. It could become a sticky situation."

With a groan, Nick pressed his hand to her waist, "Come on. Let's go mingle."

She sighed. She knew she was nervous when she started being corny. It was like an affliction. Sometimes she couldn't seem to stop.

Nick introduced her around the room, and Danielle's nervousness abated. Tears of laughter filled her eyes when one woman told about the dog who thought he was a cat. One funny animal story begat another, and soon everyone was laughing and chatting like old friends.

"Glad you came?" Nick asked, his arm draped loosely around the back of the sofa behind her. "Yes, but I am disappointed."

"Disappointed? Why?"

Motioning around the room, she replied, "There's no microphone for me so I can tell them about the Great Dane in your closet."

Before he could reply, a honeyed voice interrupted them. "Why, Nicky, I believe you've been a bad boy."

This time it was Danielle who choked on her water at the pained look on Nick's face.

A tall redhead in a beautiful green dress that exactly matched her eyes stood in front of Nick. "You didn't introduce me to your date."

He stood, obviously uncomfortable. "Hello, Sasha." With a smile that looked forced, he motioned to Danielle. "Sasha, this is Danielle Delacourt. Danielle, Sasha Courtland."

Danielle, who suddenly felt as frumpy as an old gardening hat somebody had stuffed down into the sofa, craned her neck to meet the cold green eyes. Struggling to reduce the disadvantage, she pushed herself off the soft cushion to her feet, wobbling a little on the unfamiliar heels.

"Poor Nicky, I heard Alexis was out of town, but I thought she'd be back by tonight." With an obviously false smile, she turned to Danielle. "Since you're here, I must be wrong."

For once Nick appeared to be speechless, and Danielle stared in stunned fascination at the redhead. Her beady eyes glittered with malevolence. As she returned Danielle's scrutiny, her thin lips pursed into a tight little wad, and lines of discontent formed around her mouth.

Determined not to make a scene, Danielle offered what she hoped was a pleasant smile. Holding out her water glass, she said, "If you all will excuse me, I need a refill."

"I'll get that for you," Nick quickly offered, but Danielle

silenced him with a look.

"Thanks, but I need to powder my nose, as well." Unable to rein in the nerve-induced jokes, she continued, "You can't do that for me, now can you?"

She swiftly turned and made her way to the bathroom. When she found the big room empty, she thanked God. With trembling hands, she sat her water glass on the counter, locked the door, then sank into a chair strategically placed in front of the vanity. Tears edged her eyes as she stared at the desolate face in the mirror.

Chapter 8

"Danielle? Are you in there?"

The masculine whisper outside the door startled her. Blinking the tears back, she leaped to her feet. "Nick?"

"We need to talk."

Her heart sank. What would he say? Alexis didn't understand him? She meant nothing to him? Unfortunately, Danielle had heard it all before from Jared. Would Nick say that Sasha was lying? Danielle knew better. She remembered the first day she'd met Nick when he'd had a phone call from someone named Alexis. "Have a good trip," he'd told her.

In spite of her misgivings, she unlatched the bathroom door and opened it a crack. The worried look on Nick's face clutched at her heart, and she stepped into the hallway.

"Let's go where it's quiet." He put his hand gently against the small of her back and propelled her through the crowded room. He opened the glass-paned doors, and she allowed him to guide her out onto the balcony where only a few couples mingled here and there.

Nick and Danielle leaned against the rail and looked out at the newly blooming garden below. Muted lighting slightly illuminated a path that meandered through the greenery and around a small pond. The croaking song of a tree frog filled the air, and in spite of her tumultuous emotions, Danielle smiled at the sound of crickets chirping a backup chorus.

"Come on." Nick took her hand and pulled her toward the stairway leading to the grounds.

Danielle hesitated, but then his eyes met hers, and the tenderness she saw there made her follow.

As they walked along the deserted pathway, Danielle wondered when they were going to "talk" as Nick had promised. Just as she'd given up, Nick slid onto a small bench beside the pond and pulled her down beside him.

With an exasperated sigh, he spoke. "Sasha is a very unhappy person. She wants everyone else to be the same."

"I can see that." Danielle hardly recognized her quavering voice. She looked down at her small hand still enclosed in Nick's large one.

"Oh, Danielle, I wish you could see inside my heart." He ran his fingers through his short, blond hair. "What a different man you'd find from a month ago." He lifted her hand up and kissed her palm, and she tried to ignore the shiver that coursed through her. "I'm so sorry you were hurt tonight. There's nothing between Alexis and me. Nothing."

In the dim light, she could see the pleading in his eyes. "She's Samuel's daughter," he explained. "We've filled a void for each other by attending functions like this together. But we've never had a relationship. . .barely even a friendship." He shook his head. His voice rang with sincerity. "Sasha knows that, but she saw that you were special to me."

Danielle pulled her hand away and searched his face, trying desperately to tell if he was lying. She'd believed Jared so many times that it was hard to trust her own judgment. "I am?" she squeaked.

Nick stood and pulled her to her feet. "Silly goose, of course you are," he said, voice thick with emotion. He wrapped his arms around her and hugged her tightly to him.

Danielle breathed in his freshly laundered scent, and her heart thudded as affection for this man flooded her soul. She reached up and smoothed his hair. When he drew back and looked at her, she nodded. "I believe you." With trembling lips, she placed a light kiss on his cheek.

"Good." He took her hand, and they walked slowly back up to the house.

Danielle forced herself to enjoy the rest of the evening. She'd never figured herself for a coward, but she avoided the redhead in the emerald dress. A few minutes before nine, Danielle was admiring a painting near the door when a deep voice whispered in her ear, "Hey, beautiful, let's blow this joint and go somewhere more private."

She did a double take and saw the laughter bubbling in Nick's green eyes.

He chuckled at her quick look. "Got you."

"Right. Next thing I know you'll be asking me to go back to your place to look at your sketchings."

"Ha. Not with my totally nonexistent artistic skills. They'd have to be stick figure drawings. But I do have some cool goldfish in soda pop bottles. . . ."

Danielle laughed and followed Nick to the door, where they thanked the host and hostess, then stepped out onto the front porch.

Another khaki-clad volunteer with a walkie-talkie stood ready. He looked up at Nick and Danielle, then nodded and spoke into the handheld instrument. "Party of two to be picked up at the house."

As they waited for the shuttle, Nick took her hand in his, "So, what did you think?"

"On the whole, they seem like very nice people." Danielle looked sideways at Nick to gauge his reaction to her oblique reference to Sasha.

"Yes, on the *whole*, they are." He smiled.

"Seriously, I had a good time." Danielle pulled her little jacket closer around her shoulders.

"Cold?"

"A little."

Nick shrugged out of his black suit jacket and draped it around her. He held up his hand at her protests. "It even matches. You have to wear it." His eyes crinkled. "Besides, you look sort of like a little girl playing dress up."

"Thanks a lot." Danielle's voice was dry, but the feel and smell of Nick's jacket, still warm from his body, seemed exquisitely intimate. She had it bad. She loved this man. Trusting him was not an option. It was a necessity.

Thankful for the distraction, she boarded the shuttle quickly. Nick sat down beside her and wrapped an arm around her shoulders. "One good thing about you having my jacket. . ." He hugged her tighter. "Now you have to keep me warm."

Danielle laid her head back against his arm and allowed herself to relax. If only things could stay just like they were right now.

Nick pulled into the driveway and looked over at the sleeping beauty in the seat next to him. She'd fallen asleep shortly after they got into the Jaguar and had dozed soundly all the way home. Oh, how he'd like to wake her with a kiss. Every morning for the rest of his life.

Startled by the swell of emotion, he studied her delicate features. Her dark eyelashes caressed fine cheekbones. The smattering of freckles was gone tonight, no doubt hidden by makeup. He missed them. His gaze fell on her bow-shaped mouth, which was curved into a slight smile. Was she dreaming of him?

Lord, please. . .please, allow me to be worthy of her love. Or at least allow me to keep trying to be. I've wasted so much time I could have been serving You, Father, and You have still blessed me beyond belief. Thank You for all my blessings, but thank You most of all for bringing Danielle into my life. Please, forgive me for my transgressions. In Jesus' name, Amen.

Nick sat for a minute longer, thinking with regret about the last few years. Then he twisted in his seat, and smoothing an errant curl back with his hand, he dropped a tender kiss on Danielle's forehead.

She woke with a start and jerked forward, bumping her head soundly against his. "Ouch!" Her eyes widened at his face so close to hers.

Resisting the urge to kiss her senseless, Nick sat back and rubbed his forehead, then grinned as she did the same. "Well, Sleeping Beauty, so much for Prince Charming awakening you with a kiss."

She jumped. "Huh? Did I talk in my sleep?" Even in the light from the streetlight, he could see her blush.

"No. Why?"

"Oh, nothing." She opened the car door and jumped out. "Just something Kristin and I were joking about earlier." She leaned back in the door. "Thanks for a great time, Nick."

He chuckled as she slammed the door and wobbled down the sidewalk, obviously still disoriented from her rude awakening. He slowly climbed out of the car and quickly covered the distance between them. Coming up behind her just as she reached the porch, he slid his arm around her waist. "You forgot something."

"Really?" She stopped and turned to face him. "Don't tell me you're one of those guys who thinks that every time they take a girl on a date she owes him a kiss."

Nick's smile grew broader. "A kiss would be wonderful if you're offering." He reached out and touched her arm. "But I was actually talking about my jacket." Danielle collapsed into giggles on the porch swing. Pent-up tension left her body, and he watched in delight as tears of laughter ran down her face. "I really am a silly goose," she said as Nick sat down beside her. Shrugging out of his jacket, she held it out to him. "I'm sorry, Nick. In my defense, it usually takes a cup of coffee to get my mind working after I sleep."

Nick leaned toward her. "At the risk of taking advantage of your sleep-befuddled brain, there was one more thing." He dropped a tender kiss on her mouth, then drew back with a smile. Caressing her cheek with the back of his hand, he said, "Go get some rest."

Chapter 9

Danielle was torn. She couldn't decide which one she liked best: the charming businessman who had swept her off her feet at the No Ball At All two nights ago or the kind-hearted housekeeping attendant who had thrown a game of horseshoes today to make Mr. Johnson look good in front of Mrs. Martin. The good thing was lately it seemed that the two Nicks were merging painlessly into one man.

She chuckled at her nonsensical dilemma as she left Mr. Johnson's room. As his physical therapist, she had questioned his horseshoe-playing, but his shoulder appeared to still be in good shape. The attention from a pretty widow hadn't hurt anything either.

When Danielle reached Mr. Spinelli's open door, she was greeted by an empty room. She checked the bathroom, and when she still couldn't find her patient, she hurried to look in the common areas, inside and out, with no success. Out of breath, she came back to his room again, hoping that he would have returned, but it was still deserted.

Her heart began to pound. When a patient was missing, the authorities must be called. The fear of getting Nick in trouble warred with the terror that Mr. Spinelli might be lost.

With trembling fingers she pushed the nurses' button. "Susie?"

"Yeah?"

"Would you page Nick Davis to Mr. Spinelli's room, please?"

"Sure."

Just seconds after the page, Nick stuck his head in the door. When he saw her, his face lit with delight. "What's up?"

Trembling, Danielle shook her head. "It's Mr. Spinelli. I can't find him anywhere."

His expression grew serious, but his voice was confident. "Whoa, now. We'll find him."

"Nick, I've looked everywhere." Panic edged her voice. "If we don't find him in the next few minutes, we'll have to notify the authorities."

"We'll find him," he repeated. "You search the building. I'll search the grounds. We'll meet back here as soon as we're done." He hurried out the door the opposite direction of her, then called, "Danielle."

She spun around. "Yeah?"

"Pray," he said, then jogged down the hallway to the exit.

Seven minutes later, a defeated Danielle came into Mr. Spinelli's room to face Nick's obviously growing despair.

His voice grim, he admitted, "We have to call the authorities. In the meantime—"

"Time for supper." Bob hurried into the room with a steaming tray and stopped when he saw Danielle and Nick and no Mr. Spinelli. "Whoa! Where's Mr. Spinelli?"

"We can't find him," Nick said, quietly to his egg-hiding partner. "We're about to call for help."

"Call for help?" Bob's voice was incredulous. "Won't that get the boss in a lot of trouble?"

Danielle could see the guilt cross Nick's face at the cafeteria worker's concern for "the boss." He looked like he would set the record straight, but she silenced him with a slight shake of her head. Now was not the time or the place.

"We can't worry about that right now, Bob. Our first concern has to be Mr. Spinelli."

"Well, I know that's right, but let's use our heads for a minute." Bob sat the tray down on the rolling table. "What's the last thing Mr. Spinelli said to you? When did you last see him?"

"I saw him this morning," Danielle said, thoughtfully. "He was talking about dancing with Naomi."

"Oh, yeah, he used to dance with her all the time in here." Bob nodded.

"In here?" Danielle frowned. "I understood that his wife had been dead for many years."

"Oh, she has been." Bob's voice softened. "But he'd turn on that antique radio, and when I'd bring in his tray, he'd be sashaying around the room as if he were holding her in his arms." His eyes were suspiciously moist. "Say," his gaze swept the window sill, "where is that old radio?"

"What old radio?" Nick asked.

"The one he always played music from while he danced. He must have moved it." He snapped his fingers. "My guess is, you find that radio and you'll find Mr. Spinelli." He clapped Nick on the shoulder. "You will find him, Man."

Nick cleared his throat, "I know we will, but we might have to get help to do it."

"I understand. You've gotta do what you've gotta do. Listen, I'd better get back to the cafeteria. I'll keep my eyes and ears opened for Mr. S. Keep me informed, okay?"

"Okay, Bob. Thanks."

Silence filled the room when the big man left. "I guess I'll go call the police. If he's left the grounds, we're wasting precious seconds."

Danielle nodded. "Okay."

"Surely he didn't carry that old radio with him, though."

Danielle shook her head. "I've been in here lots of times, and I've never seen an old radio. . ." As Danielle said the words, a vague memory niggled at her mind. She had been trying to avoid Nick's eyes in the mop closet. She'd glanced at the paper towels, and sitting beside them had been. . .an antique radio. "Oh, wait. Nick! Hurry—come with me." She took off at a run down the corridor, not looking to see if he followed. She came to a sudden stop at the mop closet door. Nick almost collided into her. "Shh." She put her ear to the door and motioned for Nick to do the same. The crooning tones of a golden oldie wafted through the door.

Nick tried the door knob. "It's locked," he mouthed and retrieved the key from his pocket.

"How did he get in?" Danielle wondered softly.

"I remember him telling me that he and his brother used to be pretty wild in their young days. Guess picking locks is like riding a bicycle," Nick whispered.

He slid the key into the lock and opened the door slowly. Sure enough, Mr. Spinelli, arms out as if holding someone, danced around the room in perfect time to the music.

Danielle's eyes filled with tears, and when her gaze met Nick's, his face was drawn.

"Thank God he's okay," Danielle said.

"I already have," Nick replied.

The couple approached the elderly man quietly. They stood silently by the cleaning supplies until the song ended.

Mr. Spinelli caught a glimpse of them just as the last note

played, and he smiled. "She dances like a dream, doesn't she?"

Danielle and Nick nodded. Nick reached over and turned off the radio, then put an arm around the old man's shoulders. "I'm sorry, Mr. S., but you can't be in here. We need to take your radio back to your room so you can listen to it whenever you want to."

Danielle unplugged the radio and picked it up. As Nick led the elderly man back to his room, he explained to him in soothing tones why he couldn't use the closet anymore. Danielle, following behind with the radio, couldn't keep from smiling when Nick added, "Danielle was worried about you."

Mr. Spinelli seemed no worse for wear after his big adventure, but taking in Nick's drawn face and feeling her own sagging spirit, Danielle wasn't so sure about the two of them.

While she was settling the elderly man in, she gasped. "We need to tell Bob we found him," she whispered to Nick.

"I'll go by and tell him right now." Nick stopped when he got to the door and turned back. "Danielle?"

She looked up from tucking the covers around a dozing Mr. Spinelli. "Yeah?"

"Thanks."

"Thanks for what?" she asked, puzzled by his fervent voice.

"For being you," he answered and then was gone.

When she left Mr. Spinelli's room, Danielle looked all over for Nick but couldn't find him. She walked on out to the parking lot alone, hoping to catch him there, but the little Bug was nowhere to be seen.

With a sudden shiver, she remembered that Wednesday was his last day to pose as Nick Davis. Was this disappearing act without a good-bye an indication of things to come?

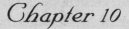

Chapter 10

Danielle stumbled into the kitchen and poured herself a cup of coffee. She'd stayed up late the night before, thinking Nick might call. He hadn't. Surely this morning he'd have a good explanation for his sudden exodus from work.

When she pushed open the door to the dining room, Kristin jumped like a robber caught with the goods and shoved something under the table.

"Kristin?" Danielle asked. "What's going on?"

"Going on?" The redhead's attempt at innocence failed. Dropping to her knees, Danielle looked under the table at the crumpled newspaper her roommate was hiding. "What's in the paper?"

"Oh, you know. Just normal stuff."

"Then why are you hiding it?" Danielle asked, irritated by Kristin's games.

"Oh, Dani." Tears filled Kristin's eyes as she put the newspaper back on the table and smoothed out the wrinkles.

Clutching her terry robe tighter around her, Danielle crossed the room in two strides. MAN ABOUT TOWN? the small headline read. Below was a picture of Nick with his arm draped around the shoulders of the most beautiful woman Danielle had ever seen. Her blond curls were tousled, and her features, absolutely perfect. Behind the gorgeous couple, a breathtaking sunset reigned over the Atlanta skyline. The caption below the photo read, "Nicholas Lancaster and Alexis Bryant enjoy the view atop the Westin Peachtree Plaza Sunday night." Her eyes filled with tears as she scanned the small bit of gossip that turned her world upside down:

> Prominent businessman Nicholas Lancaster surprised everyone by escorting a mystery lady to the No Ball at All Saturday night. Apparently the brunette beauty was just a temporary diversion, since he was on hand at the Sun Dial Restaurant Sunday night to welcome Alexis Bryant home from her recent trip to Europe.

So, Nick wasn't different from Jared after all. Pain sliced through her heart at the realization. Just as Jared had used her for a steady date, Nick had used her to pass the time while performing an unpleasant task. Or maybe there was another explanation. Her mind skittered back to the day of their first confrontation. "Are you threatening me?" he'd asked. Apparently, he believed that old adage about keeping your friends close and your enemies closer.

Before Danielle could finish the thought, great gulping sobs enveloped her body, and she collapsed into a chair. She put her head in her hands and cried until she couldn't breathe. Tender moments with Nick flashed through her mind, and she shook her head angrily to force them away. How could he treat her this way? The answer was simple. She'd meant nothing to him. It had all been an act. She should be used to this by now.

"Twice-rejected," people would whisper. Danielle suddenly realized she didn't care what people said. With Jared, her pride had been battered and bruised. As soon as she was away from the pitying looks, she'd made a quick recovery. Nick's betrayal had ripped her heart out, and somehow she knew the earth wasn't big enough to provide her with a haven from the pain. Raising her head to meet her roommate's mournful expression, Danielle pressed her hands to her stomach.

Oh, God, help me handle this pain. You are the master of my soul and the ruler of my destiny. Lord, please, help me to live each day for You. I know that even though I feel like I'm dying, I'm not, but, oh, Lord, it hurts so bad.

As if a dam had burst, new tears gushed down her cheeks, and she looked at Kristin and shook her head helplessly.

"Honey." Kristin's normally teasing voice was tender. "Maybe a nice hot shower will help you feel better." Danielle nodded and followed her to the bathroom. Handing her a plush towel, Kristin continued, "I'll call in sick for you."

"No!"

Kristin swung around and faced Danielle. "Dani, you can't go to work."

"I have to." Danielle turned on the hot water, hoping it might be a catharsis for her heart. But when she was clean and dressing for work, the empty feeling inside seemed only to have grown.

She assured Kristin she'd be okay and made her way slowly to Lancaster Manor. An unbidden hope sprang to her mind as she approached the parking lot. Could there be an explanation? Would Nick Davis be able to make the betrayal go away?

The Volkswagen wasn't there, but she hurried into the facility anyway. Maybe he'd rented a different car. The sight of

Susie hurrying to hide a newspaper dashed her hopes. Pride could not be considered, though, with so much at risk. Walking straight up to the perky nurse, Danielle asked, "Hi, Susie. Did Nick show up today?"

Sympathy shone in the woman's eyes. "No, he didn't. I'm sorry."

"Yeah, me too." Danielle turned on trembling legs and walked toward her office. Not only had she lost her heart, she'd lost the battle for more help at Lancaster Manor as well. The unfairness of the situation swept over her like an ocean wave, and like a piece of driftwood caught in the tide, she turned and washed back out the door to her car. She may have lost personally, but professionally, these people still deserved more.

As she navigated the interstate and took the familiar exit, she realized she'd come full circle. With one exception. Before when she'd bearded the lion in his den, she hadn't realized how dangerous he could be. Now she knew.

Forsaking the glass elevator, she hurried in the revolving door and took an interior elevator to the twenty-second floor. Nothing but the best for the big man, she thought scornfully. In spite of the photo caption, she bet Nick hadn't even noticed the view at the top of the Peachtree. Probably only had eyes for Alexis.

The efficient receptionist was away from her desk, probably making the mighty Mr. Lancaster's morning coffee. Danielle hadn't intended to be announced anyway. At least she would have the element of surprise.

As she neared the heavy door, loud voices drifted out to greet her. Taking a deep breath, she reminded herself again that this wasn't personal. She was here on behalf of the residents of Lancaster Manor. As their advocate, she'd do well not to antagonize the one man who could help them. So if he was in a meeting, she'd wait patiently. Well, she thought, fidgeting as she sunk into a small serviceable chair right outside the door, she'd wait. Patiently was another story.

She regretted her impulsive choice of resting places as soon as it became apparent she could hear the conversation inside. But since the topic was the one she'd come to discuss, she couldn't force herself to move.

"All I'm saying is we need to put more money into the operations of the facilities. The staffing is inadequate. And you know what else? It wouldn't hurt to do a little decorating."

"Decorating?" Danielle heard a loud snort. "Are you kidding? When you don't know who you are, a pretty picture on the wall isn't going to help."

"Samuel, there's more to it than that, and you know it." She recognized Nick's warning tone and wondered if Samuel did as well.

Apparently not. "All I know is I've been looking out for your interests, Nicky. I'd think you'd appreciate that."

Nick's tone was dry as he replied, "My interests?"

"Point taken. But I've been looking out for both of our interests. Not just mine. How do you think you got to be who you are?"

"Let me tell you something I've remembered these last few weeks, Samuel. It's not who you are that matters, but whose you are." Danielle's eyes clouded with tears.

"Oh, no, here we go again. I thought you got over all that years ago, Boy. It's good to go to church now and then. . .stay active in the community, support a few charities. . .but anything beyond that and you cross the line. People start avoiding you. Nobody likes a fanatic."

"Samuel, don't you get it? I don't care what people think. I'm not ashamed to be a Christian." Nick's rueful chuckle drifting out to Danielle told her he was thinking of their conversation in the Volkswagen the night they went to the Varsity. "Maybe I used to act like I was, but if I did, my actions then are what I'm ashamed of."

"You call yourself a Christian?" Anger raised the volume of Samuel's voice, and it reverberated down the hallway. "What kind of Christian would break a girl's heart like you did my Alexis's Sunday night?"

"Samuel, if Alexis was hurt, I'm really sorry. But you know, as well as I do, that we've never had a romantic relationship." Danielle couldn't contain the gasp that burst from her lips. "Our association has always been a business one of sorts. . . convenient for both of us. I only went to see Alexis Sunday night so I could tell her that I've met someone. Until Alexis found out there was a woman I cared for, she had no desire for me whatsoever."

This time the tears were joyful ones. Danielle's heart thudded in her chest as the man she adored declared himself openly and without shame.

"You also know, as well as I do, that she and her friend, Sasha, are behind the gossip in today's paper. Their childish actions may have cost me the woman I love. So don't expect me to feel sorry for her."

"I don't need this, Nicky. You ungrateful. . ." The door swished open, and a short, balding man in a black suit came barreling out, almost colliding with Danielle. He turned back toward the room and yelled, "I quit!" then rushed off down the hallway.

Danielle rose and stepped to the doorway of Nick's office.

He stood much as she'd left him that first day, back to the door, staring out the window at the world below. The vulnerability in his stance pierced her heart, and she was more proud of his firmness, knowing the cost. Clapping her hands together in soft applause, she whispered, "Bravo. Bravo."

He spun around and his eyes lit up. "You came." He rushed toward her, then stopped. "Have you seen the paper?"

She nodded, and he shook his head.

"It's not what it looks like."

"I know. I heard." She motioned toward the chair in the hallway.

"Can you ever forgive me?"

"Forgive you for what?" She counted off on her fingers. "For seeking the truth? For caring about people? For being honest and good? Oh, wait, you must mean for loving me." She rushed into his embrace, then lifted her head to meet his adoring gaze. "Is that what I need to forgive you for? 'Cause if it is, guess what? I need to ask your forgiveness too." She ran a hand along his cheek and smiled when he turned her open palm against his mouth, dropping a light kiss there. "Because I definitely reciprocate."

She watched in dismay as his eyes filled with sadness again. He released her hand and sank down in his chair. "I've been so blind. How could I have ever thought that success in business was the way to happiness? I should have been putting those elderly people ahead of money all along." He shook his head in disbelief. "I feel like the prodigal son. And just like the son's father, my heavenly Father has been incredibly patient and forgiving with me." He smiled as if the thought were new, and fierce determination shone on his face. "I know I'll stumble, but I don't intend to ever let Him down again." He reached out and took her hand again. "He also answered a prayer that

I'd long ago given up on."

Danielle opened her mouth to speak, then gasped when Nick eased out of his chair down on one knee in front of her.

Still holding her hand, he spoke in a solemn voice. "I used to pray that God would help me to find someone. Someone who would share my faith. Shortly after I met you, I came to realize you were that person."

Danielle tried to blink back the tears, but they poured down her face as he continued.

"But the extra blessing, the one I never thought to ask for, is this indescribable happiness I feel when I'm with you, the wonderful love I have for you. In light of that immeasurable love, Danielle Annette Delacourt, will you do me the honor of becoming my wife?"

Tears clogged Danielle's throat, and she barely managed to croak out a yes.

Nick rose to his feet and gathered her into his arms. They stood in silence for a few minutes, then he touched her chin with his finger and tipped her face up to meet his gaze. "Danielle? You do love me, don't you?"

Danielle grinned at the hint of insecurity in the normally unflappable man's voice, but she rushed to reassure him. "Nick, when I was a little girl, my mama let me plant sunflowers one year. Every day, I'd run out and look at those flowers. And you know what? Every day they were bigger. I could almost see them grow. That's how my love for you is."

An impish gleam shone in his eyes. "Could be worse, I guess."

"What could be worse?" she asked, peering at him suspiciously.

"You could have compared me to an eggplant."

Her giggle was cut off as he lowered his mouth to hers.

CHRISTINE LYNXWILER

Christine and her husband, Kevin, live in the foothills of the beautiful Ozark Mountains of their home state, Arkansas. They've been married for twenty years and have two daughters. In addition to writing, Christine runs their chiropractic office and homeschools the girls. She also teaches Bible studies at a women's correctional facility.

Her hobbies include reading, volleyball, chatting with other authors and her family on the Internet, and spending time with both her and Kevin's close-knit families.

Christine set "Beneath Heaven's Curtain" in Atlanta in fond memory of the years she and Kevin spent attending college there. The *City Dreams* anthology is near to her heart because the Delacourt sisters and their deep affection for each other remind her of her special relationship with her own four sisters.

She loves to hear from her readers. You can e-mail her at Christine_Writes@yahoo.com or write her at Christine Lynxwiler, Author Relations, P.O. Box 719, Uhrichsville, OH 44683.

IN THE HEART OF THE STORM

Linda Lyle

Chapter 1

S abrina Delacourt cringed as she watched the yacht dip and sway at its moorings. The thought of trying to step onto it made her stomach roll even worse than the boat bobbing in the wake of the giant ships leaving the harbor. Maybe getting on this boat wasn't such a good idea. Maybe coming to Hong Kong at all wasn't a good idea. She looked around at the night lights of the city rising up around her and wondered what had ever led her to leave her home in Nebraska. Home, safe home.

"Come on, Sabrina," Dianna called. "It'll be better once we get away from the dock. I promise." Dianna gave her a reassuring smile. "Jason will help you onboard. Just wait 'til the next time the boat comes by."

"Okay." She tried to sound confident, but her shaking knees belied her nervousness. Nervous, nothing. She was terrified. She watched until the boat glided in on another wave and then jumped on. At that moment another boat came perilously close, sending a barrage of waves that rocked the yacht. Sabrina felt herself falling forward until strong arms grabbed her and set her on the deck of the ship.

"That was a close one." Sabrina looked up into a pair of dark eyes. Her heart skipped a beat, and her mouth refused to work.

"Hey, are you okay?" The eyes had a voice to match, deep and velvety.

"I'm. . .I'm fine," she stuttered.

"She's just a little nervous about boats." Sabrina jumped at Dianna's voice. She hadn't noticed her boarding. How long had she been staring? Mortified, she turned toward the cabin to hide the warmth in her cheeks. She felt a strong hand grip her elbow.

"It is a bit rough here at the dock, but we'll be underway in a moment. Let me help you inside the cabin so you can sit down."

She was grateful for his support as they traversed the slippery deck with only a small rope separating them from the water. Inside, she could still feel the waves as the yacht seemed to turn on its side, but it was better than being so close to the water.

"By the way, Sabrina, this is Jason Wilkes. Jason, this is Sabrina Delacourt, our new arrival."

"Hi, Sabrina. Welcome to Hong Kong." Jason held out his hand. She held out hers and watched it disappear into his. The warmth of his hand sent a tingle up her arm.

"Thanks," she murmured.

"Where are you from?" Jason asked.

"Nebraska." She tried to think of something else to say, but her brain had turned to mush. She felt like a thirteen-year-old at her first dance. Then again, when it came to men, she always felt that way.

"Sabrina is going to teach English as a second language at the church," Dianna added.

"Great! We've been needing someone to help reach out to the different language groups here, and ESL is the best way to get an opening." Sabrina felt her stomach tighten as she looked at the excitement on his face. How could she ever live up to the expectation she saw in his eyes? What was she doing here?

The yacht began moving away from the dock, and soon the rocking weakened to a steady sway. Sabrina relaxed a little. She only half-listened to Dianna and Jason catch up on news. Most of it made no sense to her anyway, names and places she didn't know. She jumped when Dianna called her name.

"Let's go out on the prow."

"I don't think so." Sabrina could feel her eyes getting larger.

"Actually, it's probably smoother up there than in here. Come on," Jason coaxed.

He held out his hand, and she found herself reaching out. Before she knew it, she was out on the narrow, slippery walk. Jason walked behind her, grasping her waist firmly, and she discovered he was right. It was much smoother. Jason guided her to a set of benches that faced forward, and they sat down. Dianna moved to a more secluded spot and stared out at the water.

"Is she okay?" Sabrina asked, motioning toward Dianna.

"I think she's just going through some hard times right now. Her husband has been away for awhile."

Jason pointed out Victoria's Peak, the highest point in the territories, in an obvious attempt to change the subject. Sabrina was curious, but she didn't ask any more questions. Instead, she stared at the skyscrapers that lit the night sky. It was like a fairyland lit up for Christmas even though it was just an ordinary night. Skyscrapers were stacked from the edge of the harbor all the way up the surrounding mountains. Each one was lit up from top to bottom. It seemed like every building had neon signs. She could smell the salt in the air, and despite her fears of being in such a strange city, she felt a thrill of excitement. Could it be just yesterday that she had left home? Or was it the day before? The trip had taken most of a day to complete, and the time difference had left her feeling dazed.

"So, what brought you to Hong Kong?" Jason asked.

She had been asking herself the same question for months and still hadn't come up with a good answer. "I'm not sure. I just felt like I needed to do something for God." She shrugged her shoulders.

"That's the best reason I've ever heard," Jason said with a smile.

She felt like a fake. Everyone kept going on and on about how wonderful it was for her to give up six months of her life to missions when she knew that she was so unworthy of praise. She tried to think of something to change the subject.

"This is great!" She motioned to the city and the ocean in a sweeping gesture. "I never thought I'd be on a yacht touring Hong Kong's harbor."

"Yeah. One of our church members arranged for us to use the company yacht to take a cruise. He said it's the least he can do for us."

"So what are you doing here?" Sabrina asked, surprised at how much she wanted to know the answer.

"I'm fulfilling my two-year service requirement so that I can apply for full-time missions status."

Sabrina smiled and said, "Oh. That's nice," but her spirit cried out. Any interest she had had in Jason was history now. She had no intention of becoming a full-time missionary. Her Sunday school teacher's many lessons on being willing to serve had prompted her to come for six months. But when she was done, her penance would be paid.

Jason felt her pull away. She didn't move physically, but he could feel her pulling away emotionally. Obviously, she wasn't interested in becoming a full-time missionary. Too bad! He already sensed an attraction. He stared at her profile, itching to tuck the curly auburn strands of hair behind her ear. In the cabin, he had noticed her green eyes and decided she must be part Irish or Scottish. She had courage too, climbing onboard when he could tell she was afraid of getting on the rocking boat. It really was too bad.

For a moment he thought he had finally met his mate, someone who would serve by his side. It had been his prayer night and day that God would either send him a mate or take away this longing for one. He had come to the conclusion that he would have to serve God alone. It was rare that the mission board accepted single men unless they were going into rough conditions, but he knew they would accept him. He had felt God's call from early on in his Christian walk, but he had never dreamed he would be doing it alone.

Maybe it wasn't that bad. One glance at Dianna proved that there were worse things than being single.

After a few moments of silence, Dianna rejoined them and steered conversation to lighter topics, like points of interest and the weather. Jason shut out the dark thoughts that threatened to ruin this wonderful trip and focused on the beautiful night.

When they reached Llama Island, Jason helped Dianna and Sabrina onto the dock. He watched as Sabrina tried a little bit of everything: the prawns, the fried oysters, even the fried squid. She was a real trooper.

On the trip back, the yacht passed a ship at anchor in the middle of the harbor. It was strung with lights from top to bottom. "What's that?" Sabrina asked.

"It's a restaurant. It's pretty famous around these parts, known for its seafood buffet," Jason answered. "You have to take a boat out to the ship."

"Sounds different," Sabrina said.

"I'll take you sometime if you like," Jason offered.

"Maybe."

It wasn't a yes, but it wasn't a no either. He knew it was dangerous to get attached to someone who wasn't committed to the same things he was, but more than anything he wanted to be there as she discovered this city. He watched her face as they rounded the point and the boat people came into view. His heart broke every time he saw these people living on tiny boats with no running water or bathrooms. Sabrina's nose curled as the stench of sewage in the water accosted her nose. This was a side of Hong Kong a lot of people pretended not to see.

Soon enough, the yacht returned to the dock at the clock tower, and Jason took his leave. As soon as he was out of sight of the others, his shoulders slumped. He prayed all the way home, but he couldn't get that auburn-haired girl out of his mind. She even managed to slip into his dreams.

———

Sabrina and Dianna walked in silence. Sabrina didn't know what to say. She wanted to know why Dianna's husband had left, but it was none of her business. They rode the double-decker bus back to the small compound. The trip from the bus stop took only moments but seemed like an eternity. Sabrina could sense the tension in the other woman and was sure she saw tears on her cheeks in the moonlight. They paused at the base of the stairs leading to Sabrina's apartment.

"Is there anything you need?" Dianna asked.

"I need to go grocery shopping soon. Where do you go?"

"There's a store not far from here. How about we go to-morrow morning? I need to get a few things too, and then maybe we can have tea and chat." Her voice took on a pleading note.

"Sure. Just call me when you're ready to go."

"Okay. See ya tomorrow."

Sabrina paused with her foot on the bottom stair. She waved as Dianna turned back before entering the apartment next door. Something was definitely wrong. She lifted up a prayer that she could be a source of encouragement for Dianna, whatever the problem was.

Chapter 2

S abrina awoke to sunlight streaming through the window, but the window was in the wrong place. She looked around the strange bedroom for several minutes before she remembered that she was in Hong Kong. She could hardly believe it even when she looked out at the skyline dotted with high-rise apartments and office buildings. On television back in the States, she had seen the scenes before her so many times that they didn't seem real. With a sigh, she turned back to evaluate her new apartment. It was small but adequate for one person. Space was a precious commodity in this part of the world.

As she went about her morning routine, Sabrina thought about her new friend Dianna. She was obviously distraught about her husband's absence, but it was the silence of the other missionaries that piqued Sabrina's curiosity. Plugging in her hair dryer, she remembered to use the adapter. There were so many little things to get used to that it boggled the mind. After she had secured her hair in rollers, she scoured the kitchen for breakfast, finally grabbing the last bagel and an apple. While she ate, she made a mental list of all the things she would need.

She had barely finished her hair when the doorbell rang.

After putting on another round of hair spray, she dabbed on lip gloss and grabbed her purse as she passed through the bedroom. Opening the door, she was surprised to find a man instead of Dianna.

"Jason! What are you doing here?" Sabrina asked.

"I was going to call and see if you wanted to go to that restaurant tonight, but I didn't have your phone number. Besides, I had a meeting with Matthew Chambers."

"Oh." Sabrina couldn't think of anything to say. She wanted to go, but she didn't want to get involved with a man who was dedicated to becoming a full-time missionary. Luckily, Dianna appeared to save the day.

"Hi, Jason," Dianna said. "What brings you out so early?"

"I have a meeting with Matt," he replied. "I stopped by to see if Sabrina wanted to go the floating restaurant tonight. Want to make it a trio?"

"That sounds like fun. What do you say?" Dianna asked as she turned to Sabrina.

"Great." She was glad to have the decision taken out of her hands. This way she could go without feeling like it was a date.

"Since that's settled, I'll pick you ladies up at six o'clock sharp." Jason gave a mock salute and jogged down the stairs. As soon as he was out of sight, Dianna tapped her arm and grinned.

"Looks like you've got an admirer."

"He's just being nice," Sabrina argued.

"I don't think so. He's all but ignored the other short-term girls that came through here. He was always business. I think he likes you," Dianna said, her grin getting wider by the minute.

"I don't think getting involved with him is a good idea," Sabrina hedged.

"Why not?" Dianna asked, hands on hips.

"Because I'm not interested in being a missionary."

"Oh," Dianna said, looking deflated. "I guess you're right then." She nodded and then motioned for Sabrina to follow. "Let's get going."

Sabrina followed Dianna to her car and headed for the passenger side. She was surprised to see a steering wheel. She heard Dianna laughing behind her.

"It happens to everybody," she said, patting her on the back. "In Hong Kong they drive on the left side of the road, so the driver's seat is on the opposite side of the car from American cars."

"Oh." Sabrina could feel the heat rising in her cheeks. She should have known that. She walked around the car and got in the passenger's seat. As they drove, Sabrina couldn't help but feel like they were on the wrong side of the road. Some of the intersections looked tricky.

"I don't think I want to drive here," Sabrina said.

"It's not that hard. It just takes getting used to and a little practice."

"Still, I think I'll stick to the bus and the subway."

Dianna laughed. "Whatever makes you happy."

The supermarket was a lot like back home, so Sabrina had no trouble picking out things from her list. Dianna pointed out the best brands, and they were soon checking out. Despite the fact that the currency was dollars, Hong Kong dollars were quite different from U.S. currency. The smallest bill was a ten-dollar bill. Everything else came in coins. The coins were of different weights and designs, and some of them were heavy. She paid for her purchases and dropped the coins into her change purse. They drove back to the apartment and separated their bags.

"When you finish putting away the groceries, come over to

my apartment, and we'll have some tea."

"Okay." Sabrina lugged the heavy bags up the short set of stairs, struggling to get her key into the lock without dropping the bags.

"Here, let me do that." She jumped. She hadn't heard Jason coming up behind her, and now, he was so close that she could feel his breath on her neck. It sent delicious shivers down her spine. She moved quickly to the side to allow him access to the lock and to get away from temptation.

In a matter of seconds, he had the door open and was reaching for her bags. Before she could say a word, he had all her bags on the counter and was headed back out the door.

"See you tonight," he called as he rounded the corner. Sabrina stood speechless, watching him go. She was going to have to be very careful. This man was beginning to look way too good.

Jason smiled as he crossed the street. Mission accomplished. She had agreed to go to dinner. He had seen the indecision on her face, and Dianna's sudden appearance had been just the thing to convince her. Then he began to argue with the voice of reason inside his head.

You're playing with fire.

We're just going as friends.

You know you want more than friendship.

I can't be a snob. She's new and needs someone to show her around.

She has Dianna. Besides, you never showed any of the other girls around.

That was different. They were all boy crazy, looking for a husband.

He shook his head, trying to dispel the argument that had

been going on ever since that green-eyed girl had stepped onto the boat and into his arms. He could tell she wasn't interested in full-time missions, but he couldn't resist being attracted to her. Maybe he had misunderstood when she pulled back. Maybe she was a little shy. He had to find out for sure, or he would never get any peace.

Sabrina quickly put away the groceries and made her way to Dianna's apartment. She knocked, then opened the door at Dianna's call. She peeked around the door. The apartment was much like hers only a little larger. Dianna was still putting away groceries.

"I went ahead and started the tea kettle brewing so it would be ready when you got here." Motioning to a small kitchen nook near a window, Dianna said, "Have a seat. It'll take just a minute."

Sabrina watched her make short work of the groceries before grabbing a platter of cookies and coming to the table. "Oops. Forgot the tea," Dianna said with a sheepish grin. "I'd forget my head if it wasn't attached." Returning to the table, she poured the tea into the cups and sat down.

"What kind of tea is this?" Sabrina asked, taking a sniff. It had a slightly bitter odor.

"Green tea."

Sabrina took a sip of the steaming liquid. The smell was a prelude to the taste. She really wanted some sugar but decided to try it straight. Maybe she would get accustomed to the taste after awhile. Dianna offered her a chocolate chip cookie, which she was grateful for. Hopefully, it would counteract the bitter taste of the tea.

"How do you like it?" Dianna asked.

"It's. . .different."

Dianna grinned and then laughed softly. It was the first genuine laugh Sabrina had heard from her since their first meeting. "It takes awhile to get used to it."

Sabrina nodded and took another bite of cookie. "So, what brought you to Hong Kong?" she asked, hoping to avoid the question herself.

"A missionary who had worked in Hong Kong came to my church and spoke to my youth group about the people here. I was fascinated. Not too much later, I felt that God was calling me to full-time ministry. So I went to college and seminary." She stopped to take a sip of tea, and Sabrina took the moment to interrupt.

"Did you meet your husband in seminary?"

Dianna's face took on a strained look. "Actually, we met in college. I went to the local state university."

"Oh. Did you go to seminary together?"

"Yes," Dianna replied. "We decided that God was calling us to full-time missions work."

"That's great. I don't think I could do this for the rest of my life," Sabrina said.

"Why not?" Dianna asked, one eyebrow raised expectantly.

"I'm just not the missionary type."

"What type is that?" Dianna asked.

"I don't know," Sabrina said, shrugging her shoulders. "Someone who is. . ." She let the words hang in the air, unable to express the feelings of unworthiness deep within her.

"Someone perfect?" Dianna asked softly. Sabrina's head jerked up. "Missionaries are just people trying to live out the Great Commission," Dianna continued. "Every Christian is called to do the same. Foreign missionaries just do it in other countries."

An uneasy silence filled the room as Sabrina contemplated Dianna's words. Dianna seemed to be lost in her own thoughts. Suddenly, Dianna sat up and dismissed the tension with a wave of her arms. "What are you going to wear tonight?" she asked brightly.

Sabrina was more than happy to change the subject. "I don't know. What do you suggest?"

After a short discussion, they both decided on something casual yet stylish. They finished their tea and cookies before separating to get ready for the evening. Despite her resolution to dismiss Dianna's earlier remarks, Sabrina couldn't get the words out of her head. Was everyone really meant to be a missionary?

Sabrina spent the rest of the day getting settled into her new apartment. She put out the rest of her pictures and rearranged some of the furniture. The last piece of furniture was barely set in place before she realized the time. With a groan of dismay, she rushed off to get ready for the evening ahead. Even though she knew that Jason was not a prospect for the future, she wanted to impress him. The doorbell rang just as she put on the last dab of lipstick. Her heart pounded as she took one last look in the mirror before heading for the door.

Chapter 3

Jason took a deep breath and tried to reason with his thumping heart. Sabrina only wanted to be friends. There was no way that this relationship could work if she didn't feel called to missions. His mind knew it was true, but the rest of him was in denial. When the door opened, his heart skipped a beat, and he knew he was in serious trouble.

Sabrina was dressed casually in khakis and a sleeveless green sweater, but he couldn't get over how beautiful she looked. The sweater brought out her sparkling emerald eyes and accentuated the mane of auburn hair. She was perfect, almost. At her puzzled look, he realized he had been standing in the door slack-jawed, like an idiot.

"I guess you're ready," he said. He tried to think of something charming to say, but his mouth felt like cotton, and his brain refused to cooperate.

"Yeah." Sabrina picked up her purse from the table in the foyer and joined him outside. By the time she had locked the door, he had regained his senses.

"Shall we?" he asked, bowing. She smiled, and his heart skipped another beat.

"Let's." She gave a graceful curtsy. He held out his arm,

and she took it with a laugh. He loved the sound.

They walked over to Dianna's apartment and rang the bell. Several minutes later the lock clicked, and the door opened. Dianna motioned for them to come in as she continued to talk on the phone. "Hold on just a minute," she said into the receiver. "I can't go tonight," she said to Jason and Sabrina as she held the phone to her chest. "Jeff just called, and he won't be able to call again for a week. You guys understand, don't you?" Dianna pleaded.

"Of course," Sabrina whispered. Jason nodded in agreement.

"I'll talk to you tomorrow." Dianna whispered, turning back to the phone. Sabrina and Jason waved and slipped out the door quietly.

"That's good that he finally called. Dianna was getting worried," Jason said as they made their way across the courtyard.

"Why hasn't he called before?" Sabrina questioned.

"He's on a mission in a closed country," Jason said quietly. "It's really better not to discuss it in public, at least until he comes back."

"Oh," Sabrina replied. He could tell by the look of shock on her face that she had misunderstood his remarks on the boat that night. She probably thought Jeff had left Dianna. He needed to pay closer attention to what was coming out of his mouth.

"Come on. We can still go to dinner," Jason said with a smile. He held out his arm again, hoping to regain the carefree attitude of moments ago. She took his arm, and her smile returned.

Sabrina felt giddy walking so close to Jason. Despite all the warnings her brain issued, her spirit kept taking flight. He was everything she wanted in a husband, except for his desire to go to the mission field. She toyed with the idea of talking him out of becoming a full-time foreign missionary. They could always do volunteer work back home. A part of her knew it was not only useless to try, but also foolhardy. She didn't want a man she could so easily manipulate. She determined to put the issue out of her mind for the evening.

It was a short trip to the restaurant. Of course, everything was a short trip in Hong Kong since it was a very small place. The restaurant was lit from top to bottom with bright lights, just like the rest of the city. The only other place that had more neon was Las Vegas. The waiter took them to a table and gave them a menu. He took their drink orders and left.

"I suggest the prawns. They are great here," Jason said over the top of his menu. "But just about everything is good."

Sabrina glanced at the menu, but she kept stealing glances at Jason from behind her own menu. He looked great in a navy dress shirt and khakis. Unable to keep her mind on the menu, she decided to take his suggestion.

"I think I will have the prawns," Sabrina told the waiter. He nodded politely and looked to Jason, who ordered the same. As soon as the waiter had taken their menus and disappeared, Sabrina could feel the tension in the air. Jason was the first to break the silence.

"So, how do you like Hong Kong so far?"

"It's very interesting but kind of overwhelming." She took a sip of her soda.

"I'm sure it is." Jason took a sip of his drink. "So, tell me about your family."

"I have three sisters."

"There are four of you."

"Yep." Sabrina nodded and smiled. "Poor Daddy is so outnumbered."

"I bet," Jason replied, smiling in return. "What do your sisters do?"

"Well, my oldest sister, Sharon, worked in D.C., but now she is married and living in Kansas." Sabrina ticked them off on her hands. "My second sister, Danielle, and her husband own several nursing homes in Atlanta. My younger sister, Denise, is getting a degree in teaching. She's almost ready to graduate."

"Wow, you guys are spread all over the place."

"Yeah, I miss having them around, but Sharon and Danielle had already flown the coop, so it was time to try my wings. What about you?" Sabrina asked. She leaned forward to listen, anxious to find out everything she could about this man.

"Well, I'm one of two children, the traditional one boy and one girl. My sister is still in college. Her name is Katie, short for Katherine, but don't tell her I told you. She has a firm aversion to growing up."

"Really."

Jason leaned forward, putting both arms on the table. "She doesn't like that she is about to turn twenty. She wants to be a teenager forever." He rolled his eyes.

"I couldn't wait to be twenty-one," Sabrina said, shaking her head in disbelief. "I have been dying to get out of our small town for as long as I can remember."

"You look pretty good for a dead girl," Jason said solemnly. She reached over and gently punched his arm.

"Cute."

"Why were you in such a hurry to leave?"

"I don't know. I just wanted to see what else was in the world. I guess this is my big chance."

"Traveling can be an adventure," Jason said with a smile.

"But so is working for God."

"What do you mean?" Sabrina questioned with a frown.

"I mean that working for God, no matter what you do or where you do it, is so much more rewarding than working for yourself."

Sabrina was beginning to get uncomfortable with the turn of the conversation, so she almost sighed with relief when their orders arrived. She ate until she couldn't eat another bite; then Jason suggested a walk along the waterfront.

Leaving the air-conditioned restaurant, Sabrina immediately noticed the warm, tropical air. She looked out at all the buildings and the boats in the harbor. It was like a movie set. Several times in the last few days she had wondered if this was all a dream. Sabrina stumbled on a broken piece of sidewalk, and Jason reached out a steadying hand. He didn't release it as they continued their stroll in the moonlight in silence.

"I guess I'd better get you home," Jason said. His voice betrayed his reluctance to go. She felt the same way.

"I guess so." They turned back toward the subway entrance. The ride home seemed even shorter than the ride to the restaurant. Sabrina didn't want the night to end, didn't want to think about the consequences. He walked her to the door.

"I'll see you around," Jason said, giving her a half wave as he turned from the door. He waited until she was inside and the door closed before he left. Standing by the front window, Sabrina watched him go. As soon as he turned the corner, she leaned back against the door with a groan. He was just so close to perfect. With a sigh, she got ready for bed.

On the walk home, Jason reviewed the night. Things couldn't have gone better if he had planned them. He stopped and looked up into the heavens. What was God up to anyway? Why had He sent such a perfect girl to his door? Her only flaw was that she didn't want to be a missionary. *What are You trying to teach me, Lord?*

When no answer was forthcoming, Jason continued walking. He prayed for guidance. Things were going to get messy if he didn't have some backup soon.

Chapter 4

Monday morning dawned bright. Sabrina rolled over and stretched. Today was her first real day of work. She was excited and terrified all in the same breath. Throwing back the covers, she tiptoed to the shower and turned on the hot water. As steam filled the room, she relaxed her tense muscles by stretching. She was ready a half-hour early, but she couldn't stand waiting in the apartment a moment longer, so she walked over to Dianna's apartment.

"Well you're ready early," Dianna said when she opened the door. She still wore her bathrobe, and her hair was in curlers.

"Couldn't help it. Nerves, I guess," she replied.

"Come in and have a bagel," Dianna said, motioning to the table. "There's coffee too if you want some."

"I thought you drank tea."

"Not in the morning. At this time of day, I need all the help I can get." She pointed to the counter. "The sugar is over there, and the creamer is in the refrigerator."

Sabrina helped herself to a bagel and a cup of coffee while Dianna dressed. Then they walked to the mission office. Even though they were early, Matt was already in his office. They knocked on the door, and he waved them inside.

"Just the two ladies I'm looking for," he said with a smile. Matt was tall with dark hair and eyes. Sabrina had thought he was an actor or something glamorous when she first met him. She had been shocked to find out that he was the mission director. Dianna took one of the two seats in front of the desk, and Sabrina followed suit.

"Sabrina, we're so glad you volunteered to come and help us. I'm going to let Dianna show you the ropes. You'll be responsible for teaching a couple of the classes at the English camp that starts next Monday. Do you have any special talents that you could share?"

"Well, I sing at church and play a piano solo once in awhile," Sabrina said slowly. "Why?"

"We usually have a talent show at the end of the camp. Also, we try to incorporate English study with other things like music and games."

"Oh. That sounds like fun." Sabrina's initial reserve disappeared. "I can't wait to get started."

"That's what we like to hear." Matt fished a blue folder from the sea of papers on his desk and handed it to Sabrina. "This is a survivor's guide to the city. It has a list of phone numbers and addresses for each of the missionaries. There's a card you can keep in your purse that has your address in Chinese and English in case you ever get lost. It also has a subway pass and itinerary, as well as a list of places to see on your time off." Matt paused. "Is there anything I have forgotten?"

"I don't think so," Sabrina said, shaking her head. The way he had read off the list left her a little dizzy.

"Great." Matt rubbed his hands together and smiled. "I'll let Dianna show you around the church where we are going to hold the camp. This week your assignment is to get prepared for the students. They'll be here bright and early next Monday morning."

The two women walked the few blocks to the church. Sabrina was still amazed by how people in Hong Kong managed to get so much use out of such small spaces. She and Dianna entered through the basement garage and walked upstairs. Dianna took her through a maze of rooms, including the sanctuary where Sabrina had worshiped the day before.

When they had made their way back to the stairs, Dianna stopped. "So, what do you think?"

"It's a very nice facility," Sabrina replied.

"We like it." Dianna smiled. "Come in the office, and I'll show you what we've worked up for the program."

The itinerary looked pretty full. The students would be doing something non-stop from morning to night, and all of it in English. Sabrina wished she could have a similar experience for learning Cantonese. She voiced her thoughts to Dianna.

"You mean you really want to learn Cantonese?" Dianna asked. Her jaw dropped as she stared at Sabrina. "Most missionaries aren't excited about language study, except for the fact that they want to be able to communicate the gospel to people."

"I majored in languages in college. One of the reasons I signed up was to get a chance to study a language up close and personal."

Dianna shook her head in amazement. "Well, if you really want to learn, I'm sure one of our tutors would be glad to get you started."

"That would be wonderful," Sabrina said. She was so excited that she wanted to jump up and down but decided that it wouldn't be appropriate. She smiled instead.

"I'll see if I can find someone."

Dianna gave Sabrina her assignment and showed her which room would be hers. They wouldn't be able to decorate and set up the rooms until after Sunday school the following Sunday. Sabrina made some notes about the room size and things she would need to bring for decorating. By lunchtime she had done everything she could, so she searched the church for Dianna. She found her in the church office, but she wasn't alone. Sabrina's heart skipped a beat as she noticed Jason's dark hair. Dianna came into the hall.

"I was just about to come looking for you," Dianna said.

"What's up?"

"Well, I found you a tutor," Dianna replied.

"Great! Who?"

"Me," Jason said from the doorway. That one word was enough to send tingles up her spine. She wasn't sure if it was the fact that she would be spending even more time with him, or if it was just the pure pleasure she got from hearing his voice. Either way, she knew it was going to be a glorious summer. She didn't want to think about the fall.

"Hope you don't mind," Dianna said, a hint of concern causing frown lines to form around her mouth. "All of the native-speakers are really swamped right now."

"I don't want to be a problem." Sabrina held up her hands as if to stop Dianna.

"It's not a problem," Jason said quickly. "I have more free time in the summer."

"Well, if you're sure. . ."

"I'm positive."

"That's settled then." Dianna clapped her hands to punctuate the finality.

"What's on the agenda now?" Sabrina asked.

"I need to go back to the mission office and work on something for Matt," Dianna replied. "I don't think we have anything else pressing right now. The work will really start on Sunday afternoon. Until then, you just need to be working up your lessons and activities for the camp and getting acquainted with the city."

"In that case," Jason interjected, "why don't we work on your Cantonese this afternoon? Then we can go out and try it in the real world." He looked eager to start.

"Okay," Sabrina replied, trying not to let her enthusiasm show too much.

"Why don't we start with lunch? I'll show you how to order."

"That sounds good. I'm starved."

"Does that mean you will make sure she finds her way home?" Dianna asked, hands on hips.

"Yes, Mommy. I'll have her home in time for dinner," Jason said, winking at Sabrina.

"Have fun, but don't stay out too late," Dianna replied shaking her finger at Jason. He laughed, and the three friends walked out together. When they got to the street, Dianna said good-bye and headed toward the office.

"Come on," Jason said to Sabrina. "I'll show you a great little restaurant."

"Little" was the key word, Sabrina decided a few minutes later. The place wasn't much bigger than her living room back home. Several small tables, most of which were full, were wedged into the small space.

Jason read the menu out loud and made Sabrina repeat the words. The sounds seemed foreign to her tongue, and her jaw hurt by the time they finished. After he explained each item, she ordered her meal in Cantonese. The waitress smiled as she took the order.

"See, that wasn't too hard, was it?" Jason asked.

"Not too bad, but my jaw is killing me."

"I know the feeling." Jason chuckled. "My jaw hurt for the first three months."

"Oh, well, that's encouraging." Jason laughed again, and she joined him.

They laughed a lot over the course of lunch. Afterward, instead of taking her to the mission office or back to the apartment, he took her out on the Star Ferry across the bay. Then they walked all over town. He took her by several street vendors and showed her how to bargain. By the time they got back to the apartment, Sabrina was exhausted but happy. It had been exciting and different. Being with Jason was like the cherry on top of the sundae. She almost hated to say good-bye.

"I guess I'd better let you get some rest," Jason said. The wry smile was proof that he didn't want the day to end either.

"Do you want to stay for dinner?" Sabrina asked, surprised at her own boldness. The minute the words were out she regretted them. They just weren't meant to have a relationship, and spending time together only put off the inevitable. He must have sensed her change of heart because just as she thought he was going to say yes, he stopped.

"I better not. You should get some rest. Besides, I need to work on some things at my place."

"Okay." She felt a mixture of relief and disappointment. He waved and then trotted around the corner. She went in and sat on the sofa. Immediately, exhaustion hit her like a sudden wave. Curling up on the couch, she fell asleep.

Chapter 5

Over the next week, Sabrina prepared for English camp. Her assignment was to teach survival skills for social situations. By Friday morning, she had several ideas that she wanted to run by Matt. For the first time, Sabrina made her way to the missions office by herself. Already she had learned some of the local bus routes and grocery stores on her outings with Jason. He had remained friendly yet aloof all week. Part of her was relieved, but the rest of her was disappointed. As she climbed the short set of stairs to the building, she dismissed the gloom that had descended on her spirit.

Matt was in his office, early as usual. "Good morning, Sabrina. What brings you out so early?"

"I have some ideas that I want to run by you."

He smiled and motioned for her to sit in the chair across from him. "Always glad to hear new ideas."

His interest encouraged her to continue. "I was thinking that since I'm trying to help the students with social survival skills, we might create realistic situations." Sabrina paused for a breath.

"I'm listening," Matt said, leaning forward slightly.

"Well, we could actually have a dinner party, say the last night of the camp. The rest of the week we could practice different aspects of a party, like introductions and polite conversation."

"Sounds interesting. We were planning to have a party for the students at the end, so it wouldn't take much to turn it into a formal dinner party." Matt paused for a moment, stroking his chin. "Sure. Let's do it."

Sabrina let out a breath she hadn't realized she was holding. For a moment, she didn't know what to say.

"Great," she finally replied.

"I'll mention it at the meeting this afternoon and give you a few minutes to share your ideas. Then we can brainstorm together and make definite plans." Matt clapped his hands as if to say it was a done deal. "Anything else?"

"No. That's it."

"In that case, I'll get back to the paperwork," he replied, patting the stack of folders in front of him.

"Sure. See you this afternoon."

Sabrina left the office in such a daze that she almost ran over someone in the foyer. She didn't have to look up to know who it was.

"Morning, Sabrina." The sound of his voice sent a shiver of delight up her spine. "You're not cold, are you?" Jason asked, concern etched in the tight line of his lips.

"No. Just one of those unaccountable shivers." They walked outside into the sunshine.

"What were you doing here this early, anyway?" Jason questioned.

"I had an idea about the last day of camp." She shared her idea with Jason. He nodded his head as she explained, his smile getting brighter with each word.

"I think that would be a fun way for the students to practice.

I can't wait to see how it works out."

"What were you doing here?"

"Checking my mail."

"Oh, well, I guess I'll head back to my place," Sabrina said.

"Lots of work to do for next week?"

"Not really. I've done all I can until after the meeting this afternoon."

"How about a trip to some place new?"

"Why not?" Sabrina smiled up at Jason, her heart suddenly lighter. She had dreaded the idea of spending a long morning alone.

Jason smiled in return and held out his hand. "Let's go."

She took his hand. Something about being with him seemed so right. They walked to the bus stop in companionable silence, neither one wanting to break the moment. She was content to just let the morning be what it may.

Jason took her to a shopping district, and they wandered around for a couple hours. Sabrina even found some souvenirs to take back to her sisters and her parents. They ate lunch at another out-of-the-way place before heading back for the meeting. At the bus stop, Jason looked at his watch.

"We'd better move it, or we're going to be late." He took off at a lope, dragging Sabrina behind him. They arrived at the mission office with five minutes to spare. Sabrina leaned against the wall to catch her breath.

"All that running for nothing," she said between gasps.

"We needed the exercise after that meal anyway." Jason grinned. One day that grin was going to be her undoing. "We'd better go inside," he said, holding the door open for her.

They weren't the only ones running a little late. Several other members of the team slipped in the conference room after Jason and Sabrina had already taken their seats. Matt opened with prayer before going over some previous business. Then he mentioned Sabrina's ideas to the group. There were nods of approval. Matt opened up the meeting for discussion, and soon they had definite plans for the last evening, including the menu. Matt delegated tasks and then closed the meeting.

"I hope everybody's ready for Sunday," he said as they stood up. Sabrina took a deep breath to calm the sudden tripping of her heart. Up until now, it had all been talk and planning. Soon, she would be standing in front of a group of students. She was excited and terrified at the same time.

Jason must have read the expression on her face because he moved closer and squeezed her arm. "You'll be great."

"How did you know what I was thinking?"

"I remember how I felt before my first day. Everybody feels nervous and unworthy about serving God when they start out. Just remember that it is God working through us and not just us doing the work." Jason touched her shoulder. "I need to talk to Matt about something. I'll see you later."

Sabrina watched him walk away and wondered how she was ever going to be able to walk away from this man.

Chapter 6

Jason waited until the others were gone before approaching Matt. With one look at Jason's face, Matt motioned for him to go into his office. He closed the door before joining Jason on the small couch in the corner.

"What's up?" Matt asked, his face unreadable.

"I'm in trouble," Jason said without preamble.

"What kind of trouble?" Matt asked, his brow wrinkling in concern.

"Heart trouble."

"Sabrina?"

"How did you know?" Jason asked.

"All you have to do is look at your face when she walks in the room. It gives you away every time." He smiled and then continued. "It's also written all over her face." When Jason didn't return his smile, Matt's face grew serious. "You don't look happy."

"I would be perfectly happy except for one thing."

"What's that?"

"She's not interested in serving as a missionary."

"At least not yet," Matt replied.

"What do you mean?"

"Sometimes people don't know what they want. I don't know how many volunteers I have seen go through a summer or short-term program convinced that this is their one-time service overseas, but then later they go on to serve in the ministry in some way. It gets in the blood."

"I hope so," Jason said. He took a deep breath. "I don't know how I'm going to be able to say good-bye otherwise."

"Give it some time and prayer. God will show you what you need to do." Matt paused for a moment. "I wouldn't give up on her yet. She's getting that look in her eye."

"What look?"

"The I'm-hooked-on-missions look."

Jason gave a weak smile. "I hope you're right. I really do."

"Let's pray about it."

The two men knelt beside the couch and prayed for God's guidance. Jason left feeling lighter. It was good to get his worries off his chest. He also had the impression that he should continue his relationship with Sabrina. Only God knew where that would lead.

———— ◆ ————

Sunday evening Sabrina surveyed her assigned room. It looked like a small living room, sort of. She grinned at the thought. The small classroom had been emptied of the table and chairs that normally occupied it. In their place, Sabrina, along with a couple strong young men, had moved in a small couch and some chairs from the church office. She had brought along some pictures from her apartment and some knick-knacks to make it look homey. Her lesson plans were ready, but her stomach was in knots.

"Looks great," Dianna said from the door. "Ready for some dinner?"

"I am starved," Sabrina replied, then grimaced as her stomach growled audibly.

"Sounds like it." Dianna laughed and pulled her arm. "I think we'd better feed you pronto."

"Where are the others?"

"Matt had dinner waiting for him at home, and Jason is getting us a table at Hard Rock Café."

"I love that restaurant."

"Me too. I just wish Jeff were here." Dianna's smile faded. Sabrina touched her arm and the smile returned. "I don't mean to be a downer."

"You're not," Sabrina assured her. "When is he coming home?"

"He should be back before you leave."

"Great! I can't wait to meet him."

The two walked to the subway stop, chatting about the coming week. Before Sabrina knew it, they were joining Jason at a table. Even with rumpled hair, he still set her heart to pounding. He pulled out a chair for Dianna and then for her.

"I hope you don't mind. I ordered an appetizer. It should be here any minute."

"Thank You, God," Sabrina said.

"She means that sincerely," Dianna said with a laugh. "I thought her stomach was going to jump out and start nibbling on me."

They all laughed. The waiter arrived with the appetizers and took their drink orders. The evening passed quickly with a lot of laughter and chatter. By the time she reached her apartment, Sabrina was ready for bed, but thoughts of the next day kept her too wired to relax. It was past midnight before she finally drifted off to sleep.

The morning sun seeped through the blinds, waking Sabrina. She sat bolt upright, sure that she had missed her alarm clock. A quick glance told her that it would be another hour before the alarm went off. Anxious to get the day started, she got dressed and headed for the church. Despite the early hour, Matt was already there registering students.

"Glad you're here," Matt said. He patted the seat next to him. "I need some help." He showed her how to fill out the forms. They were so busy for the next hour that she didn't have time to think about her class.

After registration, all the students met in the sanctuary for orientation. Sabrina joined Dianna, Jason, Matt, and a couple other volunteers on the stage. Matt welcomed them and opened with prayer. Then Dianna taught them a couple choruses, which the students seemed to enjoy.

Finally, it was time. Sabrina stood at the door as her first group of students came in. The students were separated into groups. Each group would take turns in the different stations. Sabrina was teaching social survival skills. Matt was giving a Bible lesson. Dianna was teaching music while Jason did games and recreation.

Sabrina felt very conspicuous as every pair of eyes turned on her, but she introduced herself and asked the others to do the same. She led them in an ice-breaker game, which created a more relaxed atmosphere. It wasn't long before she found herself enjoying the students immensely. Jason caught up with her during break time.

"How's it going?" He looked at her so intently that she almost didn't answer.

"Great! I'm really enjoying it." His face relaxed into its usual grin.

"I thought so. Are you officially hooked yet?"

"Maybe," Sabrina said, surprising herself. Jason didn't have a chance to reply because Matt was calling for the next round. Sabrina went back to her room and greeted the next group of students with more confidence.

The groups ate their meals together and met up again for the evening service. When it was over, the students dispersed to their assigned sleeping quarters, and the leaders met in the church office to go over the day's events.

"Things went pretty smoothly today," Matt said. "Any problems?" No one spoke, so Matt continued with some announcements and schedule changes. "Okay. Let's get some sleep. Tomorrow will be another long day."

Everyone groaned, but smiles covered all the faces. It had been an exhausting day, but at the same time, Sabrina felt exhilarated.

The rest of the week followed the same pattern until Friday morning. As the students practiced their polite conversation in pairs, Sabrina walked around the room, listening in to see how they were doing. But she was startled by a conversation between two of her Buddhist students.

"You are very lucky to be accepted by such a distinguished college." Sabrina smiled at the way the girl accented every syllable, trying to use big words. Her smile faded as she heard the other girl's reply.

"My mother went every day to the temple and prayed. She fasted and brought gifts to the temple. She says that fate has smiled upon us. My best friend was not so lucky. Her mother did not go every day, and she was not accepted."

Sabrina continued circling the class, but she couldn't get her mind off what the girl had said. At lunch, she sat alone in the office to think.

"A penny for your thoughts," Jason asked from the doorway. When she didn't reply, he came in with his plate and drink. "Is this seat taken?" he asked, motioning to the chair next to hers.

"It's a free country."

"Are you going to eat that, or just look at it?" Jason asked, pointing at her suspended sandwich.

"Oh." Sabrina took a bite, but her mind was still thinking about the girls.

"Okay, I give. What's up?"

"Hmm?" Sabrina asked.

"What's got you so occupied that you can't even eat? Is it a guy?" he asked, narrowing his eyes to slits.

"I was just thinking about a conversation between two of my students this morning."

"And?"

"Well, one of them was describing how her mother went to the Buddhist temple every day and performed rituals so that the girl could get into a good college. She said the reason another friend of hers didn't get into the college was because her mother wasn't faithful enough."

"Sounds typical."

"It just seems so sad that they think that you have to follow some kind of strict regimen in order for good things to happen to you.

"I know. It's all about works, not faith." Jason took another bite of his sandwich before continuing. "That's why these English camps are so good. It exposes students to the gospel, to a new way of thinking."

Sabrina nodded her head in agreement. They finished

their lunch in silence. Sabrina prayed silently for the two girls and for the rest of the students. Even as she went back to class, their conversation haunted her. How could she ever make a difference?

Chapter 7

Jason watched Sabrina walk away. Her concern for the students reinforced his feeling that Sabrina was called to be a missionary, to be his wife, to be his partner. *Lord, open her eyes and heart.* He jumped when he felt a hand on his shoulder.

"You look serious."

Jason turned to see Matt standing behind him. "Just saying a little prayer."

"I see," Matt said. "How is the situation coming?"

"There may have been a breakthrough."

"Oh, really." Matt smiled. "What kind of breakthrough?"

"Well, let's just say her heart might be opening."

Matt slapped him on the shoulder and smiled knowingly before walking away. Maybe Matt had been right all along. Just maybe.

Sabrina prayed all afternoon for the two girls in her morning class. She couldn't remember their names because she couldn't pronounce them, but God knew who they were. She felt the Spirit urging her to witness to them, so she waited for an opportunity. Her break came when the girl who had mentioned her mother's faithfulness to the temple volunteered to help Sabrina decorate the dining room for the upcoming dinner party.

"Thanks for your help. . ." Sabrina hesitated.

"You may call me Ling. It is easier to pronounce than my whole name," she said with a smile.

"Thanks, Ling." Sabrina nodded her head and motioned for Ling to work on the tables.

"Where would you like these?" Ling asked, holding up pair of candlesticks.

"The candle holders go on the buffet table," Sabrina replied.

"Buffet table?" the girl repeated carefully.

"The long table where the food will go."

"Oh!" She smiled with understanding, then walked over and placed the candles. "You work very hard."

"Thank you," Sabrina answered awkwardly. It seemed strange to accept a compliment for something she should be doing. *Lord, send me an opening.*

"Your God is pleased by hard work also?" she questioned.

Sabrina inwardly flinched at the way she said *your* God. Sabrina prayed for the right words before she answered. "Yes, God is pleased by hard work, but He's more pleased by a right spirit."

"What is a right spirit?" the girl asked, obviously confused.

"Our attitude when we work should be one of gratitude. . . you know. . .thankfulness."

"Thankful for what?"

"For Christ dying on the cross."

"Who is Christ?"

"Haven't you been studying this in the Bible class?" Sabrina asked, turning from the tablecloth she was unfolding.

"My English is not so good. Sometimes I do not understand," Ling replied, her face turning red.

"Then you should ask questions. That's why we're here."

Sabrina pulled two chairs out from the table and motioned the other girl to sit down. "Do you know who Jesus Christ is?" When the other girl shook her head no, Sabrina pulled a witnessing tract from her pocket and began reading through the gospel with the other girl, allowing her to read the Scriptures in her own language.

"First of all, God loves you and wants you to experience peace and life—eternal and abundant. That's what John 3:16 and John 10:10 say." She pointed to the verses, and Ling nodded.

"Next, we have been separated from God and that abundant life by sin. The Bible says we are all sinners. Do you believe that?"

"Sinners?"

"That we've all done wrong things, that we're not perfect."

"I believe this," Ling replied.

"God showed His love by sending Christ, God's Son, as a man to bridge the gap between God and man. Christ died so that we could all have a personal relationship with God."

Tears flowed down Ling's face like a fountain. She looked up at Sabrina. "You mean someone loves me," she pointed to herself, "so much they die for me?"

"Yes. Jesus loves you more than anything."

"I think I want to know more."

"Good. Let's go talk to Matt. He can explain it in your own language."

Sabrina gave the girl a tissue. Putting an arm around her shoulders, Sabrina walked with her to the office. She explained to Dianna what had happened, and Dianna took Ling into Matt's office. Sabrina waited in the outer office, her heart thudding in her chest. She had witnessed to someone, and they wanted to know the Lord. The knowledge left her awed and inspired to do more.

Sabrina waited outside the office for what seemed like an eternity before a smiling Matt and a glowing Ling came out, followed by Dianna. It was obvious that Ling had asked Christ to be Lord of her life. On impulse, Sabrina hugged Ling, which obviously both pleased and embarrassed the young girl. Dianna did the same before slipping into the hall to answer a student's question.

"Ling and I are going to go over some Scriptures this afternoon. Do you think you can handle the decorating alone?" Matt asked.

"Not a problem," Sabrina said with a grin. She watched Matt and Ling walk down the hall, sharing the good news with all of the staff as they went. With a sigh of satisfaction, Sabrina turned in the opposite direction.

She went back to the dining room and finished the decorations in a fit of energy. Looking at her watch, she was shocked to see that she only had an hour to get ready for the party. It was a good thing that she had brought a change of clothes, because she didn't have time to go back to her apartment before the party.

Grabbing her bag, she headed for the ladies' room to change into an emerald green pantsuit and dress shoes. She touched up her makeup and fluffed her hair, the most she could do given the situation, then slipped into her dress shoes. When she returned to the dining room, some of the church members were arriving with food. Between setting up the food and greeting students, Sabrina barely had time to breathe, much less eat. Her stomach growled in protest.

"There it goes again," Jason said, shaking his head. "How can you keep forgetting to eat?" he asked in mock seriousness.

He held two plates of food in his hands.

"Just busy, I guess," Sabrina said with a wry grin. Tilting her head, she smiled coyly at him. "Is one of those for me?"

"Hmm. I don't know." He shifted the plates as if weighing them. "I was holding them for the prettiest girl in the room, but since she's not here, I guess you can have it."

"You're lucky you're holding food, or I'd get you for that one." She shook a warning finger at him.

"I'm so afraid." His grin showed just how afraid he really was. "Come on. Let's go somewhere a little quieter."

She followed him into the now-quiet office. They cleaned off a corner of the desk and pulled up two chairs, then Jason blessed the food. Sabrina hadn't realized how hungry she was until the first bite touched her lips.

Jason smiled. "Enjoying the food?"

"Immensely," she said between bites.

"Good. I wouldn't want you to go hungry."

"Sorry," she said, slowing her intake of food.

"Don't be. I like a woman with an appetite. Nothing makes me madder than to buy a woman dinner and watch her pick at it."

"You know, we always seem to be eating when we're together."

"I guess you're right. I hadn't thought about it."

They finished the rest of the meal in relative quiet. It was a nice break from the cacophony of sounds coming from the dining hall. Sabrina was suddenly tired beyond words. The week had been draining, both physically and mentally.

"Don't take this the wrong way, but you look tired."

She could see the concern in his eyes.

"I guess it's because I am tired. I think we all are."

"These camps can be draining. At least we have the rest of the weekend to rest before the next one starts. But it won't be as draining as this one because it's a sports camp."

"How can a sports camp be less tiring?"

"Well, for you anyway. Since you're not one of the coaches, your schedule will be less hectic. You can take a break and watch us play."

"Why am I not a coach?" Sabrina asked.

"You want to be a coach?" Jason asked, obviously surprised.

"No, not really," she said with a smile. "I just don't like you making assumptions, that's all."

"Sorry. I did not mean to imply that you are incapable of being a coach based solely upon your gender." He gave a deep bow. "Actually, Dianna will be coaching the girl's team. I just hadn't seen your name on the roster."

"I'm doing the Bible study, which makes me a little nervous."

"Why?"

"I haven't actually taught a Bible study before, and teenagers aren't known for their kindness to their teachers."

"These kids will be. They're taught to show respect to their teachers."

"Good," she said emphatically. "I need all the help that I can get."

"You'll be great."

"Thanks for the encouragement. It really means a lot to me."

Jason leaned forward in his chair until his face was mere inches from her own. "You mean a lot to me."

Sabrina's heart pounded in her chest. She waited for him to close the distance between them, but he didn't. He stood up and held out his hand. "I think we should get back to the party."

Disappointed, she took his hand and stood up. Releasing

her hand, he grabbed the plates from the desk. They walked back to the party in silence. Jason put the plates in the kitchen and began to mingle with the students. She did the same, but her eyes kept wandering back to Jason.

After all the food had been cleared away, they took down all the decorations and put the rooms back in order. By midnight, the building looked like a church again. Jason hopped on a bus back to his place with barely a wave. Dianna and Sabrina rode with Matt back to their apartments.

Sabrina forced herself to go through her nightly ritual, falling into bed at one o'clock. Even though she was exhausted, she kept running Jason's words through her mind. Was Jason the man God wanted her to marry? Could she really be a missionary's wife? The questions swam together until they were blotted out by blissful darkness.

Chapter 8

Sabrina blinked and tried to roll over, only something seemed to be holding her. She opened her eyes enough to see the covers were entwined around her legs, immobilizing them. Unwrapping them proved difficult since her eyes were still filled with sleep. Once free, she flipped over and squinted at the clock. Ten-thirty. It had been a long time since she had slept this late. In college, all of her classes had been early so that she could get to work. With a groan, Sabrina crawled out of bed and stumbled to the bathroom. There was only one cure for this kind of hangover: a hot shower.

Coming out of the bathroom, she felt like a new woman. She went into the kitchen and put on a pot of coffee. The four-cup coffee maker was perfect for a single person. While she was waiting for it to brew, she hooked up her laptop computer to the phone line and checked her E-mails. More than thirty messages were waiting, not surprising since she hadn't been able to check them all week. She scanned the list and noticed one from her sister Sharon.

Hi ya Sis,
How are things going in Hong Kong? I'll bet you're

asleep as I write this. Wish we were closer so we could see each other more.

Guess what! It looks like our second wedding anniversary is the last one Rory and I will share alone. Our first baby is due in August! I've got everything planned. We're changing the little room Rory uses for his office now into a nursery. We decided to paint it mint green to be safe. I'd love to name the baby Felicity Delacourt Ford if it's a girl, but I'm having a hard time selling Rory on Felicity. He wants to name a boy Philemon Delacourt Ford.

Gotta run. Little Felicity or Philemon is taking a lot of energy from Mommy. Think I'll take a nap.

Love,
Sharon

Sabrina poured a cup of coffee before writing a response. She thought a moment and then typed a reply.

Congratulations, Sis,

I'm happy for you and Rory. I can't believe Rory doesn't like Felicity. I think it's a beautiful name. However, what was he thinking, wanting to name the baby Philemon? It's a great Bible name, but the kid would never hear the end of the teasing. It's nice to include our family name.

By the way, I met a guy. He's handsome, charming, sweet, thoughtful, a Christian, and single. The only problem is he feels called to the mission field—foreign missions. I don't know what to do. Could you see me as a missionary's wife?

Lots of love,
Sabrina

Sabrina hit the send button. Then she glanced through the remainder of the E-mails, reading a few short ones from friends back home. Somehow their concern about which haircut to get just didn't seem important. She couldn't forget the feeling she'd experienced when she'd shared Christ's love with a lost soul.

Grabbing her Bible, Sabrina sat down at the makeshift desk and flipped open to the marked page. She reread the Great Commission. Everyone was to be a missionary wherever they were. Yesterday, she had been a missionary. The thought hit her like a speeding train. Missionaries were just ordinary people doing what all Christians should be doing, witnessing the love of Christ.

She leaned back into her chair and pondered the thought for a moment. It was an overwhelming discovery, something she wanted to share with others. Turning back to her computer, she typed in the verse and her thoughts and sent an E-mail to everyone in her address book.

Taking out a notepad and pen, she started making notes for a Bible study. It wouldn't be useful next week because most of the camp attendees would be non-Christians, but it would be great for when she got home.

Home? The place seemed like a vague dream. Her apartment in Hong Kong seemed so much more real than the family home in Nebraska. She didn't feel homesick at all, which was strange. Her first night at college had been a tearful one. Several times she had almost called her parents and asked them to come and take her home. But here she felt at home, relaxed, despite the fact that it was a foreign country. Could she spend her life in a foreign country?

She puzzled over the idea. Somehow it didn't seem as

strange a thought as it had her first day here. But Jason had suddenly started avoiding her last night. Maybe he had changed his mind about her. Maybe he had never really been attracted to her. With a sigh, she turned back to her Bible study.

Jason mentally kicked himself over and over again. The more he thought of his conversation with Sabrina during the Friday evening dinner party, the more he couldn't believe what he had done. How could he have blurted out to Sabrina that she meant a lot to him? The look on her face had been one of pure shock. How would they ever be comfortable around each other again? She would probably avoid him the rest of her stay here.

He would have to learn how to get a grip on his feelings before they got totally out of control. He made a promise to himself that he would pray before he opened his mouth again. The Bible was right when it said that man could tame a horse with a bridle, but he couldn't bridle his own tongue.

Jason decided to give Sabrina room to breathe. Pushing too hard could send her running for cover and home. On the other hand, if he didn't say anything, she might think he wasn't interested. He groaned in frustration. What should he do? The answer was so obvious that he thumped himself on the forehead. Prayer was always the answer.

"Lord, what do I do? I'm falling in love with her."

Do you really love her enough to let her go?

The thought sent a chill down his spine. He didn't want to let her go, but how many times in Scripture had God said that His ways are not our ways. True love meant doing what was best for the other person. Was he willing to let her go if that was what God asked? He prayed that God would make him willing. It was the best he could do at the moment. Sabrina had to find her own way; he couldn't force her to choose the ministry if she wasn't called. They would both be miserable then.

With a sigh, he sunk back into the couch and prayed for strength. He would have to let Sabrina decide for herself what God's call for her life was and then abide by that decision. From now on, he would let God do the leading and get out of the way. It was going to be a long couple of weeks.

Chapter 9

Sabrina watched Jason from across the church. Instead of sitting with her and Dianna as he usually did, he had moved to the other aisle. She told herself that it was his obligation to sit with the students and not a sign that he wasn't interested. However, even the appearance of Dianna's husband hadn't brought him near, which was a bad sign.

"So, Sabrina, how do you like Hong Kong so far?"

"Excuse me," she said, turning in her seat.

"You look a thousand miles away," Dianna said. "Jeff asked how you like Hong Kong."

"Oh, it's wonderful. I never imagined that I would enjoy it so much."

"If you didn't think you would enjoy it, then why did you sign up?" Jeff asked.

Sabrina considered the question for a moment and shrugged. "I hadn't really thought about it before. I guess I felt it was my duty to do missions work at least once."

Jeff stopped to return a greeting before he replied. "Why didn't you just work at a local mission?" He held up his hands. "I'm sorry. I just met you, and here I am throwing all these questions at you like you're at the Inquisition or something."

"It's okay," Sabrina said, smiling to put him at ease. "Nobody's ever questioned my motives, not even me."

"I guess the reason I'm so interested is that so many people do things or hold positions in church that they are not really called to. They do it because no one else will do it." Jeff shifted positions in the pew. "I was one of those people."

"What do you mean?" Sabrina asked, openly curious.

"I taught Sunday school because I felt it was my duty to serve in the church. I didn't stop to ask God if that was what He wanted." Jeff's brown eyes filled with emotion. "I almost missed out on God's call for my life.

"How do you know what God's will is for your life?" Sabrina asked.

"First of all, you have to pray for God's guidance, and then you have to learn to listen to that still, small voice in your heart." He patted his chest with one hand for emphasis.

Sabrina was about to ask for more information when the pianist started playing the prelude. She spent the rest of the service pondering Jeff's words. Obviously, he and Dianna were happy in their position here. It was written all over their faces. She passionately wished for the same experience in her own life.

After church, Jason came over to greet Jeff. He thumped him on the shoulder, and the two exchanged a warm hug. When Dianna invited Jason to go to lunch with the three of them, he politely declined, walking away, barely acknowledging Sabrina's presence.

"That's odd," Jeff remarked.

"It's not just odd; it's downright rude. What's up with him anyway?" Dianna asked.

"Maybe he had pressing business," Sabrina suggested.

"Still, he could have said something." Dianna watched

Jason's retreating figure, hands on hips. "I'm going to have to have a talk with that boy."

"Now, don't go interfering, mother hen." Jeff put an arm around his wife's shoulder. "He's a big boy and can make his own decisions."

Dianna colored at the remark, which Sabrina thought was strange. She shook off the thought and followed Jeff and Dianna down the aisle. They chose a western restaurant not far from the church and chatted over soft drinks.

"I wanted to talk to you some more about our previous conversation," Sabrina said, turning to Jeff. "How do you know when God is speaking to you?"

"It's hard for one person to tell another when God is speaking because it is a very personal thing." He moved his glass to the side and leaned forward. "Sometimes He speaks through the Bible, sometimes through a Christian friend, and sometimes through our circumstances."

"I'm just not sure what God wants me to do. I graduated from college last month, but I don't know what I want to do."

"Well, I think Jeff's earlier question is a valid one. Why did you sign up for an overseas assignment?" Dianna asked.

"I'm ashamed to admit it," Sabrina replied, the heat rising in her cheeks. "I wanted to get away from home and see the world."

Jeff chuckled. "You wouldn't be the first, but is that the only reason?"

"No," Sabrina said, shaking her head for emphasis. "Our Sunday school teacher is always talking about how we should be witnesses and how so few people are answering the call to ministry. I guess I felt guilty."

"Was it guilt or the tugging of the Holy Spirit?" Jeff asked quietly.

Sabrina stopped for a moment to let the idea sink in. Had it been God speaking and not her conscience all along? Just then the waiter appeared with their order, and Jeff let the topic drop. They spent the rest of dinner enjoying each other's company and getting to know one another better. After dessert was served, Dianna tapped her glass with a fork.

"I have an announcement to make. I was hoping to tell both you and Jason at the same time, but since he's being rude, he can find out later."

"What's up?" Sabrina asked.

"I'm going to have a baby," Dianna said. Jeff grinned like the Cheshire cat.

"Congratulations!" Sabrina squealed, clapping her hands. "When?"

"Well, I'm only six weeks, so it'll be awhile yet."

"Oh, I'll miss it," Sabrina said, frowning at the thought. "You'll have to E-mail me pictures," she commanded.

"Yes, Sir." Jeff gave her a sharp salute. Dianna playfully swatted his arm.

"Of course I'll send you pictures, but we may be back in the States at the time. We're supposed to go on leave this fall."

"Maybe I can come visit."

"I'd love it," Dianna replied.

The rest of the meal was spent talking about the coming birth and names for the baby. Sabrina was excited for Dianna, but a twinge of jealousy reared its ugly head. She wanted a family of her own, and her choice candidate for marriage had just brushed her off. Squelching the thought, she turned her attention back to Dianna.

Jason walked home in a gray funk. More than anything, he

had wanted to go to lunch with Sabrina. Sure, he wanted to visit with Jeff, but his main desire was to see Sabrina. That was exactly why he had chosen to leave. He had wanted it too much. And he was afraid he might have offended her by being so abrupt.

At his apartment, he made a quick sandwich and ate it without tasting it. He pulled out his Bible and tried to study, but his mind kept wandering. In desperation, he fell on his knees and prayed for peace. If Jesus could calm the stormy seas, He could calm the storm in his heart. Peace was slow in coming, but it finally made an appearance when he released his will to the Father. Afterward, he opened his Bible again and began to read. God was in charge of the universe, not him. He had to let God move in Sabrina's life no matter how hard that was to practice in everyday life.

Jason spent the rest of the day in prayer and Bible study. His final prayer before he went to bed that night was that God would show Sabrina His plan for her life and help him not interfere with those plans. Sleep was a long time coming.

Chapter 10

Sabrina went into the next week with more confidence than the previous one, but a tinge of doubt still triggered her racing heart. Although she stumbled through her first Bible study, the students didn't seem to notice her inadequacy for the job, probably because of the language barrier. Their questions near the end of class revived her failing confidence, allowing her to continue on with a calmer spirit.

Jason's attitude, on the other hand, left her totally bewildered. He had practically stopped communicating with her except for polite greetings and discussions of mission business. There was no more chitchat, no invitations to go sightseeing. He had even said that he couldn't tutor her in Cantonese anymore because of his schedule. It was an excuse; he was avoiding her. It hurt more than she wanted to admit.

Despite her strained relationship with Jason, the week went smoothly. Several of the athletes accepted Christ, and Sabrina was learning a sense of independence that she had never known. She didn't need Jason or Dianna around to feel secure when exploring the city. Several times that week she had ventured out alone, ordering lunch and shopping. It had been a freeing experience.

During that time, she had allowed her thoughts to consider the possibility that God had called her to foreign missions for more than just this summer. The students tugged at her spirit; she was growing to love them and be concerned for their spiritual well-being with a depth of feeling that surprised her. Even the city with all its pollution and crowding called to her. This place was beginning to feel like home.

"Penny for your thoughts," Matt said from behind her.

"Kind of cheap, aren't you?" Sabrina teased.

"Okay. A dollar, but that's my limit," he replied firmly. He put his hands on his hips and squared his shoulders as if anticipating a fight.

"Sold."

"Okay, give it up."

"I was just thinking about how much I felt at home here. I never thought such a strange place would feel so familiar." She smiled up at Matt, who was grinning like a hyena. "What?"

"I don't know what you're talking about," Matt said with a shrug of his shoulders.

"Come on. You've got that look."

"What look?" he asked, the picture of innocence.

"Matt," Sabrina warned.

"I give," Matt said, raising his hands in defeat. "I just had a feeling that you were going to get hooked on missions this summer."

"Really? How?" Sabrina tilted her head in confusion.

"You just had that look. I could tell after the first day that you were going to enjoy this kind of work."

"You're not just saying that, are you?" Sabrina asked.

"No. Ask Jason. He can vouch for me."

"Jason?" Sabrina's head jerked up. "What does he have

to do with this?"

"I mentioned it to him not long after you got here."

Just then Dianna called to Matt from across the room. "Oops. Duty calls. Let's talk more about this later," he said as he walked away, still wearing that goofy grin.

The idea that the two men had been talking about her felt strange, somewhere between irritation and a sense of confirmation. Sabrina was irritated because they were talking about her behind her back, yet she felt a sense of confirmation because she had been thinking the same thing herself. She knew that God had brought her to Hong Kong to show her His will for her life.

But then if Jason had sensed that God was calling her to mission work, why hadn't he said anything? Why was he avoiding her like he couldn't stand the sight of her? Maybe he had never really been interested in her as a girlfriend. Maybe he had just been trying to encourage her to follow God's calling. If so, no wonder he was avoiding her. Her face burned at the way she had been acting. She vowed to be friendly but cool to Jason from now on.

The vow worked for the remainder of the camp. Sabrina did her work, and Jason did his. She could have sworn that she caught him staring at her several times, but it must have been her imagination. She was pleased with the amount of self-control she had shown, but in the next second it all disappeared.

"Want to see Victoria's Peak?" Jason asked Friday afternoon.

"Sure," she replied without thinking.

"Great. We'll go tomorrow before the typhoon settles in."

"Typhoon?" Sabrina could feel her eyes widening.

"Don't worry," Jason reassured. "It's just a big rainstorm." He patted her on the shoulder. "I've got to get back to the game. See ya tomorrow."

Sabrina stood in place, shocked by this turn of events. She didn't know if she was more stunned by the invitation or by the idea that she was about to live through a typhoon. She stared after Jason's retreating back and once again wondered what she had gotten herself into.

———◆———

Jason tried to concentrate on the game, but his eyes kept wandering toward Sabrina. He hadn't been sure if she would agree to go with him after her cool attitude the last few days. Then again, he hadn't exactly been friendly lately himself. He wiped the sweat out of his eyes and focused on the player with the ball.

At least he still had a small chance of winning Sabrina's heart. He had prayed every day that God would show him what to do, and this morning when he'd prayed, he'd felt the go-ahead to court Sabrina. Now he just had to figure out how. The trip to Victoria's Peak seemed a nice romantic start. His attention was drawn back to the game when the ball nearly flew past him. Grabbing it at the last moment, he dribbled down the court.

When the game was over, Jason found Matt in his office. He knocked on the door, and Matt looked up from the stack of papers on his desk. Jason leaned against the doorjamb and smiled. "Drowning in paperwork, I see."

"Always," Matt replied, returning the smile. "Is that the Cheshire cat I see?"

"I don't know what you're talking about."

"Oh, really? I don't suppose it has anything to do with a certain red-head?" Matt asked, pretending to pick an imaginary piece of lint from his shirt.

Jason rolled his eyes before coming in and closing the door behind him. He plopped into a chair across the desk and sighed.

"So it is about a certain red-head."

"Busted," Jason replied. He ran his fingers through his hair, then leaned forward to rest his forearms on his knees.

"That bad?" Matt asked.

"Well, it could be worse. I asked her to go to Victoria's Peak with me tomorrow, and she agreed."

"Then what's the problem?"

"She could be going just to be sightseeing." Jason looked up sharply at Matt's chuckle. "What?"

"Young love." Shaking his head, Matt continued to laugh.

"This isn't funny," Jason said sternly.

"I was just remembering my younger days," Matt said with a grin. "Jason, nothing in this world that matters is easy to obtain. There's always a risk involved, but I'd say this is a pretty sure thing."

"You really think so?" Jason looked up hopefully.

"Yeah, I really think so." Matt thumped the desk for emphasis. "You'll never win the race if you stay in the stables."

"Thanks, Matt."

"Don't mention it."

"I'm sure I won't have to. You're bound to bring it up again the next time you need a favor," Jason said with a grin.

"Smart boy," Matt replied, nonplused. Wrinkling his nose, Matt added, "Another word of advice. . ."

"Yeah?" Jason said, turning around.

"Take a shower first."

With a laugh, Jason left the office for home to do just that. Twenty minutes later, he emerged from the shower clean and refreshed. He headed for his source of strength, his quiet corner, for more Bible study and prayer. This was one of the biggest decisions of his life, and he didn't want to make a rush judgement. He prayed that God would guide his mind and heart and that

He would open Sabrina's heart. Although he knew that God was in control, Jason still felt nervous and on edge. He passed the night in fitful dreams, some good and some bad. At dawn he wondered which dream would become reality.

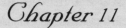

Chapter 11

The ring of the telephone jarred Sabrina from a restless dream. Disoriented, it took her two rings to realize the phone was making the noise, not her alarm clock, and another ring to find the phone. She put the receiver to her ear, only to realize that she had the mouthpiece to her ear. Turning it around, she mumbled a greeting.

"Sabrina?"

"Jason?" Turning to look at the clock, she asked, "Do you know what time it is?"

"Not really. I've been up studying for awhile."

She groaned into the phone.

"Were you asleep?" He sounded contrite.

"Not anymore," she mumbled.

"I'll call back later," he said.

"Wait! I'm awake now. If you call back and wake me up again, I won't be responsible for my actions." She took a deep breath and tried to speak in a calm voice. "Now, what did you need?"

"I was just going to set a time to pick you up to go to Victoria's Peak."

"Oh." Sabrina thought for a moment. "What do you suggest?"

"I thought you might like to see it at night when all the buildings are lit up and the moon is out."

"Sounds good to me." She twisted the cord between her fingers, praying he would finish the conversation soon so that she could go back to sleep.

"How about I pick you up at five and we have an early dinner before we go up?"

"Fine." She stifled a yawn. "Five will be just fine."

"Great, I'll pick you up at five."

"Okay." She hung up the phone without saying good-bye and was asleep before the connection was broken.

———◆———

Jason stared at the phone in disbelief. She had hung up on him. He put the phone back in the cradle and looked at the clock. Six-thirty, no wonder she hung up. It was way too early to be calling a girl for a date. He slapped his forehead, trying to clear the cobwebs. What had he been thinking? He had been up most of the night thinking about today. Finally, he had gotten out of bed and started studying his Bible. It beat tossing and turning in bed.

With a sigh, he returned to his studying. It was the only way to get his mind off Sabrina and tonight's date. Maybe this way the time would pass faster. A sudden burst of wind blew through the kitchen window, scattering his papers. He jumped up and closed it. Looking out, he could see the clouds moving in and trash blowing around in the alley. He was glad that he could take Sabrina up to the peak before the storm. There was no telling how long the typhoon would last, and he only had a short time left before she returned home. Gathering his papers, he prayed that it would be enough time.

———◆———

Sabrina awoke the second time to a tapping at the door. She

groaned, wondering if God had it in for her. The clock read a few minutes before nine. Wrestling free from the sheet, she stumbled across the bedroom and grabbed her robe on the way out. She repressed a squeal as she stubbed her toe on the chair and limped the rest of the way to the door.

"Good morning," Dianna said. Her pert smile faded as she took a closer look at Sabrina. "Maybe not."

"Can I help you?" Sabrina asked, squinting in the glare of the sunlight.

"I just thought you might like to go to the grocery store before the storm lands," Dianna replied, looking contrite. "I woke you up, didn't I?"

"You're not the first person," Sabrina said, rolling her eyes. "Come in." She stepped aside for Dianna to enter.

"I can come back later," Dianna suggested.

"No. I might as well get up. I don't think God wanted me to sleep in today anyway." Sabrina walked over to the coffeepot and fumbled through the cabinet looking for the coffee.

"Why don't I put on the coffee while you take a shower?" Dianna offered.

"Great idea." Sabrina motioned her toward the offending machine and stumbled toward the bedroom.

"You're not a morning person, are you?" Dianna asked.

"Nope." Without another word she closed the bedroom door.

The tantalizing smell of fresh-brewed coffee tickled her nose as Sabrina opened the bathroom door a short while later. Revived by the heat from the shower, she walked out into the living room fully dressed and coherent.

"You look alive."

"I feel much better," Sabrina replied. "Now where's the coffee?"

"Right where you left it." Dianna pointed toward the kitchen. "That's a good place for it."

Dianna giggled. Sabrina ignored her, pouring herself a cup of coffee. She pulled out a bagel and cream cheese. She offered Dianna one, but her guest declined with a wave of her hand. Downing it in a few bites, Sabrina swallowed the coffee and motioned for Dianna to go.

"That was fast," Dianna exclaimed.

"My taste buds are still asleep. I didn't want to wake them."

"You're a riot," Dianna said, laughing out loud.

"Whatever," Sabrina replied. "Let's just go."

By the time they reached the store, Sabrina's normally happy personality was back in full swing. The store was crowded because of the impending storm. Dianna helped her pick out the things she might need for emergencies, such as extra batteries and bottled water. Due to the crowd, it took two hours to make a few purchases and get back to the apartment. As she stepped out of the car, Sabrina looked up at the sky.

"The clouds are getting pretty thick and low," she said. A gust of wind blew her hair around her face and into her mouth. She pulled it loose and held it at the nape of her neck.

"Yeah," Dianna replied. "This is just the beginning. It could last for days." Sabrina must have looked as scared as she felt because Dianna smiled and patted her arm. "It will be okay. It's not a big one."

"Sure." Sabrina tried to sound reassured, but she was only fooling herself. Knots were already forming in her stomach. "Do you think it's okay to go out tonight?"

"Probably. The forecaster said the storm won't hit until late."

They separated the groceries and went to their apartments. Sabrina still didn't feel comfortable about the upcoming date, if you could call it that, but her nervousness probably had more to do with being alone with Jason than with the coming storm.

She spent the afternoon watching an old video, then prepared for the evening. She was ready and waiting when the doorbell rang at five o'clock sharp. Jason looked more handsome than ever in black slacks and a black button-down shirt.

"Ready?" he asked, pointing to her bag and the umbrella she had in hand.

"Yeah. Let's get going before the storm moves in."

"Sounds like a plan." He took her umbrella and held out his arm. Sabrina took it, and they walked to the subway station arm in arm. They went to a western restaurant for dinner. Conversation waned over the meal until Sabrina's nerves felt taut like a bow.

"Why does it seem so hard to keep a conversation going?" she asked.

"I don't know," Jason replied with a sheepish grin. "Maybe we're trying too hard."

"I guess." She looked out the windows. "I don't think the typhoon is helping matters either."

"Nervous?" He reached out and took her hand, gently stroking the back of it with his thumb.

"Yeah, a little." The heat from his touch sent warmth all the way up her arm to her face. Suddenly, it felt right to be there together.

"I'll protect you." Jason patted his chest with his free hand. "Me, heap strong man."

Sabrina laughed. After that, conversation flowed freely through dinner. Then Jason led her to the subway station that would take them to the foot of Victoria's Peak. He grabbed her hand as they fought the gusty wind. As yet, no rain had fallen, and the sky was still pretty clear. Clouds scudded across the moon and disappeared just as quickly.

There were two ways up to the peak, the fastest being the incline railway. They clambered aboard, making their way down the sloped car. Sabrina didn't notice much on the ride up since the warmth of Jason's body was so near. She wanted to snuggle into his arm and stay there forever, but was that what he wanted?

At the top, they went into the observation tower and out to the wall. If not for the storm, they could see for miles. The light of the stars was being snuffed out as the clouds piled in. During the short ride to the top, the storm seemed to have worsened. Jason looked like he was about to ask her a question when a raindrop landed on her nose. Other drops soon followed, until Jason and Sabrina were forced to pull out the umbrella. The gusty wind tore at the flimsy protections, sending them running for better shelter.

"I think we had better head back," Jason said. "The storm is coming in sooner than expected."

Sabrina nodded wordlessly. She licked her dry lips and followed Jason's lead. He squeezed her hand.

"Why don't we take a taxi home? That way we don't have to worry about getting drenched going from the subway to the bus."

"Okay." Sabrina followed him to a sheltered parking garage where there was a queue for taxies. Several people were already waiting.

After five minutes of waiting with no sign of a taxi, Jason spoke. "I think we'd better go down the incline railway and get a taxi at the bottom. I don't think they're coming up the mountain anymore."

Sabrina nodded and followed him back to the train station. He held firmly to her hand as they walked, giving her a sense of security. They purchased two tickets and sat in the train, waiting anxiously for it to finish loading the other passengers. Sabrina could see several of the people who were waiting in the taxi queue getting on the train. She sighed in relief as the train inched forward. At the bottom, they moved quickly to the door, but few taxies were nearby, and most of them were either full or off-duty.

In silent agreement, they ran for the subway station. Halfway there, the wind turned the umbrella inside out. Jason threw it into a nearby trash can as they ran down the street. Sabrina felt a near panic setting in, so she had no reservations about running through the subway station. Their speed paid off. They slid through the doors just as the train was getting ready to leave. Breathless, they sank onto an empty seat and tried to wring out some of the water from their clothes. Sabrina was soaked to the skin and shivering in the air-conditioning.

"We'll be home soon, and you can change," Jason reassured her.

That thought kept her going on the long train ride. At their stop, they exited the train and made their way up the labyrinth of escalators that led to the surface. Sabrina counted four levels going up. They stood outside the station under the overhang in amazement. The streets had turned into small rivers. Traffic was non-existent, especially buses.

"We'll never make it to your apartment. We'll have to go to mine and wait out the storm," Jason yelled.

Sabrina's heart skipped a beat. They were going to run three blocks to his apartment in this. The full impact of what he was saying didn't hit her at first, and then she realized what he meant. They were going to be stranded together for who knew how many days. She stood rooted to the spot in fear.

Chapter 12

Jason could see the fear in her eyes, and he knew that it was from more than the idea of running three blocks in a downpour. He squeezed her hand and pulled her closer so that he could look into her eyes.

"It will be okay," he said firmly. She nodded, but he could still see the tension in her body. He tightened his grip on her hand. "You ready? Let's go."

They sprinted down the street, splashing through puddles. The good news was that they couldn't get any wetter than they already were. In a way, Sabrina was lucky. She was wearing open sandals so the water simply ran off her feet. Jason, on the other hand, was wearing dress shoes and socks that weighed down his stride. When they finally reached his apartment, he struggled with the latch to the gate. Inside, he pulled Sabrina under the awning while he unlocked the door. At least they didn't have to climb upstairs, like his neighbor had to.

Jason ushered Sabrina in first and then stepped into the foyer. Closing the door, he leaned against the door to catch his breath. Sabrina seemed unsure what to do. Water dripped from their clothes onto the ceramic tile floor. He pulled off his shoes and socks, leaving them behind the door, before he tiptoed quickly to the bathroom.

"Wait right there. I'll bring you a towel," he called.

"Okay."

Sabrina pulled off her sandals and nudged them next to his shoes. He could see her shivering. Grabbing a thick towel, he ran back to her side and started rubbing her shoulders and arms dry.

"I can do it," she said between chattering teeth.

"I know, but I can do it faster." He rubbed vigorously for a few more moments before wrapping the giant towel around her shoulders. He picked her up and carried her to the bathroom amid arguments from Sabrina.

"There you are," he said, putting her down on the bathroom floor.

"I am perfectly capable of walking."

"Yes, and perfectly capable of dripping all over my carpet," he said with a smile. He bent over the tub and turned the hot water on full blast.

"Just what I need, more water," she said dryly.

"Hot water. It'll get you warmed up." He pulled two more towels from the cabinet and put them on the vanity. "I'm going to put on some tea and pray that the power doesn't go off."

"Amen."

"Get those wet clothes off and stick them in the hall, and I'll put them in the dryer." He stopped and looked her in the eye. "I mean everything."

She blushed but nodded. "What can I wear in the meantime?"

"My robe is right here behind the door," he said. "First, I'll take your clothes and put them in the dryer, and then I'll get the tea started." He went out, closed the door, and turned his back for good measure.

Sabrina stripped off her wet clothes and slipped into the robe. Instantly she felt warmer. She wrung out the excess water from the clothes into the sink before she handed them out to Jason. Then she closed the door, hooked the latch, and stepped into the hot tub of water, turning off the faucet. The heat enveloped her, sending warm waves coursing through her veins. In a few minutes, the shivering stopped. She soaked in the tub for awhile, unwilling to face the cold air again. Eventually, she got out and wrapped her hair in the smaller towel Jason had put out. Then she took the other and rubbed the rest of her body dry. As soon as she pulled the plug on the tub, Jason knocked on the door.

"Yes?"

"Are you finished?"

"Almost," she called through the door.

"The tea is ready and your clothes will be dry in about half an hour. Come on out when you're ready."

She heard his footsteps retreating. Taking the robe off the hook, she brought it to her nose and sniffed; his cologne still lingered in its folds. Hesitantly she pulled it on; it felt a little too intimate. It was warm though, so she pulled it as tight as she could and tied the belt in a knot. Turning, she caught her reflection in the mirror and laughed. The sleeves hung below her fingertips and the hem was nearly to her ankles. She rolled up the sleeves and wrapped her arms around herself before unlatching the door.

"What was so funny?" Jason asked from the kitchen.

"Just look," she replied.

He turned around and smiled. "I see what you mean." He motioned to a barstool across the counter from him. "Have a seat."

She was grateful for the space between them. It was awkward enough wearing his robe without having to be in close proximity to him. Gratefully, she took the mug of tea and sipped it.

"Feel better?"

"Much. And you?"

"All dry now," he said pulling at a gray sweatshirt. He had changed clothes while she was in the bathtub. He wiggled his toes, and she looked at them in envy.

"I totally forgot socks," Jason exclaimed, tapping his forehead. "I'll be right back." He came back with a thick pair of socks that looked brand new. "Don't worry, I haven't worn these, so there aren't any cooties."

"Thanks," she said and smiled. She slipped them on while Jason returned to his side of the counter. "Do you think we should call someone and let them know that we're okay?"

"Good idea," Jason said. "I forgot." He picked up the phone and dialed. It was obvious that he was talking to Matt. After a few noncommittal responses, Jason said good-bye and hung up. "Matt said to hang tight and stay dry, and as soon as the storm lets up a little, he'll come get you in the car."

"How long do you think it will take?"

"No less than twenty-four hours according to Matt. Nothing will move except the subways for at least that long."

"Oh."

She felt Jason take her hand. "It will be okay. We'll play card games and eat just like we did in college." Jason squeezed her hand, then turned to the cupboard behind him. "Let's see what we've got. Chips, dip, and drinks in the fridge, chocolate cookies, and ice cream for when you're all warm again." He pulled the chips and cookies out and put them on the counter.

"Comfort food," he said, patting his stomach.

"I see cookies, but where's the milk?"

"Got milk, but aren't you a little cold for that? How about hot chocolate?"

She grinned. "Double the chocolate, double the fun."

Just as Jason finished preparing the hot chocolate, the buzzer rang on the dryer. Sabrina hopped off her barstool to go check. Her underclothes were dry, but everything else was still damp. She pulled out the underclothes and stuffed them in the pocket of the robe before turning the machine on for another twenty minutes.

"Are they dry?" Jason asked, peeking around the doorway.

"Part of them," she said, trying not to blush. "Do you have any more sweats?"

"Sure do, a pair that shrunk in the dryer and are too small for me. They should be perfect for you." He disappeared into the bedroom and came back with a set of dark green sweats. She grabbed them and headed for the bathroom.

"Don't eat all of the cookies," she warned.

"You snooze, you lose," he called back.

Jason watched her until she turned the corner out of sight. The sight of her in his bathrobe seemed so right. He knew that he wanted to spend the rest of his life with her, but was she ready to commit to serving as a missionary overseas? Maybe, maybe not, but he had to know for sure. She came back to the kitchen, rolling up the sleeves on the sweatshirt.

"Can I ask you something personal?" Jason asked. He saw her hesitate, but she nodded for him to continue. "Since you've been here, I've noticed that you really seem to have a gift for this type of ministry." He paused. "Do you think God might be calling you to mission service abroad?"

He watched her face as she thought about the question. Holding his breath in anticipation, he waited for her answer.

"I do think God has been dealing with me in that area," she said quietly. He released his breath as she continued. "I'm not really sure what He wants me to do, but I do know that I want to work with international students in some way."

"Would you be willing to go to a foreign country?"

"If that's what God wants me to do, then yes, I would."

Jason's heart soared. God had answered his prayer, and he knew that she was the woman God had designed just for him. Now he only had to figure out how to tell her. He would wait until the perfect moment before he popped the question. He wanted it to be just right, and besides, one more matter needed to be cleared up.

"I'm glad you've made that decision," he said. "Believe it or not, it had a lot to do with how I've been behaving the past week or so. I think I owe you an explanation."

"Yes?"

"From the moment we met, I could see how right you were for this type of work," Jason said. "And as time passed, I began to fear I was pushing you to become an overseas missionary rather than letting God lead you. The only way I could see to stay out of the way was to do just that—stay out of the way. I'm afraid that's caused me to be rude and a little standoffish. Will you forgive me?"

"Of course I will, Jason, although I must admit you did have me confused there for awhile."

"Thanks." He smiled. "Now how about I beat you at a game of Uno?"

"Beat me?" Sabrina put her hands on her hips in defiance. "Like you could."

237

"You're on," he replied, shuffling the cards. He pushed the hot chocolate and cookies within her reach and started dealing the cards.

———————•————————

Sabrina looked up at the clock and was shocked to see it read midnight. They had been eating and talking and playing cards for three hours. She stretched and yawned.

"Sleepy?"

"Not really, just stiff. I haven't stayed up this late since finals," Sabrina replied.

"The last time I stayed up this late was a lock-in for the youth at church." He groaned. "Talk about your long nights."

"Why don't we see what's on television?" He grabbed a couple drinks out of the refrigerator and the chips and dip before heading for the living room. She followed his lead. They found an old action drama on one of the stations that they both agreed on and then settled in with the food. Halfway through, Sabrina could feel her eyes getting heavy. Jason put his arm around her, and she settled into his shoulder and drifted off to sleep.

The movie ended, but Jason wasn't paying any attention. All he could see was Sabrina. Curled up in his arms, she felt so right. His heart nearly beat out of his chest as he watched her sleeping. Just then her eyes opened and looked straight into his. In that moment, he knew that this was the time to ask her.

"Sabrina?"

"Yes?" she whispered.

"I have prayed for a long time for God to send me a soul mate. Someone who would be a partner in my life and in the ministry God has called me to." He paused for a moment, swallowing past the lump in his throat. "Sabrina Delacourt, I have fallen in love with you. Will you be my soul mate, my partner, and my wife?"

Sabrina stared into his eyes in shock. She thought she had sensed that he had feelings for her, but she had never expected a declaration of love so soon. She was too surprised to speak. The hope in his eyes began to disappear, and he turned his head.

"I guess I jumped the gun, didn't I?" Jason asked.

She tried to clear her muddled brain. Was this what she wanted? Could she be a missionary's wife? She opened her mouth to answer, but the words wouldn't come. In desperation, she grabbed the front of his shirt and pulled him close. She answered in the only way she could, with a kiss.

When they parted, Jason sat still with his eyes closed as if in a trance. She waited for several minutes before he opened his eyes again.

"God in heaven above, let that be a yes, because if it isn't, I'm in real trouble."

"It's a yes."

He grabbed her in a bear hug and then rained kisses on her face before locking her in another long kiss. They jerked apart at the ringing of the doorbell.

"Talk about being saved by the bell," Jason mumbled as he stood up.

"Is there a damsel in distress here?" Matt asked from the doorway. "Because the cavalry has arrived." When they didn't answer, he looked from one to the other. "What?"

Epilogue

Sabrina stood in the doorway of her church in Nebraska and looked at the ones she loved. All of her sisters were waiting at the altar. Jeff and a very pregnant Dianna were sitting on the aisle right behind her mother. Matt, who was on furlough, stood behind the altar, waiting with his Bible. However, it was the man at the end of the aisle who captured her attention just as he had her heart. Jason was handsome in his full tuxedo, but she hardly noticed what he was wearing. It was the look on his face when he took her hand at the end of her long walk.

"I'm happy for you, Princess," her father whispered before he stepped back to join her mother. In the background, she heard the cry of Sharon's baby, who had come into the world just in time for her wedding. It was perfect.

After a beautiful ceremony, they walked downstairs to the reception, hand in hand, greeting all their friends and family. Sabrina and Jason were separated for a time by well-wishers and photographers. She found him later, talking to Sharon.

"So, when are you guys going back to Hong Kong?" Sharon asked.

"It'll be at least a year," Jason replied. "I've finished all the requirements, but they like couples to have been married for at least a year before they go overseas. Adjusting to marriage is hard enough without having to adjust to a new culture and the challenges of language study."

"I would think you had already adjusted," Sharon said with a grin.

"True, but this will also give Sabrina a chance to take some seminary courses before we ship off, and we have to go through training before we can be commissioned."

"All I can say is that you better take good care of my little sister," Sharon said, poking him with her index finger.

"I promise," Jason replied, holding up his hands as if protecting himself. Then, his face turned serious. "You know I love your sister very much."

"I can see that," Sharon said, nodding in agreement. "Exactly when did you fall in love with my little sister?"

"That's hard to answer. I guess from the time she fell into my arms," he said with a chuckle.

"And I can tell you when I knew I wanted to be with you forever," Sabrina said, coming up behind him and taking his arm.

"When was that?" Jason asked.

"In the heart of the storm," she said with a smile.

LINDA LYLE

Linda hails from her native state of Alabama. She is single but is very thankful for a close Christian family in which she is the youngest of five. She is an avid reader who at age thirteen decided she wanted to try writing a story, and before she knew it she had one hundred pages written. She put writing aside to focus on her education, but she took every writing course she could and experimented in writing short stories and journalizing ideas. She finished her first book less than a year before it was published. Linda is very happy to be able to write wholesome and entertaining fiction that portrays her Christian values.

THE
ARROW

Kathleen Paul

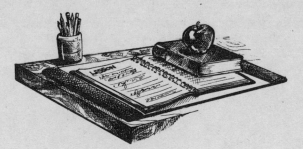

Dedication

To Peggy M. Wilber, author of *Reading Rescue 123*, who taught me how to teach those struggling readers who just don't "get it."

Chapter 1

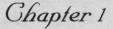

Denise Delacourt rested her forehead against the cold metal door and twisted the deadbolt, locking out the students who had ruined her day, ruined her teaching career, ruined her dreams. Jamie Jack Jordan had been the last one sauntering out to the hall without a backward glance. Of course he didn't care that they'd reduced her to tears on the very first day of school. None of them cared. They weren't normal. They weren't children. They weren't human.

Denise sniffed and reached in the pocket of her denim jacket to pull out a tissue. She hadn't let the tears fall, the ones that had been stinging behind her eyes since third period that morning. She'd remained stoic. But she figured they knew. They knew they scared her to death.

She slumped against the door, then rolled around so that her shoulders pressed hard against the unyielding surface. Surveying the shambles of her English classroom, she felt the last vestige of pride in her first assignment vanish.

Spit wads! They'd thrown spit wads. She didn't know kids still did that. She didn't know spit wads were so nasty. She hadn't known they stung when they hit bare skin. She hadn't known they stuck to material like her skirt and jacket. Tears coursed down her cheeks.

Even with the air conditioning on, the muggy room smelled of old disinfectant and mildew. Denise suddenly longed for a clean Nebraska breeze to freshen the atmosphere and maybe lift her up, whipping her out of Houston, taking her back home. Kind of like Dorothy of Oz in reverse. The munchkins Denise had discovered in this land far away from home had piranha teeth, and they'd been nibbling on her all day.

A sharp knock on the door interrupted her pity party. Quickly wiping away the tears, Denise peered through the narrow slice of glass that served as a window to the hall. Beyond the tiny wires criss-crossing the glass, Ed Meecham's smiling face appeared. "Let me in."

She barely heard his muffled voice through the security door, but she nodded and unlocked it, glad to see an adult.

"So, Snow White," he said as he stepped into her room, "did the dwarves devour you on the first day in the big city school?"

He looked at her face and then around the room.

"Phew-ee! I guess that's not a joking matter," he amended.

Spit wads clung to the ceiling, the posters on the wall, and the barred windows. A bookcase stood precariously tipped at the back of the room and volumes spewed out of its shelves. The bulletin board on English poets sported tattered edges and graffiti.

"You got to hand it to 'em." Ed grinned sardonically and shook his head in mock admiration. "They work fast."

"I couldn't catch them," whined Denise. She heard the whimper in her voice and cleared her throat. She must at least act like an adult even if she wanted to run home to Mama. "Most of this happened in the first three periods. I quit turning my back to write on the board about then."

Ed's smile took on a genuine reflection of humor. "Hey, this isn't a lost cause. Look how much you've learned in a day. Number one rule: Don't turn your back on the enemy."

"I don't want to think of them as the enemy." Denise moved over to her desk and collapsed into the hard metal chair. Ed made himself comfortable in a front row, battered desk.

"I think I lost all my idealism in the first hour," moaned Denise. "I thought I was going to be a light for these kids, make a difference, lead them to the better things, show them the Christ who lives within me, demonstrate the love God has for them."

The look of utter astonishment on Ed's face tickled Denise's sense of humor in spite of her disillusionment. Laughter bubbled within her, breaking through her despair.

"Wow!" he said. "And all I aim for is to teach them a little math."

Denise laughed. It felt good to release the tension. "You don't teach them 'a little math,'" she protested. "You teach them algebra. I'd rather tame tigers for a circus act than tackle one A plus B equals C minus D."

Ed shook his head, laughing with her. "The titles on the course list says algebra one and two, but I teach survival math. That's all they can handle."

"Survival math?"

"Cash Register 101, Checkbook 101, Sentencing 101."

"Sentencing?"

"Sure. If you get eighteen months for this misdemeanor and eight months for another, six months for that misdemeanor, minus five months probation, how old will you be when you're clear?"

"Ed, that's awful." Denise sighed, no longer finding any

humor in the situation.

"I can't teach them algebra, geometry, and the other high school classes they're slated for. Most of them can't recite a multiplication table. Some of them can't add and subtract two digit numerals. Most of the students you had today can't read at a fourth-grade level. Why should they be interested in Shelley and Keats when they can't read the newspaper?"

"You think I'm pretty naïve, don't you?" Denise asked.

"Fresh from the cornfields," agreed Ed. "But hey, country girl, you may be just what this system needs. Look at you, you don't fit the mold around here. You dress like it still matters what your image is."

Denise involuntarily looked down at her denim suit, long flared skirt, pale yellow blouse, country-tailored jacket, soft leather ankle boots.

"I didn't choose this for an image, Ed. It was on sale."

"But you wouldn't have bought it if it were a sleazy, purple, shimmery, foo-foo dress."

Denise couldn't help laughing. "Foo-foo dress, Ed? What's a foo-foo dress?"

"Hey, give me a break. I'm a guy. Foo-foo, you know, something fluffy and slinky, and you wouldn't be caught dead in it."

"Thanks, I think," said Denise, still laughing.

"The point is: your hairdo, even though I know that fancy braid thing is stylish, is conservative too. And your face isn't caricatured by tons of makeup."

"How is all this going to help me teach these juvenile delinquents?" asked Denise soberly.

Ed scratched his head. "Once you get your feet on the ground, I think you'll enjoy these kids. They'll like you too. I've taught in several schools in Houston. And I didn't choose Milton

High for the combat pay. When I taught in the ritzy neighborhoods, the kids didn't appreciate anything I gave them, whether it was extra help or just attention. They figured they had it all. Here, the kids may be gruff and hard to read, but they like a teacher who likes them. Give yourself time, Denise."

"You're good for me, Ed. Thanks."

"Good for you?" asked Ed, with a gleam in his eye. "Then how about dinner Friday night to celebrate your making it through your first week?"

"If I make it."

"You'll make it. I'll take you to someplace soothing, atmosphere exotic, quiet music."

"Are you married?" asked Denise, pointblank.

"Divorced. No children," answered Ed. "Who said you were naïve?"

She ignored the question and asked her own. "And what do you think about God?"

"I heard He's a nice guy, but we've never socialized."

With regret, Denise shook her head. "No, Ed. Thanks for the invitation, but I take my relationship with God seriously. Going out with someone who doesn't share that faith would complicate both our lives unnecessarily."

"You could convert me," Ed offered with a winsome smile.

Denise grinned at his foolishness, but in her heart it saddened her that to him it was just that—foolishness.

"No, Ed, dating a guy with the intention of leading him to salvation is backward. And who in this life ever got anywhere running the race backward?"

He shrugged and, with an exaggerated sigh, gave up his quest. "You realize you're forcing me to go look for a sleazy woman in a purple foo-foo dress."

"Well, you can tell me all about it, at least the parts that are repeatable, on Monday."

———◆———

Dear Mom and Dad,

My first day at school was a disaster! My attitude had sunk to below sea level, and I was ready to retire. I have eight English classes. The largest one has six students and the smallest, two girls. One girl is Carlotta Mendez. Pray for her specifically, Mom. She says she's been a prostitute since she was thirteen. She calls herself Lot. It has such a hard sound to it. I call her Carlotta, and she rolls her big beautiful brown eyes at me, and I want to cry.

I knew when I signed the contract to work at a juvenile delinquent alternative school that it wouldn't be like anything I'd ever seen before. At the end of the day I locked my door and bawled. Dad, I am so naïve. How can I help these kids? They know more about a hard life than I can even guess. But I'm not giving up. I'll learn.

Ed Meecham, the math teacher, came by and cheered me up. No, he's not a Christian, and I won't let myself become interested, even though he's cute, funny, and intelligent. Not necessarily in that order. Bet that gives you something else to pray about for your baby girl.

I heard of a place where the kids hang out. It's some kind of club called the Arrow. I think I'll investigate that. Ed says he doesn't think it's gang related because the probation officers haven't put it off-limits.

Hey! It could be a lot worse. Ed says so. We only had

one lockdown this week. Ed says that's some kind of record for the first week of school.

Stay on your knees, Mom, Dad.

Your youngest, prettiest,
most adventuresome daughter,
Denise

Chapter 2

Denise carried an umbrella. She put her money in a wallet, not wanting to brandish a purse in this scary neighborhood. She jammed her keys into her jeans' pocket and clutched a small cylinder of Mace. And she carried the umbrella—big, black, heavy, and ready to clobber anyone who threatened her. She looked at the painted yellow arrow on the pavement and skeptically searched the alley it pointed to. Could the door to this club, the Arrow, be among these warehouses?

Saying a prayer for safety and guidance, she warily proceeded into the deserted passage between two-story industrial buildings. The crudely painted yellow arrows directed her to an ordinary metal door. A sign said, "Enter at your own risk. Only weapon allowed—the Sword of Truth."

Denise wrinkled her brow. *The Sword of Truth? Do these kids even know that refers to Scripture?*

She tested the handle and found it gave under the pressure of her thumb on the metal tab. She pulled it open slowly, expecting to hear the long, drawn-out creak indicative of a haunted house.

Lord, she prayed, *if this is dangerous, tell me now so I can turn tail and run.*

She peered into the gloom. A plywood wall painted purple stood just three feet beyond the doorway. An orange arrow pointed to the right, a rather useless sign since another wall cut off a turn to the left.

"Hello." She cleared her throat and tried again. "Hello." Muffled music answered her. She felt the heavy base beat as she placed her hand on the frame of the door. "This must be the right place."

She stepped inside and took a few steps down the narrow hallway. The door closed behind her, cutting off the outside light. The area around her dimmed to the gloom of a barn in the middle of the night. She put a hand on the wall to orient herself. As her eyes adjusted she saw another arrow a few feet away, pointing down another corridor. She peered up at walls extending only a few feet above her head. Fifteen feet beyond, the tin roof, interlaced with steel crossbeams, looked dark and foreboding.

"Great," she muttered. "This is a maze." Scattered along the walls, small painted arrows and large neon-lighted tubes pointed the way. "I hope there isn't a gag in here, nothing popping out in my face like a carnival haunted house." *Lord, was this a good idea? You are my strength and my tower of refuge. Put Your angels all around me, Lord. My knees are buckling.*

To the muted sounds of a rock group, Denise followed the course laid out for her, climbing over barriers and scrunching down to pass through four-foot high tunnels as well as walking through the constantly-turning minihalls. "Someone went to a lot of trouble constructing this." *Lord, did anyone think about a quick exit in case of fire?*

Finally she emerged in an open space illuminated by ultraviolet tubes lining the walls. Teenagers lounged on huge pillows, a boom box emitted caterwauling with loud percussion and strident melody, and a pop machine dominated the center of the room. Along the back wall, motorbikes and a beat-up VW bug were parked inside the building in front of huge garage doors. *The fire exit. Good.*

Denise blinked as her eyes adjusted to the weird lighting.

Three boys and a girl hovered near a pool table. Around the Foosball table, the most active humans in the room slammed the back of one of the players in congratulations over a point made.

"Miss Delacourt." A familiar voice called her name above the wail of electric guitars. She turned to be confronted by one of her students. The black light illuminated his eyes and teeth eerily in his coal black face. Standing eye-to-eye with him, she felt the restrained energy in his muscle-bound compact frame. She didn't feel threatened.

Oh, thank You, Lord, someone I know. "Henry—"

"Aw, Miss Delacourt, not here," he interrupted with an urgent whisper. "We're not in class. Can't you call me Hobe like everyone else?"

"Sure, Hobe. Will you introduce me to some of your friends?" She looked around the room, noticing many of the occupants had stopped what they were doing to stare at her.

"Whataya doing here, Miss Delacourt?"

"I heard this was a place where my students hang out. I wanted to visit and maybe get to know you better."

In the unnatural light, she saw his face turn to stone, all feeling, all expression wiped out.

"Miss Delacourt." Carlotta Mendez walked over and took her elbow. "You shouldn't be here. Some of the kids won't like it." She tried to turn Denise back to the opening of the maze, but Denise dug her heels in.

"Is there someone I can talk to, Carlotta? Your leader?"

"He's busy."

"I can wait."

Movement in the room alerted her. The teens massed together and surrounded her. She searched the serious faces, looking for a spark of friendliness.

"Whadja come for, to look at the freak druggies?" A voiced hissed at her.

"No." She looked around, trying to locate the accuser.

"Curiosity killed the cat." Another disembodied voice. Denise shivered. Not being able to see which one spoke unnerved her. She swallowed and shot up a prayer for help.

"I really just wanted to know more about my students. I want to help but don't know how."

"Leave us alone."

"Get outta here."

Denise felt fear swell in her chest, making it hard to breathe. She silently recited, *Neither fear ye the people of the land. . . . The LORD is with us: fear them not.*"

"No!" Denise stamped her foot and glared around the circle of intimidators. "You stop acting like this right now. I didn't come here to hurt you. I don't deserve to be treated like this. Why can't you be a little nice? How about offering me a pop?"

Confusion flickered across several faces. Encouraged, Denise continued her performance of bravado.

"I'm not leaving until I've made at least one friend here." She nodded her head in emphasis, crossed her arms over her chest in defiance and narrowed her eyes, trying to look tough and determined.

"Is she for real?"

"Yeah, she's my English teacher. Clueless. Leave her to the Rev."

Denise recognized Henry's voice and felt a mixture of comfort and anxiety. He hadn't disclaimed any connection with her. That was good. But evidently she would be turned over to their leader. Henry wouldn't stand with her against his peers. She shouldn't expect that.

The song from the boom box ended abruptly, leaving an uncomfortable silence hanging around them. The next song kicked in, jolting Denise's nerves with its blast.

The Rev? Did that have some connection with a big motorcycle? Did it refer to his temperament? Revved up? What did that portend for her?

"So," said Denise, noticing the group had relaxed at the mention of their leader, "are there any diet drinks in that machine?"

The side of the circle nearest the center of the room shifted and a path opened so that she could move forward. Denise swallowed the fear that plagued her, sent up another prayer for safety, then one for accomplishing what she came to do.

She walked over to the machine, trying to relax and move casually, not as if she were edging her way through a prickly hedge. Sticking two fingers into the coin pocket of her jeans, she pulled out a couple quarters and made a selection, Diet Pepsi. The can clattered to the opening and she retrieved it, grateful that it was cold and she hadn't had to fight the machine for her purchase. To lose a battle to a pop dispenser in front of this antagonistic crowd would have been another humiliation.

She pulled the ring on the top of the can and looked around with a satisfied smile. The smiled dropped into oblivion. The teens had deserted her. Just as she had been the center of their attention a moment ago, now she was as studiously ignored. They'd gone back to their various occupations, and their body language clearly stated, We are not acknowledging your presence.

I haven't come this far to give up. I'll just roam around and watch. But I better not single out the kids I know. I don't want to bring any condemnation down on them.

She followed her instincts and approached the pool table. She'd played pool in tournaments during college, but concluded showing off wouldn't promote her acceptance. She didn't receive a cold reception from the pool players; they simply ignored her existence.

Discouragement reared its ugly head as she moved from group to group, getting no response. They ignored her presence, ignored her comments; she could have been a microscopic dust mite.

"Hey, Rev," she heard a voice behind her raised over the din of the boom box. "We got a visitor."

"So I see." The deep male voice sounded adult.

Denise turned and spotted him immediately. Thirtyish, dressed in faded jeans, old scuffed cowboy boots, a tattered cloth jacket, and a T-shirt. The T-shirt caught her eye. The front said, "My boss is a Jewish carpenter," in letters formed of wooden beams.

She looked up and noticed his stubbled chin, dark brown hair badly in need of a cut, and blue eyes full of mischief.

Dear Mom and Dad,
 I have met a man. Make that—I HAVE MET A MAN. My heart actually went pitter-pat. His name is Rev. John Slann. He's about three inches taller than me. I'd say he's around thirty. Solid build. Like he could pitch

hay all day, Dad. Not married. Works out of one of the big churches here in town, Houston Evangelical Fellowship. He's opened this place for the downtown teens. I told you about it in my last letter. The Arrow. I'm going to help the kids make banners for the main room. They just pulled down all the posters and painted, so they're ready for a new look.

I'll try to get him to clean up a bit before I send you a picture. And oh, he rides a Harley.

Love you,
Keep praying,

Your reenergized daughter,
Denise

P.S. God is so good!

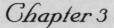

Chapter 3

Y ou've got to admit she's got nerve," said Rev to his three-member teen board. They sat for their council on the cement floor of the main room.

"She doesn't belong here," griped Sashquita.

Rev stood and put a hand on his heart and pointed over their heads to an imaginary figure. "And Jesus said to the man possessed by swine, 'You don't belong here.' "

Turning, he faced another nonexistent figure. "You, lowly fishermen, quit following me. You don't belong."

He turned again, but before he could cast off any more sinners, Sashquita interrupted. "Okay, okay, you made your point."

Rev sat down. "This is our opportunity to help someone besides ourselves."

"I don't get it," said Mic, a lanky kid with way more freckles than muscle. "Jesus helped the thieves, hookers, the poor. This Miss Delacourt. . ." He said her name with pure mockery in his tone. "She's not needy. First you make out like she's gotta be included 'cause Jesus woulda, and then you say *we're* gonna help *her?*"

"Mic," said Abraham, the teen board president, "you don't ever get it. Rev says *all* have sinned. She's a sinner. You can't look at what people look like on the outside and make a decision about their insides."

"But what do you mean by us helping her?" asked Sashquita.

"Couple of things," said Rev, leaning back into the pile of huge colorful pillows stacked against the wall. "She really doesn't have a clue about living in the city. We need to educate her. Slowly, so she doesn't get shocked to death. Then she needs a place to fit in, just like you do. A place where she feels accepted and needed. We can do that for her."

"Come on, Rev. She'd fit in anywhere," said Mic.

"Does she fit in here?"

"Well, no."

"That proves my point. We're the ones she wants as friends, and she doesn't fit in. So we should help her."

"What do we have to do?" asked Abraham.

Rev shrugged.

"You told her she could help with the banners." Sashquita's narrowed eyes spoke her annoyance.

With palms up, Rev gestured his helplessness. "Hey, I don't know how to sew."

Mic sat rubbing his lean jaw with an outsized hand. Deep thought lines creased his brow. "She works at the school. We could tell the guys to give her a break." He grinned at the others. "You know, make 'em know we mean it."

"That might backfire," said Abraham. "We don't want our enemies targeting her for revenge."

"What enemies?" asked Rev, raising his eyebrows and only allowing a hint of a smile to reach his lips.

"Enemies left over from the past, Rev," said Abraham.

"We ain't been making no new ones, Rev," claimed Mic.

"Okay," said Rev, sitting up and pulling a pen from behind

his ear. He grabbed his ragged clipboard, overstuffed with various sizes, colors, and shapes of paper. "Let's go over the gains we've made this week and plan for next Friday night."

Denise showed Angelica how to make the blanket stitch around the two-foot-tall satin egg, fastening it to the rich purple cloth background. Several other girls drew around the cardboard pattern of a chick that had been placed on cloth printed in various yellow designs.

Rev had done a Bible Study on Colossians 2:8, "Beware lest any man spoil you through philosophy and vain deceit, after the tradition of men, after the rudiments of the world, and not after Christ." He explained Satan clouded the issues by bringing brilliant minds to argue over pointless problems, thereby distracting them from the more important activity of worshiping God.

Out of that grew the concept and design of this banner. They planned to attach bold letters spelling out, "Question: Which came first, the chicken or the egg?" and "Answer: God."

"Are we going to cut the letters out of cloth or paint them?" asked Denise of her coworkers. A half dozen different answers bombarded the air.

"Whoa!" She laughed. "Okay. Who said fabric paint?"

"Me," said Georgy, raising a hand.

"Okay, what are the merits of fabric paint?"

"By the time we get to the letters, we're going to be tired of all this cutting and stitching."

"Good point," conceded Denise. "Who said applique? What did you mean by that? And why would that be to our advantage?" Denise led the discussion. At first she could hear that her questions sounded stiff, but the girls soon giggled over each other's ideas, and the atmosphere loosened up. She found it easy to like these teens once they let down their guards.

"Miss Delacourt, may I talk to you?" Rev called from his office door.

"Sure." She put aside her scissors and jogged across the cement floor.

The office had a half wall with glass above, making the small area anything but private. When Rev shut the door, he indicated she should sit in the cushioned chair beside his desk. He lounged in his own office chair, swinging back and forth, and rolling it occasionally.

"How's it working out? Do you feel they're beginning to accept you?"

"Yes," Denise answered enthusiastically. "Abraham, Mic, and Sashquita paved the way. When their glacial reserve melted, the others began to thaw. Then I beat your pool champion, Quirk, and suddenly I was just a little bit cool."

Rev smiled at her, and Denise made a mental note to tell her three sisters about the devastating dimple that flirted with her whether the good minister knew it or not.

"I do have something I'd like to ask you about," she said.

"Shoot."

"These kids can't read at a useful level."

"I know that."

His pleasant tone relieved Denise's apprehension. She didn't want to push into his territory, but the idea she'd uncovered in researching how to help her students compelled her to take the initiative. Giving these kids a fighting chance at academics excited her. She bubbled over with the new phonemic reading techniques she'd found on the Internet.

"I think I've found a way to help them, but my principal is reluctant to try something new."

"Spell it out for me. Remember my field is not education, as in reading, writing, and 'rithmetic."

"These kids are used to failure in reading. Nobody likes to fail, so they avoid situations where they know from past experience that they will fail. What they need is practice, but they avoid practice to avoid feeling inadequate. We can turn that around by giving them opportunities to succeed. Success breeds success."

Rev nodded, and she needed no more encouragement than that to plunge on.

"First we have to give them something to read that they are capable of reading. Only the books at that level are insulting to their intelligence. They're smart even if they can't read."

"I believe that."

"So we emphasize not the reading but the opportunity to nurture their younger siblings."

"How?"

"We pick a book at the third- or fourth-grade reading level. We prime our kids to read these books fluently. On Saturday, or even an evening, we have the families come in, and we perform the books. Costumes, acting parts, and the reading."

"You think this will work?"

"There are case studies where students' reading levels increased by as much as two-grade levels in twelve weeks. Once you see how it is done, you'll be a believer."

Rev's grin spread across his face. "I'm a believer now."

Denise nodded. She knew from a week of working beside this man that he lived his faith. She wanted to share with him how much she'd felt God's leading in her search for ways to rescue these illiterate kids. "I believe God has given me a tool to help my teens. Will you give me the chance to implement it?"

Rev sat forward in his chair and picked up a pencil. He twirled it between his fingers as he thought. "Let me run it pass the board."

"How long will that take?"

"Two days. I propose it. We pray. We vote."

"May I start looking for suitable books?" Denise stood with the intention of returning to the banner project.

"No harm in that as long as you remember that your plan has to meet with the teen board's approval."

She paused with her hand on the door knob. "The teen board?"

"Yes."

"You don't have to run it by your sponsoring church board?"

"No, this is a program I can spearhead. It doesn't affect the budget. It doesn't involve transportation, new personnel."

"Oh."

"What's wrong?"

Denise squirmed under his penetrating gaze. "It's a big deal to me. It just doesn't seem like a big deal to you."

Rev smiled in that relaxed way that always drained the worry and tension from her. She'd noted before that the peace around this man affected her. She couldn't help responding with a half-formed smile as the doubts eased out of her heart. Her spirit always moved to harmonize with his tranquility. She treasured the feeling.

"I see the potential, Denise. I recognize your enthusiasm. That enthusiasm will go a long way to energize the project. But today it's a possibility, not a reality, and there's no reason to rush ahead of God. When He gives me the go-ahead, then I'll pour all I've got into it. That's a promise."

She beamed. She could feel the intensity of her smile and turned quickly to the door before he could read her transparent feelings.

Oh, Father in heaven, she prayed as she left the room, *I do like this man.*

Dear Mom and Dad,

I'm making progress at school. I'm reading the selections to my students instead of requiring them to read for homework.

Hey! That training in the drama club has paid off. I did a dramatic rendition of Silas Marner. *They were supposed to follow along in their books. Yeah, right! I looked up, and all eyes were glued on me. That threw me for a sec, but the old ham at heart rose to the occasion. I got up from my desk and moved around the room. Everyone that came that day aced the oral test.*

That's another thing to pray about. No one's in danger of securing the perfect attendance award. And the truant officers go out in force each day. Because the kids are in this school, they are required *to show up. Most of them are on probation, and if they don't come, it's a violation. That is unless they can prove they got run over by a truck or something equally debilitating.*

Let's see. Please pray that the reading program I'm starting at the Arrow will really help. Pray for Enrico's father—no details I can share but a very serious situation. Pray for my car; it's coughing. Please pray that Rev notices my sparkling personality.

I love you so much.

Your humble daughter,
Denise

P.S. Why hasn't Danielle answered my E-mails? Is she too busy reforming the nursing homes of Atlanta to bother with a little sister? Get after her, Mom.

Chapter 4

Rev slapped the folder closed with a feeling of satisfaction. So far this project had been under budget every month, allowing for luxuries such as pizza and movie night. He stood and stretched, looking out his cubicle office to where the kids clustered around Denise Delacourt. What an unexpected blessing she'd been.

"Thank You, Lord, for replacing Jennifer Coolidge so promptly."

He opened the door and leaned against the frame, listening now to Denise instruct her players in the reading theater.

"Listen to me read these two lines. You follow in your books."

She read them off with great emphasis.

"Now I'm going to read those same two lines again."

She did, delivering the words with just as much vigor.

"Now you all are going to read the same lines aloud with me. I'm not going to slow down, but don't get discouraged. We'll read them over until you sound great. Keep your eyes on the words in the book. You must look like you are reading to the audience."

"Miss Delacourt?"

"Yes, Quirk?"

"Why do we all have to read? Some of us are going to be acting it out?"

"Well, for one, I don't know who's going to read what yet, so we are all going to learn it. And, if somebody gets sick—"

"Or thrown in the slammer," added Hobe.

Denise grinned at him, recognizing his wry humor. She rephrased his comment. "Or unfortunately detained, then almost anyone can step in and fill the gap."

Rev watched her, poised before these tough kids. She looked like a flower blooming in a cactus patch, and it looked right.

Yep, Lord, she's much better suited to this than poor Jennifer.

Miss Coolidge had graduated with a degree in social work from a fine Bible college back East. She'd had all the right credentials, sterling references, and was the second cousin of somebody's nephew's wife. The somebody was on the mission board of the church. Rev had been appalled when the church hired the girl, sight unseen, no interview, no formal application. She'd lasted three days.

Denise had none of Jennifer's intellectual savvy, but she possessed something more important: a true gut instinct. Rev watched with admiration as she read. Her enthusiasm flamed and spread through the room, igniting the usually placid teenagers. Even Sullen Sol looked interested.

"Thank You, Lord," Rev prayed again.

Denise's earth-shattering screech reverberated off the aluminum walls. Rev gave up his nonchalant observation and started forward, only to stop in his tracks as she descended on Matt, a 250-pound, six-foot-three giant.

"You can't hold the book like that," Denise squealed. She removed it from his club-like hand and held it with considerable respect. "This is what will break the cycle of poverty for your siblings."

A snort followed an unbelieving laugh.

Denise spun around, her eyes wide, her face earnest, every ounce of her determined to make these young people listen to her. "Don't you dare make fun of books." She held the book aloft. "This is the way you can climb to the top of the heap with no one snickering, no one watching your mistakes as you learn. Books hand you dignity on a platter. Who's going to make fun of you when you know the great themes of literature and apply them to what's going on around you? This is a stepping stone for some and a winch for others. Do you know what a winch is? It's a contraption that can grab hold of something and pull it out of the mire. When you inspire your younger brothers and sisters to read, you're giving them a gift that will last forever.

"And the first thing you have to do is show them. You're going to show them you think reading is great. If you just tell them, they won't get it. They look up to you. You're the older, wiser kids in the family. Not some adult trying to cram things down their throat, but another kid, just older. If you show them, they'll believe."

Rev put a hand over the lower half of his face. The smile hidden behind it grew bigger. Miss Delacourt's passion for literacy overwhelmed her small audience. Rarely had Rev seen his unflappable teens with their mouths hanging open. He also wondered how much of that tirade they had actually taken in. They certainly understood the gist of her high-sounding speech. She handed the book back into Matt's huge hands, and he held it like a newborn baby.

"Page six, second paragraph." Denise had the rehearsal underway again.

Denise slowed her steps as she came into the alley and saw her students gathered around the door of the Arrow.

"Hi, guys," she greeted them. "Why aren't you inside?"

"Door's locked."

"Rev's not here?"

"Nope."

Lord God, what's going on? They look mad, no, disappointed.

"What happened?"

They shuffled their feet, cast sideways glances at each other, but no one answered.

Okay, Lord, how do I relax this situation?

"I know," said Denise. "I have fourteen dollars in my purse. Let's walk down to that ice-cream place on the corner and get a cone. We can rehearse there."

"There's eight of us, nine with you," said Matt. "Fourteen dollars wouldn't buy a cone apiece."

"Don't they have kiddy-cones?"

"Sure, but. . ."

"Well, a little bitty kiddy-cone is better than no cone at all." Denise turned to walk away, praying that they would follow. "Come on. It's air-conditioned."

Ancient Mr. Luechen looked askance at her party of teens as she ordered the nine cones. They behaved well, although picking out the exotic flavors she wouldn't touch with a ten-foot pole. She chose butter pecan, herded the kids to a corner of the old shop, passed out text sheets, and started the reading recital before anyone had a chance to complain.

The frowning owner made swipes at his counters and busied himself behind the freezer showcase. Toward the end, he stopped pretending he wasn't listening and leaned over the serving shelf. As the teens chorused the last line with enthusiasm, Mr. Luechen broke into applause.

"It's good," he said, beaming at his customers. "It's for children, right? You will teach them a moral while they listen to the story. This is good. This is what they did in my school when I was a boy. It's good."

"You thought they did a good job?" asked Denise. She nodded to her students and noted the anxious looks on their faces. They wanted to be praised.

"Excellent," said Mr. Luechen. "They read well. The story is alive. It is good work."

"We have another one," said Mic. "Do you want to hear it?"

"Sure, sure." Mr. Luechen came around the counter and sat down at one of the tables.

The students lined up and began without a word from Denise. She fought tears. God had given her so much more than she had hoped for. As they read the Tale of the Country Mouse, she praised God for the teens' progress.

Half an hour later, they stepped out the door of the ice-cream shop with Mr. Luechen inviting them back. The teens dispersed except for Chipper, a girl with incredibly short hair and equally bizarre long fingernails. She tagged along as Denise walked back to her car.

"Can you tell me why the Arrow is closed?" asked Denise.

"There was a fight."

"Oh, dear." Denise sighed. Fights erupted at her school often enough. They scared her. None had occurred in her classroom, and she prayed at the door every morning for safety and peace for all. "Tell me about it."

"Enrico came in yelling at Carlotta, and before Rev could get to him, he'd slammed her against the wall. She hit her head, and there was blood everywhere. Rev and the other guys pulled Enrico off of her, but not before he hit her a couple of times. They pinned him to the floor."

"Is Carlotta all right? Where is she?"

"They took her to the hospital."

"Did someone tell her parents? Did Rev go with her?"

"Yes. No. Rev called her home. Sashquita went with her in the ambulance. Rev made the EMTs take her along. Then Rev and Abraham went to the police station to be with Enrico." Her tone chilled with bitterness as she continued. "Rev called an ambulance *and* the police. Everyone was mad at him for calling the cops."

"But why?"

"He's supposed to be one of us. You don't turn in your friend to the police."

"That's not true, Chipper." Denise stopped in the street and waited until Chipper turned to face her. "Friends take care of friends. They do whatever it takes to help a friend. You know that thing about friends don't let friends drive drunk. It's for their own safety, right?"

Chipper nodded.

"This is the same. Rev wouldn't let Enrico barrel through life, hurting others and himself. Rev did what he thought was best for Enrico. He had to be held accountable for his actions."

The teen looked off into the distance.

Denise chewed her lip as she studied the young face buried under a ton of somber hues of makeup. *Are you considering what I'm saying? Does it make any sense to you? At least you aren't arguing with me. But I don't know what you're thinking.*

They started walking again.

"I don't get it, Chipper," Denise said after they'd passed

several dilapidated storefronts. "Weren't the kids angry at Enrico? Weren't they mad because he hurt Carlotta? Didn't they want justice done for her sake?"

"Sure, but they would have done the justice themselves. We didn't need the cops to settle the score."

"Oh."

They drifted down the street, carefully negotiating the broken sidewalk and avoiding piles of garbage. Denise looked up at the Texas sky, cloudless and pure blue. The discrepancy between God's beautiful creation and man's refuse strewn at her feet twisted her heart. The task of loving these kids and guiding them to a better future had just been handed a liberal dose of reality.

"I have to admit something, Chipper." Denise put a hand on her companion's arm. "I'm glad I wasn't there. I've never seen violence, except on TV. I don't know how I would handle it."

Chipper patted her hand as if consoling a young child. "You'll do okay, Miss Delacourt. When something like that happens, you just act from what's inside you. You got good inside you."

Dear Mom and Dad,

Who is teaching whom? I was feeling pretty successful. My students are actually learning to read. They are much more cooperative.

I wish I could put them in a van and take them out into the wilderness. We could roam together for forty years, learning what God wants us to learn for survival. But even when the Israelites crossed the Jordan, they still didn't have it down, did they?

This must seem pretty rambly to you.

I'm upset.

One of my students, Carlotta, is in the hospital with a concussion and broken ribs. Enrico beat her up. He's in jail.

I've cried buckets tonight. If I could take these kids away from downtown Houston, would they learn without the distractions of their ugly world? In the ideal setting, would they feel God's love? Why do these precious children have to live in squalor, terror, and ignorance? Can I make a difference?

I guess you better pray that I can see how great God is. Eyes off of me, eyes off of circumstance, eyes on Jesus. Think I'll reread The Hiding Place.

Nothing is impossible with God.

Thanks for loving me, Mom and Dad. You don't know how much your strength comes through for me every day.

Love,
Denise

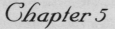

Chapter 5

E d Meecham sat in a front row desk, popping his gum and looking like one of the students instead of the math teacher. Denise enjoyed his friendship, and since he never tried to be romantic except in an exaggerated, off-beat, humorous way, she encouraged his daily visits after school.

"I was impressed by your students' performance last night, Denise." Ed leaned over and scooped up a handful of paperbacks to give her as she put her bookcase in order.

"I want to thank you for coming, Ed. That meant a lot to me. I was plenty nervous."

"You didn't act it."

"Well, you're not supposed to act nervous when you're telling the students they will be great. Might give them the impression you don't really believe what you're saying. I can tell you I was muttering prayers all day, though."

"Too bad more of the parents didn't come. That Asian fellow sure made up for the lack of adults with his enthusiasm."

Denise smiled as she remembered the ice-cream shop owner's unexpected appearance. "Mr. Luechen. I don't even know how he found out the time and place." Denise sighed and leaned back to sit on her heels. "Maybe the parent attendance will pick up after a couple more performances. I suggested we do it once a month, but the teens voted for every other week."

"You'll be busy."

"It's worth it." She moved over to straighten the next set of shelves.

"The talk your friend gave after the second story, the one about the country mouse, that stuff isn't in the Bible, is it?"

"About being a sojourner in a foreign land? Sure it is. Christians are like aliens to this planet. Our citizenry is actually with God and in His kingdom."

"That sounds pretty bizarre."

Denise laughed. "I suppose it does when it's a new concept. But I think Rev did a great job of relating the country mouse to people looking for 'home.' The mouse didn't feel comfortable in the city, and humans don't feel comfortable in their state of sin."

"And it all ties into the relationship with our creator."

Denise sat back and looked at Ed's face, searching for his usual flippant attitude.

Ed shrugged his shoulders. "Well, it's all a very interesting philosophy."

"It's not philosophy, Ed. It's truth."

"Right, in your book, not in mine."

Denise shot up a quick prayer for wisdom, but before she could speak, the moment passed. Ed plunged into a different area, one more comfortable for him. Denise recognized the tactic and gave his questioning heart over to the Holy Spirit, knowing God would draw Ed closer and maybe give her another opportunity to witness.

"I've started doing that little thing you do with my students as well."

"What little thing?" Kneeling beside the second battered bookcase, she stacked magazines in two piles.

"I read the word problem to them twice, then another two times with them reading out loud in chorus."

Denise stopped to look up at him. She grinned at his sheepish expression. He'd scoffed at her technique when she first tried it.

"And?" she prompted.

"And their comprehension has gone up in just three weeks. Their level of confidence has soared, and now I wish I had formally tested their level of performance before I started this haphazard experiment." Ed leaned over the desk, his face just inches away from Denise's. "Would you be interested in coauthoring a paper for *JOT?*"

"JOT?"

"The Journal of Teaching. We can give a report on the new research put to work in the classroom."

Denise thought of the wonderful gains her students were making academically and the resistance in collegiate circles to implementing the phonemic techniques that had born startling positive results in research.

"Oh, yes, I'd love to," she exclaimed.

"Ahem!" Someone cleared his throat from the doorway.

Denise shifted to look around Ed. Rev stood just inside the classroom with a scowl hardening his face.

Now what is stuck in his craw? wondered Denise as she rose to her feet and went to greet him.

"You wanted to go with me to visit Carlotta?" he asked.

"Sure, I'm almost ready." She turned to grab her purse and found Ed standing directly behind her. Scooting around his body blockade, she went to her desk, shuffled papers into a semineat stack, and shoved them into her carryall, then slung her purse strap over her shoulder. The sight of her two friends silently eyeing each other brought her to a dead stop.

What on earth? What's up with them? She studied the cold expressions and the stand-off body posture of the two men for a moment. *Oolala, jumping jiminey. They're taking each other's measure, and the only reason they'd be doing that is me. Rev is actually interested in me!*

Feeling herself glow with pleasure, Denise tried to wipe the delight off her face. She approached them with a carefully casual air.

"You didn't get a chance to meet last night? Ed, this is Reverend John Slann, director of the Arrow. And Rev, this is Ed Meecham, math teacher and my first friend in the big city."

Their hands went out to meet in a traditional shake, but Denise wondered what information transmitted between them during that physical ritual. They each muttered some customary words of greeting while she fought to keep from giggling. Echoes of high school and the thrill of knowing two guys found her attractive bubbled in her heart. But this time the thrill had an added edge. This time one of these men attracted her. She'd had numerous "discussions" with her heavenly Father over her eligibility to be a proper minister's wife. So far she'd had no indication she shouldn't apply for the job.

She put a hand on Rev's arm. "I'm ready to go."

He grunted and stepped out in the hall.

"Oh, I forgot something. Could you wait by the empty trophy case for me?"

He grunted again and ambled down the deserted hallway. Denise turned back to her teaching buddy.

"Now, Ed Meecham, I told you I would not become involved

with you romantically because you aren't a Christian. You stop acting territorial."

"I just wanted the guy to know you had someone looking out for you. A big brother image."

"Sure you did." Denise's voice dripped with skepticism.

"Anyway," Ed continued after clearing his throat, "I just might take an interest in this Christianity thing with you hanging around being a shining light and all. I might give up my hedonistic stance for you and convert."

"Well, you can't do that for me. You have to do it for yourself. But even if that did happen, I think we'd still be destined to be friends and nothing more."

"Not even best friends?" asked Ed with the old twinkle in his eye.

"My best friend is Jesus."

"I don't see how you can say corny things like that and not sound corny."

Denise had no explanation either, so she patted his arm and gave a little wave as she parted. She caught up with Rev as he stood gazing into the empty trophy case.

"Our school isn't big on competitions," she explained.

He nodded without looking at her.

"I believe in honesty," she said. He turned his face so she could see the seriousness in his hazel eyes, but he made no comment. "Ed is a friend. He's helped me a lot in getting adjusted to the big city and the school rules and the realistic expectations of the job. But I've told him before and I just reminded him, I'm not interested in anything more than having him as a good friend or big brother."

"When I walked in, you were looking up at him with a much warmer expression than friendship."

Denise crinkled her brow, trying to remember the conversation. Light dawned. "Oh! He'd just asked me to cowrite an article about the technique we're using to help the students. Rev, this method is not being accepted, and it is such a shame because it works!"

She put her arm through his in a natural and comfortable gesture. They talked as she guided him to the office, where she checked out for the day, and then out to the car.

When they pulled into the hospital parking lot, Rev changed the subject.

"On the papers you filled out to volunteer for the Arrow it says your birthday is this weekend. May I take you out to celebrate?"

"Yes, oh, yes," she agreed. "I was dreading my birthday without my family. I can't think of anything I'd like better. Unless. . ."

"Unless?"

"We could hire a jet and whisk around the world to visit my kith and kin. I have a sister in Hong Kong, one in Atlanta, one in Kansas, and my folks are back in Nebraska."

"I'll try to put that into the budget for next year."

———————⋅◆⋅———————

Dear Mom and Dad,

First, Carlotta is doing much better and got to go home the day after Rev and I visited her in the hospital. Enrico is out on bail and in foster care because his dad beat him up as soon as he walked through the door. Pray, pray, pray. I don't have a notion as to how that is all going to work out.

My birthday was great. Thanks for the light winter coat. I can't believe it will ever get cold enough for me to wear it here in Houston. It was eighty degrees yesterday, in October! But people tell me when it gets cold it feels really cold because of the humidity.

Sharon sent me home-canned green beans from her garden. But you probably know that. Imagine our cosmopolitan Sharon putting up her own canned goods.

Danielle sent me a cookbook with Southern recipes from Georgia. She still remembers my disastrous cooking adventures from high school. When will she ever believe I've learned a thing or two over the years?

Sabrina sent the most gorgeous modern kimono-type, silk dress you ever saw. Pale pink with gold and silver threads outlining darker pink flowers. I wore it on a date with—are you ready?—Rev!

He even borrowed a car so I wouldn't have to ride on the back of his Harley. He hasn't kissed me yet. Dad, he acted like a perfect gentleman.

Very disappointing.

Just kidding, Dad.

You both will love him. I can't tell you how much I've grown to admire the way he handles the kids. I'm learning a lot from watching him. That is, when I can beat down these girly tingles of adoration. And his longest sermon so far was fifteen minutes. No wonder the teens think he's tops. He jumps in, makes his point, and challenges them. That's it. No flowery speeches, no monkey business.

Love and Kisses,

See you at Christmas,

Your undaunted daughter,
Denise

Chapter 6

Denise stood with her hands in a sink full of soapy water. Five minutes before, the large basement kitchen of Rev's supporting church had bustled with workers. Even though they had used mostly disposable dinnerware, feeding more than three hundred Thanksgiving suppers made for a lot of washing up. The cheers of the crowd in the fellowship hall announced a touchdown. Almost fifty viewers sat enthralled by the football game on a large screen television. Down the hall another TV ran children's videos. In the room next to that, people of all ages played board games, and the nursery held a dozen infants and toddlers. Only Denise and Mrs. Olsen remained in the kitchen.

"Well now," said the older lady in charge of organizing the necessary after-dinner scrubbing, "it's true. Many hands make light work. You're the last of the volunteers." She rattled on as she moved around the kitchen, tidying the last few things. "Everyone has been so helpful. Another successful year. The biggest disaster was when the fresh bowl of cranberry sauce tipped into the dressing. Poor Hazel! She was in such a dither, and it really was a minor accident." She shoved a handful of tea towels into the laundry receptacle. "I'll start the dishwashers and be on my way. My Carl wants his nap."

"You and your husband have earned one, Mrs. Olsen. I've never seen so much food served with such efficiency."

"This church has served Thanksgiving dinner for twenty-five years, Dear. We ought to have it down by now." She reached for her purse and sweater. "Are you almost done?"

"I just pulled the plug on this sink. Once it drains, I'll rinse it out and then go join the kids in the TV room."

"Don't you want to be with the adults?"

Denise laughed and shook her head. "I'm not much of a football fan. I'd rather see the movie."

The older woman smiled with understanding before she turned to go. Her shoulders drooped with weariness, and she waved a hand half-heartedly. "No one should be in here for the rest of the afternoon. There's a snack bar set up in the fellowship hall. The light switch is right here, Dear. Turn it off as you leave. And thanks for helping."

"My pleasure, Mrs. Olsen. Have a good rest." Denise asked a blessing on the white-haired daughter of the Lord as she watched her trudge down the hall. This member of the older generation truly demonstrated a servant's heart.

It took just a few seconds before the water made a last slurping noise as it eddied out of the huge sink. Denise turned the faucet on and splashed away the suds and the last of the grainy sediment clinging to the bottom.

"Hi."

Rev's voice made her jump.

"Oh, you're back." She turned to look at him and thought he grew more attractive every time she saw him. Today he wore traditional clothing, slacks and a polo shirt rather than tattered blue jeans and a T-shirt. Earlier he'd had a chef's apron on and looked dashing with gravy smeared down his front and his hands encased in clear plastic serving gloves. *I've really got it bad, Lord. Are You going to do anything about his showing some interest in me? I really have tried to be patient.*

"Yep, I'm back." Rev hung the van key on the Peg-Board in a cabinet and swung the door shut, locking it. "Seventeen senior citizens all delivered safe and sound." His strong voice boomed over the clatter and swish of the dishwashers. He surveyed the nearly empty counters. "Georgy met me in the hall, saying you need help putting the coffee urns into the closet."

"I do?" She looked over to the four monster serving canisters. "I didn't even know they belonged in the closet. Mrs. Olsen must have remembered on her way out and asked Georgy to deliver the message." She wiped her hands and hung the tea towel on a rack. "Which closet?"

Rev crossed the room and opened a door, revealing a small walk-in lined with shelves. Boxes and huge storage cans cluttered part of the floor. They had to squeeze in to clear a space wide enough for the four coffee pots. With that done, they each carried in one of the urns and made a second trip for the others.

"Hold it," said Rev. "I've got to scoot these tablecloths over for that last pot to fit." He picked up a stack of white linens and quickly deposited them on the shelf below with some others. He turned to take the last pot from Denise. "Hey!" he shouted and reached past her, knocking her against the shelves.

The door shut with a thud. Rev grabbed the knob, twisting it and shaking the door at the same time.

"What's wrong?" asked Denise.

"We're locked in." As he spoke, the lights went out. The room had no windows. Darkness surrounded them, obliterating the shelves. "And when you turn out the lights in the kitchen," said Rev in an annoyed undertone, "this light goes out as well."

"On purpose?" Denise heard the irritation in her voice. "Someone locked us in here on purpose?"

"I heard a giggle right before the door swung shut. On the basis of that alone, I would say, yes, this is a deliberate prank. You wouldn't happen to be carrying a cell phone?"

"No, I don't have one. Take this thing. It's getting heavy."

His hands touched her arms and moved slightly to grasp the big pot. She felt the weight ease and let go as he took it.

"Can you help guide it into the slot?" he asked.

"Sure."

In a minute they'd stowed their burden on the shelf.

"Now what?" asked Denise.

"Well, it won't do any good to bang on the door and shout."

"Why not? The church is full of people."

"The dishwashers are running, and they make noise aplenty. The kitchen is off-limits once it's shut down for the day. And if our conspirators are as good as they usually are, they have a lookout to head off any staff member coming this way."

"So what are we going to do?"

"Make ourselves comfortable and wait until the dishwashers have finished and the game's over. Then people will be milling around in the halls again."

"Couldn't we bang on the door just in case someone happens to be passing by?"

"We could, but us banging on the door and yelling would give our captors a great deal of satisfaction. Right now I don't feel like giving them anything remotely pleasurable."

"Why, Rev Slann, you almost sound angry."

"Annoyed," he admitted. His deep voice rumbled in the tiny space.

"Aggravated?" Denise asked to keep her mind on his mood, not his masculine presence doing odd things to her equilibrium.

"Agitated."

She heard him chuckle and imagined his familiar grin framed by lopsided dimples. Pulling in a deep, stabilizing breath of air, she tried to forget how this man attracted her like no other. She put aside his generosity, his sense of humor, his logical approach to problems, his kindness, his warm hazel eyes, his hair that often needed someone to brush it out of his face, his compact body, his. . .

Oh, Lord, help! Her mind searched for a safe topic.

"Well," she said, grasping the first thought that came through her befuddled brain, "at least we won't starve to death. Our bodies could probably live off that Thanksgiving feast for a week."

"Oh, I don't think we'll be in here that long."

Rev moved to reach behind her. She felt his breath on her cheek and the warmth of his arm extended over her shoulder.

"What are you doing?"

"I'm looking for candles. I know there are some in here."

"Is there any air coming through here?" she asked. "I'm feeling very warm, kind of closed in."

His supportive arms closed around her immediately.

"Are you going to faint? Are you claustrophobic?"

"Not usually." She wasn't about to explain to this wonderful, caring man that he was the cause of her dizziness.

"Can you sit down? There's a vent up there, but I bet it's closed." He moved away from her to allow her body to sink to the floor.

She slid from his arms and sat awkwardly in the jammed floor space.

"How do you know so much about this place?"

"I was associate pastor here while I was in seminary. Associate pastor meant assistant janitor on many days." His feet shifted and then the area next to her was empty.

"Rev?"

"I'm standing on a box looking for those candles."

She heard the shuffling of things as he sorted through the contents on a shelf.

"Here!" he exclaimed.

"Candles?"

"Matches."

A flare of light followed a scraping sound.

"Found them."

Denise craned her neck to watch him light one, place it on a metal stand, fit a decorative hurricane glass over it, and set it on a shelf. He lit a second. The closet filled with a soft glow. She found the lumpy bag she leaned against was rock salt for de-icing the sidewalk. Next to her knees someone had squeezed three electric ice-cream makers into a small space. Rows of canned goods lined the shelf by her head. *So much for a romantic atmosphere.*

Rev fiddled with something near the ceiling out of her sight.

"I've got the vent open," he announced and sat down on the boxes. "Shall we play twenty questions?"

"Is that where you think of an object and then the other person asks twenty questions to narrow down what it might be?"

"Hmm, that's the original game. I pick you as my object and I want to ask questions to determine who and what you really are."

"That's sounds interesting, and I get my turn to ask you questions, right?"

"Right."

Dear Mom and Dad,

I spent five hours of quality time with Rev on Thanksgiving. We were trapped in a supply closet at his church and didn't get out until the pastor noticed his Harley in the parking lot and came looking for him.

While we were trapped, we talked a lot and laughed even more. I'm surprised nobody heard us carrying on before Pastor Griggs rescued us. My voice box squeaked by the time we got out, so Rev took me to a diner where we had coffee to lubricate our tired throats and talked for another three hours.

We conversed intellectually on such diverse subjects as books, God's claim on our lives, the fate of pennies, world peace, goldfish, and lizards. We compared siblings, teachers in grade school, favorite hymns and choruses, summer camp, and eccentric relatives. We discovered similar tastes in architecture, hobbies, not to mention suntan lotion and insect repellent. Rev. John Slann even understands the merits of asparagus over broccoli.

I'm in love.

I think he's coming to visit at New Year's, then he'll bring me back to Houston for the second half of the school year. I know you'll love him too.

He still hasn't kissed me, Dad.

With my feet on the ground (honestly),

Your happy daughter,
Denise

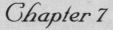

Chapter 7

W e can have the wedding here," Chipper said as she handed Rev two more cans of pop to slide into the opened machine. She and Sashquita were in charge of the vending machines at the Arrow that month and had proudly brought in ten cases of pop at incredibly discounted prices. They had entered the expense in the right column of the accounts book and filed their receipt. Now they loaded the machines with a giddiness that made Rev shake his head in amazement. These teens never ceased to befuddle him. In some ways they reflected the mores of the average American woman. His mother got giddy over fantastic bargains.

"Who's getting married?" he asked.

"You are."

The can in his hand missed the slot, hit the concrete, and exploded into a fount of fizzy brown liquid. The can careened crazily at his feet until enough pressure had been released for it to sputter to a stop.

The girls dissolved into giggles, collapsing on the pile of pillows against the wall.

Rev picked up the half-empty can and pitched it into a barrel. Marching across the room, he grabbed a handful of rags from the utility room and came back to toss them down on the spreading amber puddle.

He then confronted the girls with his hands on his hips. "Whom am I marrying?"

The girls exchanged glances, and the brief moment of sobriety disintegrated once more into uncontrolled twittering.

Definitely akin to every other adolescent female in the United States of America.

Rev shook his head in disgust. Usually this type of silliness reassured him. He spent all his working hours trying to penetrate the hard protective shell these kids wore so effectively. It got discouraging. This behavior, so normal and so unguarded, blessed him as a glimpse into their hearts.

But not now.

"Okay, girls, let me in on the story."

Chipper wiped her eyes and nose across her shirt sleeve. Sashquita used her shirttail.

"I'm waiting," said Rev, trying to sound nonchalant between gritted teeth.

"Miss Delacourt, of course," said Chipper.

Rev felt his jaw fall and his cheeks warm. *Well, Lord, so much for the private talks we've been having over my future with Denise.*

Sashquita's face fell into that worldly wise expression that pushed Rev's buttons. He hated it when the kids looked hard and calculating. She smiled slyly and crooned, "Well, you are in love with her, and she's yours for the asking."

Father, help me with my temper here.

"I can't joke with you about this, girls. I am considering asking her to marry me. But marriage is something I don't take lightly. Until I'm finished praying about it. . ." He felt his throat tighten and knew anger fought to get the rein on his tongue. He carefully chose his words. "I'd appreciate not being the butt of anyone's humor nor the center of any gossip."

He turned on his heel and walked out, crashing into the release bar on the back door and plunging into the cold damp air outside without his jacket. He needed to cool off.

He left the teens unsupervised in the building. Something he never did. He left the mess on the floor. Something he never did. He left a conversation with the children under his influence without closure or a definite arrangement for further discussion. Something he never did. He broke into a jog, determined to clear his mind and get his emotions under control as he ran around the block of warehouses.

Father, keep peace in the building until I return. I leave it under Your watchful eye. Tell me why I'm so upset. I need Your wisdom here.

As his feet pounded the pavement and his blood surged in rhythmic cadence to feed the extra demands he made upon his body, his mind reached out to God, asking for and receiving the extra serenity he needed for his soul.

So what if the kids' speculation exactly matched what had been on his mind? The delectable Miss Delacourt inhabited most of his thoughts. Since Thanksgiving afternoon spent in a closet, she popped into his mind's eye with regular frequency. Rev clenched his fists as he pressed his body to run at an even pace, as he forced his breathing to be controlled.

Invasion of privacy. That's what he objected to, but only because he felt vulnerable. He didn't know if he had God's blessing, and he didn't know for sure that Denise felt as strongly as he did.

Five minutes later, he opened the warehouse door to the club and found the overhead lights out, the black lights on, the boom box throbbing, and more teens gathered. The girls must have cleaned up his mess. A quick survey of the room reassured him that no disaster had occurred in his brief absence. *Thank You, Lord.*

He could join the boys at the foosball table or play pool with Hobe, Jamie Jack, and Georgy. Instead he decided to hang the second banner the girls had made. In metallic silver letters, it said "Rock On" and quoted Jesus from Matthew 16:18, "And upon this rock I will build my church; and the gates of hell shall not prevail against it." Many of the teens had signed the gray rock which stood as the only emblem on the black background. To them this symbolized a commitment to Jesus and a willingness to be used by God.

As Rev ran the pole through the cloth sleeve at the top of the material, his thoughts turned to how much these kids had gained in the two years he'd worked with him. Denise's program for boosting their reading frosted the cake. God had sent the perfect person to give his teens the practical edge they needed to keep working toward a fulfilled, useful life. While Rev had tried all sorts of motivational techniques to get the kids to do better in school, nothing had worked like Denise's enthusiastic approach to reading.

Abraham and Mic approached him.

"Hey, Rev, need a hand?" Abraham spoke his words in perfect sync to the background beat of the music.

"Sure," he answered and hoisted the ladder onto his shoulder, gesturing for the two to follow. Mic grabbed the banner while Abraham scooped up the ropes they would use to suspend it from the rafters. As Rev climbed the ladder and worked with the two boys to secure the newest banner, he chatted with them about the upcoming basketball game. He reached to tie a knot in the last rope, trusting Mic and Abraham to steady the ladder.

"Hey, that looks good!" said Denise.

Rev shot a glance over his shoulder, and the smile that sprang to his face disappeared as soon as he saw Ed following her through the back door, his arms laden with flat square boxes.

"Pizza!" The word chorused above the music. Rev hurried down the ladder before the two helpers stabilizing his descent could desert him. He watched as the teens swarmed around Denise and Ed and the alluring incense of Italian cuisine. He also noticed the amazement on Ed's face as the kids stopped to give thanks and then remembered to thank the teachers for bringing in dinner.

Later the two men sat together on the floor as Denise ran the kids through one of their Reading Theater rehearsals.

"So what prompted you to bring pizza?" Rev asked.

"It was an excuse to escort Denise." Ed popped the last bite of pizza in his mouth, made a wad of his napkin, and tossed it in the trash can. "She wouldn't have let me come along just to protect her. I knew better than to suggest it."

"Why would she need protection tonight when she's been coming down here for months?"

Ed shifted uncomfortably against the stack of pillows. Rev had noticed all evening how the man alternated between agitation and fatigue—one minute keyed up and the next weighed down by the problems of the world.

"Why don't you get some chairs in here?" Ed asked.

"The chairs are in the closet. You want one?"

"Not those rickety folding chairs you use for the kids' performances. They're downright scary."

Rev waited, refusing to ask his question about Denise's

safety again. Ed sat with his jaw tense and a furrow across his brow. Finally he rewarded Rev's patience with an explanation.

"Speaking of scary, Enrico's father visited the school today. That man has been on and off drugs all his life, more on than off, and his brain is far beyond fried."

"Why did he come to the school?"

"To stir up trouble. Our security is pretty tight, but he slipped in. He barreled down one hall after another, shouting for Enrico. Any other day, he would have found him, but our school nurse had taken Enrico to get his cast off. That cast was the result of Enrico's last encounter with his father."

"I've never met Mr. Resmondo. He's never been at home when I've visited the family."

"That figures."

"What does this have to do with Denise's safety?"

"Resmondo is not a rational man, and some of the notions he takes are dangerous. He thinks the school, the teachers, the authorities have stolen his son. He's blazing mad at the whole establishment, and he's likely to take it into his head to do something about it."

Rev's gaze shifted from the weary math teacher to the lovely lady gliding in and out of the group of teens as she imitated a fish. Who would want to hurt such a wonderful woman? A madman. Unfortunately that was just who they were dealing with. A shiver of apprehension coursed down Rev's spine.

"I appreciate you guarding her," he said quietly, almost under his breath. "I guess you've figured out I'm in love with her."

"Sorry to say I came to the conclusion I didn't have a chance as long as you were around." Ed shrugged. "Well, actually, I didn't have a chance as long as Jesus Christ is around. And from what Denise tells me, He always has been and always will be."

Rev grinned. "Well, praise be to God, in my circumstances, He's not competition but part of the team."

Ed shook his head as if to clear it. "You do it too."

"What?"

"Say corny things that sound legit."

Rev laughed.

Dear Mom and Dad,

We had a staff meeting today after school. Joseph Resmondo, Enrico's dad, has been put under a restraining order, keeping him away from Enrico, the school property, and any employee of the school. Pray for this man. He carries around a lot of hurt and anger. I know he is not in his right mind.

Rev did a talk on the only men who are in a right mind are righteous with God. Everyone else suffers from sin and is therefore in a wrong mind-set. The teens ate it up. They seem to understand everything he says. He has a knack for phrasing things in their language.

We have done six Readers Theaters now. All but two of the parents came last time. The downtown theater director came with a reporter from the paper. How in the world did they get wind of it? She (the theater director) is going to give us some old costumes and is talking about our group doing a production next summer at the theater. Can you believe that? She says she has some public funding through the library to do something with inner-city kids. I am flabbergasted. But why should I be? Our God does some pretty wild things, doesn't He?

I'm spending more and more time with Rev. He helps me with my projects, and I help him with his. Then we do fun things that are almost like dates when we can grab a spare minute. He took me to see the Battleship Texas and the San Jacinto Monument last weekend. We were heavily chaperoned though. Nine teenagers. But he held my hand right in front of the whole group.

Now if I can only get him to kiss me in private. You don't suppose he has some weird lip disease, do you? I may have to ask if this goes on much longer.

Yes, I did get your E-mail, Dad. I would never *be pushy.*

Your patient daughter,
Denise

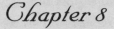

Chapter 8

Denise pushed the curtain aside, exposing the night. She looked again at the pouring rain sheeting down her apartment window. Five more minutes and she would call Rev's cell phone. He was never late, or at least he called if he couldn't make it on time. She padded to the kitchen in her slippered feet and stirred the stroganoff sauce. She turned down the heat again and went back to the window.

Down by the safety gate she caught a glimpse of a man. Too tall and lanky to be Rev. And Rev would just drive in since he knew her security code. The man standing so still in the dark spooked her. Why would anyone be hanging around in the cold rain? Should she call the police or the apartment management?

"Hurry up, Rev," she whispered. Her breath left a circle of fog on the window. She went back to stir her sauce once more. After fiddling with the table arrangement and checking her hair and makeup, she went back to the window. The man was gone.

A knock on the door startled her. She jumped and spun around.

Finally.

She hurried across, but right before she twisted the dead-bolt, a flicker of caution stayed her hand. She peered through the peephole. No one was there. The light from her front porch reflected an orange glow in the puddles. The bare limbs of the small bush hovering by her walkway couldn't conceal anyone. Several cars parked at the curb. She recognized them as belonging to the other tenants.

Someone is there. I didn't imagine that knock.

Without a qualm, she sped over to the phone and dialed 911.

She quickly explained who she was, where she was, and why she was scared.

Again the knock, louder this time, echoed through her tiny living room.

"Don't open the door," instructed the emergency operator.

"Don't worry. I won't," whispered Denise. "But I am going to peek."

She put the phone down on the end table and tiptoed across the rug. Holding her breath, she put her eye up to the peephole. Nothing. Absolute darkness. She frowned, blinked, and looked again. A loud crack against the wooden door hurled her back. She let out an involuntary screech and grabbed the phone.

"He's right outside the door," she reported.

"The squad car is just three blocks away," said the soothing voice on the other end. "Hold on."

"If this is my students' idea of a practical joke, I'll flunk them all."

"Don't assume it's a prank. Don't open that door."

"I won't."

Denise clutched the phone as if it truly were a lifeline to safety. She swallowed and tried to form some sensible prayer, but her thoughts remained riveted to the closed door, and fear paralyzed her mind.

"Denise," said the operator.

"Yes."

"I have one of your neighbors on another line. She's watching the man from her apartment. That betters our chances of catching him."

Denise closed her eyes.

Yes, dear Lord. Catch him. I don't want anyone to get hurt. Please, help the police catch him without any violence.

"Denise." The voice spoke sharply over the line.

"Yes?"

"You didn't answer. I was afraid you had gone to the window or the door. Just stay where you are. Our men are on the premises now, but the intruder has slipped off into the bushes. Don't open the door until you know it is the police."

"I'm not going to open the door." *Who in their right mind would open the door?*

Denise checked the clock. Rev was more than an hour late. Slowly the minute hand moved. She watched as it ticked off three more minutes.

"Denise?" The woman on the phone.

"Yes?"

"The police are coming to your apartment now. They didn't find the man."

In a moment a knock sounded, and Denise ran to answer, first checking through the peep hole. The uniformed cops looked wonderful to her.

The first one through the door walked over to the phone and spoke for a moment before hanging up.

"Oh, I didn't tell her thank you," objected Denise.

"That's all right."

"Will you tell her for me?"

"Sure." The officer pulled out his small notebook and flipped it open. "You'll need to answer some questions."

A movement at the door caught Denise's attention. The other policeman blocked the door and spoke to someone outside.

"Excuse me, Sir, you can't come in just now."

"What's happened?" Rev's frantic voice reached Denise, and she bolted past the man beside her. "Where's Denise?"

"Here." She scooted by the other man, who seemed determined to protect her, and flung herself into Rev's arms.

"What happened? Why are the police here?" he asked as he held her in a viselike grip.

"Someone tried to come in here. I don't know who."

The same policeman who had hung up her phone darted into the kitchen. He came out a second later, holding the saucepan she'd left on the stove.

"I think I caught it in time." He sniffed over the pot. "Maybe not."

Denise moved to salvage her dinner. The policeman let Rev come in and asked him a few questions. The other officer followed Denise into the kitchen and asked her to go through the events of the evening step by step. He kept asking question after question. A third officer eventually joined them.

"I have a description of the man from two neighbors," he said. "Approximately six feet tall, very thin, Hispanic, shoulder-length black hair. Dark baseball cap, denim jacket, jeans, and cowboy boots."

"Joseph Resmondo," whispered Denise.

"What can you tell us about this man, Miss Delacourt?"

Denise quickly outlined the situation with Enrico and his father and the restraining order put on the man.

"Good," said one of the men. "We'll have a place to start

looking for him. I'd suggest that you spend the night somewhere else. We can't guard your door."

"She can stay with our pastor and his wife," said Rev. "But I think I better add something to what you've already written down."

Denise and the three policemen turned expectantly to the youth pastor.

"It's the reason I'm late. I did try to call, Denise." He gave her halfhearted smile. "I guess you were busy talking to 911. Resmondo cornered Carlotta outside the Arrow and threatened her. She managed to get away from him and ran. She didn't go home, and my teens and I have been looking for her. We found her. We've been busy filing a report on that incident." He turned to the officers. "I sure would feel better if Joseph Resmondo were behind bars."

One of the men nodded. "We'll see what we can do. May I have a number where we can reach you, Miss Delacourt?"

After the policemen advised her once more to take a few things and go somewhere else, Rev assured them he would escort her to the pastor's home. They left, and he bolted the door.

When he turned, Denise tried her best to keep the tears at bay. But when Rev opened his arms, she lost all the control she'd mustered so far. Once in his arms, she laid her head on his chest and cried. Rev stroked her back and led her to the couch.

After some time and a dozen tissues, she was able to speak.

"Do you know what is going on with Enrico, Carlotta, and Joseph Resmondo?"

"I learned more of the story tonight," admitted Rev.

"Can you tell me, or is it confidential?"

"I can tell you. Carlotta isn't keeping it a secret." He paused for a moment, tightening his hug and urging her to rest her head against his shoulder. She relaxed in his embrace and waited.

"Carlotta is pregnant. She told Enrico's youngest sister that the baby belongs to Enrico. Carlotta wanted Estella to tell her mother, but she told Enrico's father instead. Of course Joseph flew into a rage. Then Enrico found out that Carlotta had told his family instead of him, and he blew his top. That's when he attacked her at the Arrow. It would seem that there has been a lot of yelling and hitting going on in their homes recently."

"Why do they have to be so violent? It doesn't solve anything."

"That's obvious to us, Denise, but Enrico and Carlotta have never seen any other kind of response. For years, one generation of their families after another has modeled that volatile temper. It's become a family trait handed down almost as faithfully as a genetic curse."

"They're in bondage to a way of behaving."

"But that bondage can be broken."

"Rev, it seems so impossible."

He rested his chin against her hair. "Am I going to have to sing you one of those kiddy choruses about nothing is impossible for God?"

"No." Denise sighed. She rested against him, listening to his steady heartbeat. The evening had turned out so different from her expectations. "I ruined the first meal I've cooked for you."

"Extenuating circumstances."

"It was Beef Stroganoff."

"With noodles?" he asked, an odd note of distaste coloring his question.

She leaned away to get a good look at his face. "Rev, all stroganoff has noodles. I think it is in the definition or something."

"Just as well it didn't turn out then."

"Why?"

"Do you promise not to be judgmental about this?" he asked, his face reflecting a seriousness which made her wonder what in the world could be wrong.

She nodded.

"I hate noodles. I loath noodles. I despise and abominate noodles. It is an unreasonable passion, a prejudice that cannot be overcome by reason."

She raised her eyebrows and fought the grin tugging at the corners of her mouth.

Rev continued to frown.

"Beans too. And rice, but not to the extent that noodles and beans provoke me."

"Why?"

"It comes from being raised by a single mom with no money and little time. We ate noodles until I had dreams of the stuff squirming in my stomach, wiggling into my veins, and sliding throughout my body. We ate beans every night we didn't have some form of cheap pasta. I dreamed beans would pop out of my nose, ears, and belly button. We didn't even have the cutesy pasta shaped like wheels or bows or shells or the alphabet. It was horrible, Denise. Promise me you won't subject me to noodles, beans, and rice."

By this time Denise couldn't restrain her giggles.

Rev feigned indignation. "You're laughing at my heartfelt request. You are a hard woman, Denise Delacourt."

Through her laughter, Denise promised to obliterate noodles from her menus.

"And beans?"

She nodded, unable to speak.

"Rice?"

"You said you could tolerate rice." She gasped out the words.

"In small amounts."

"Okay."

"I think I have found the perfect woman. If you weren't laughing like a hyena, I'd kiss you."

Denise immediately sobered. She looked into his eyes and saw seriousness returning. He did kiss her, and she thought she would explode with happiness until she heard his stomach growl. With their lips pressed together they both began to giggle. He released her.

"You're hungry," he said.

"That was your stomach," she returned.

"No, I made a deep throaty growl of passion. It was your stomach that gurgled."

"Passion?" asked Denise.

Rev looked at her seriously for a moment.

"Yep. Passion. It's time we got you over to the Griggses' house."

Dear Mom and Dad,

I am much calmer than when I called you. I'll be staying the week with the Griggses, and I won't go anywhere alone. The police will put Joseph Resmondo in jail when they find him.

Love,
Denise

P.S. Rev has no weird lip disease.

Chapter 9

Rev rolled his shoulders back in an effort to release the tension. He propped the broom he'd been using against the wall and dug in his pocket for coins. At ten o'clock, the Arrow was officially closed, but he and one confused teenager remained in the building.

"Enrico, you want a pop?"

Enrico nodded once. The boy lounged on one of the bigger pillows, his shoulders slumped and his gaze fixed on nothing.

For three days they'd waited for something to give in the Resmondo situation, and Rev felt useless. Enrico had been at Rev's heels like a well-trained dog. Yet he wouldn't talk any more than an animal would. Grunts were the major part of his communication.

The police hadn't found Joseph Resmondo, and Rev wondered how much time they'd been able to devote to the search. If Resmondo'd murdered someone, then they'd pull out all the stops. As it was, Enrico's dad had harassed Denise and nothing more. Of course the police took it more seriously because his action was in violation of the restraining order. Still, the police force had murders, rapes, grand larceny, drug deals, and a long list of hideous crimes to keep them busy. Rev thought menacing his sweet Denise was a heinous crime.

He plunked his coins in the slot and got himself a Pepsi, and a Mountain Dew for Enrico. He handed the pop to Enrico as he collapsed into the pillows and stretched out in a comfortable position. Minutes of silence followed. Rev finished his drink. Enrico had opened the can but hadn't taken a sip.

"Tell me," said Rev, "just what is the most bothersome thing on your mind?"

"What did I do when I got mad at Carlotta?"

Rev strained to catch Enrico's soft words.

He answered without any quibbling. "You hit her."

Enrico nodded almost imperceptibly. "And what did my dad do when he got mad at me?"

"He hit you."

"I'm just like him. I hate him." His voice took on the strength of anger. A deep, cold chant of rage ensued. "I'm tall like him. I'm skinny like him. I'm mean like him. I'm just like him." A pause. "I hate me."

Ah, a chink in the armor. Thank You, Lord, and help me have the right words.

"Right now you're seeing yourself as created in the image of a very sinful man. You're sinful yourself. But that can change. You can rip off that image just as some insects tear out of an ugly cocoon. God planned for the change."

"A new life?" Enrico snorted. "A new beginning? You've preached that one before, Rev. It don't make sense for people like me."

"It doesn't make sense for anyone. God didn't design it to make sense for us. All that matters is that it makes sense to Him."

"In school, they are always telling us, 'Use your brain. Figure it out.'"

"You've been coming here for over a year, Enrico. I don't have any new words to tell you. It's the same message you heard the first day you came. The thing is: it was the same message around two thousand years ago. It isn't going to change."

Rev could hear them both breathing in the quiet room. A fluorescent light hummed. So did the pop machine. He heard the wind tapping metal against metal somewhere on the outside of the building. The teen lay still.

Enrico closed his eyes. "He ain't going to change."

"Your father or God?" asked Rev.

"God."

"You got that right."

"And if I don't change?"

"God will still love you, wait for you, and push you, and pull you closer until you finally change."

"Or die," said Enrico.

"Or die."

Another long minute ticked by.

"I guess I'm ready, Rev."

Rev swallowed against the lump in his throat and blinked rapidly to stop the tears. He nodded and stayed quiet, listening to his young friend talk to God about sin and salvation.

"Thanks for coming with me, Rev." Enrico led the way up the narrow stairs of the tenement apartments. Graffiti marred the walls in between the cracks and peeling paint. Remnants of a shredded rug muffled their footsteps on the creaking stairs. One bare bulb at each landing cast its shabby surroundings in sharp relief. The blare of TVs and radios intruded on the isolation of the stairwell.

"No problem," said Rev as he stepped over a pile of garbage destined to go out in the morning, or so he hoped.

Enrico bound up the last few steps and swung open the door to the right of the landing. "Ma!"

Rev followed, smiling at the scene he came upon. Enrico's mother and two little sisters hugged the lanky boy, completely encircling and hiding his thin frame.

Suddenly, Mrs. Resmondo released her son and stood back, her hands still on his shoulders. "You have permission? You haven't run away from the foster home?"

"No, Ma, we called." He jerked his head in Rev's direction. "I got thirty minutes and Rev will see I get there, but I had to tell you."

"Tell me what?"

One sister swung on his arm. "You look like you won a lottery. Are we rich?" She laughed even as she said it.

Enrico ruffled her hair. He said something rapidly in Spanish. The girl's face went blank and then her eyes grew big and her mouth fell open.

The other sister squealed and danced around the room.

"Is this for real?" asked his mother. She looked beyond her son to the youth pastor standing in the doorway.

Enrico and Rev nodded their assurance at the same time. But instead of the mother's face showing joy, her features twisted in horror. The two little girls froze for a second and then backed toward the bedroom door. Enrico turned to face Rev.

"Papa," he said.

Rev turned to find Resmondo in the doorway. With a glare at everyone in the room, the brutal man stepped in and quietly closed the door behind him.

Mrs. Resmondo gathered the girls together, propelling them into the bedroom. "Go to bed. Go to sleep," she said and firmly closed the door. She turned and faced her husband.

"I don't want any trouble, Joe. It's not good that you're here. The police are looking for you."

"I'm leaving, Gloria, but I'm leaving with my son. We'll go to New Mexico or maybe Arizona. Maybe even California. I want my son with me."

"I don't want to go, Papa," said Enrico, standing straight, his eyes at the same level as his father's and only a few feet separating them.

"You will do as I say," Joseph growled.

"Mama will need a man to help. I can get a job and help pay the rent. If you're gone, she'll need my help."

Joseph's eyes shifted from his son to the woman who stood just behind his shoulder.

"Your mother needs no one. I don't give her the money for the rent. When I'm gone it'll be the same as always. If you stay she'll have to feed you. If you want to do something good for your ma, you'll get out of her house. You'll come with me."

His mother placed a hand on Enrico's arm and said one word. "No."

Without warning, Joseph took two quick strides across the room and pushed Enrico aside. He grabbed Gloria as Enrico hit the wooden kitchen table, stumbled, and fell to the floor. Rev started forward but stopped when he saw the thick shining knife blade at Mrs. Resmondo's throat. She began to cry.

"Mr. Resmondo," Rev said, intently watching every twitch in his face. The man's appearance said "drugs" just as clearly as black print on a white page. "I think we should slow down here and talk. You don't want to hurt your wife."

"Shut up." Joseph looked around the room as if a solution would jump up, something that made sense. "You just shut up.

I know what I'm doing."

Enrico eased himself to a stand.

"I'll go with you, Papa. Let Ma go."

Joseph moved away from Gloria and gestured with the knife for Enrico to move to the door ahead of him.

"I want to get some clothes and things," objected the teen.

Rev watched as the man's expression changed from suspicion to outrage. He saw the tension spread through Joseph's body, saw him clutch the knife and turn the blade toward his son, saw his stance change to that of a cat about to pounce.

"Liar!" screamed Resmondo.

"No!" hollered Rev.

Resmondo catapulted at his son just as Rev leaped to intercede. He tackled him in a full body hit, and they both sprawled across the table. The wood swayed under the strain and crashed to the floor with the deafening crack of splintering boards. An old chair fell victim to the collapse and added to the noise.

Rev lay stunned with the older man motionless beneath him. A searing pain across his stomach and side took his breath away. He must have been scraped by the shards of wood. He heard Mrs. Resmondo's screams, the sound of sirens, Enrico calling out words he did not understand. He shifted away from the foul odor of Resmondo's unwashed body, thinking he was going to vomit. Moving his hand to his side he noted the stickiness. What had been on the table that spilled? The odor overwhelmed him. He gagged and fell back on the floor. He brought his hand up to his face and saw the blood. The knife. His blood. The pain. Was the knife still in him?

Oh, God, help.

Chapter 10

L oud knocking roused everyone in the Griggses' house from their Saturday morning sleep-in.

Pastor Griggs called up the stairs, "Denise, some of your students are here." He turned to the small crowd in the doorway. "Come in. I'll put some coffee on. My wife will be making pancakes in a bit. Would you like to stay for breakfast?"

"No, Sir, we can't," said Chipper, distress evident in her quivering words, and her face on the verge of collapse.

"Well, if you change your mind, you're welcome."

He went down the hall to the kitchen as Denise came down the stairs, fastening the belt around her robe. "What's wrong?"

"You have to come with us," said Georgy.

"These are for you," said Mic. He pushed a bouquet of flowers from the grocery store into her hand.

"Thank you," Denise responded automatically as she looked from one distraught teen to the next.

"They're from Rev," said Sashquita.

"Sort of," added Quirk.

None of them looked directly at her. The boys stared at the floor and shuffled their feet. The girls looked like they'd spent

311

the night at a funeral, eyes puffy and makeup washed away.

"What is going on?" asked Denise.

Georgy sniffed. "Rev wanted to ask—"

"Don't!" interrupted Sashquita. "One of the guys should say it."

The two boys exchanged glances and made it quite evident that neither wanted the job, whatever it was. Mic, whose posture always resembled a wet noodle, slumped even more than usual. Denise crossed her arms over her chest and very nearly counted to ten aloud.

"Mic's got the ring," said Chipper.

"Mic, do it," said Quirk.

Mic dug in his pocket, pulled out a small object, and cleared his throat.

"Get down on one knee," ordered Sashquita.

Mic's backbone finally got some stiffening. "I won't! You wanna do this?"

"It's by proxy," pleaded Georgy. "You gotta."

"I don't gotta. I don't even know what that proxy stuff is."

"Just do it," said Quirk.

Mic gathered up his nerve again, straightening his oversized shirt and rubbing his hands over his jeans.

"Miss Delacourt," he began.

"Denise," hissed Chipper.

Mic glared at her and turned back to his teacher. "Miss Delacourt, would you do the honor of becoming Rev's wife?"

A murmur of disgust went through the witnesses.

"He said it wrong."

"It doesn't matter."

Denise stomped her slippered foot.

"What are you kids doing?" she demanded.

"We're asking you to marry Rev," explained Sashquita.

"He loves you," said Chipper. "He said so. He was going to ask you. He hadn't finished praying about it yet."

"And now he won't be able to." Georgy began to cry.

"Why?" gasped Denise.

"He's in the hospital," said Sashquita. Tears coursed down her cheeks.

"Dying," said Chipper and fell against Mic, sobbing.

Quirk peeked over the crowd in front of him and raised his voice to be heard. "Enrico's father slashed him with a butcher knife. He's in jail. Tore open Rev's belly. Bled a bucket before the—"

A grunt ended his announcement, and Mic shoved him out the door.

Denise had never fainted, and she wasn't about to now even though her throat closed, preventing her from breathing, and her legs wobbled, and the room spun. She would get dressed and go to Rev. Maybe she'd get there in time to say good-bye and "I love you."

Pastor Griggs drove them in the church van to the hospital. The five teens had come in Mic's vintage VW bug, a car that usually sat inside the back doors of the Arrow with its engine in pieces on the floor. Rev and the boys were always "fixing" it.

As soon as the elevator doors parted and they stepped into the waiting room, Denise spotted the rest of the teens grouped together in a solemn huddle. Abraham came forward.

"Room 1357, Miss Delacourt." He gestured down a hall. "That way. Hurry."

Denise took off at a fast walk. Her head swiveling from side to side as she passed the rooms. 1362, 1361, 1360. She ran the last few yards and stopped in front of the wide, heavy door marked 1357. Taking a deep, shaky breath, she pushed it open.

The darkened room had a light over the head of the hospital bed. Rev lay still among tubes and machinery. His arms rested on the outside of the covers, which were pulled up and neatly tucked over his chest. A dark stubble accentuated the paleness of his face. With his eyes closed, he looked to be peacefully sleeping.

"Oh, Rev," Denise whispered. With tears blurring her vision, she tiptoed into the room and stood beside the metal guardrail. Reaching down, she touched his hand, surprised to find it warm. She slipped her fingers under so she could clasp it in a gentle grip.

"I don't know if you can hear me, Rev. It's Denise. I came to tell you, 'Yes, I will marry you. I love you and have for a long time. I've even told my parents I want to spend the rest of my life with you. They want to meet you. You have to get better, Rev. You have to."

His hand closed around hers, and he squeezed with only a slight pressure. His eyes flickered open, and he stared at her.

"Do you think I'm dying or something?" he asked, his voice thick and sluggish.

Startled, Denise shook her head vehemently. "No, no. You mustn't think that. You're going to get well. You must try, Rev. I don't want you to die."

His lips curved up, and a hint of his dimples flashed.

"I'm not planning on it." He took a couple slow, careful breaths. "Have you talked to the doctor?"

"No, the teens came and got me."

He closed his eyes and gave a slight nod.

"Rev, I do love you. Chipper and Georgy said you were planning to ask me to marry you. They had Mic ask me, and they even got a ring out of Quirk's uncle's pawn shop. See?" She held her left hand in front of him.

He opened his eyes and looked. The laugh lines like crow's feet deepened, his lips twitched, and then he grimaced in pain. His eyes closed again.

Denise laid her left hand on his pale cheek.

"We're engaged, John Slann." She sniffed and forced herself to continue, trying to infuse her words with cheerful optimism. "And you just better hurry up and get well so we can get married. I don't believe in long engagements."

Rev smiled without opening his eyes. "I love you, Denise," he whispered. "We'll get married soon. It's only a nasty flesh wound."

Denise considered the meaning of those last words.

"You're not dying?" Her voice croaked.

Stunned, Denise tried to remember just exactly what she had said in the last five minutes. With a certainty, she'd made a fool of herself. She stood up and tried to pull her hand out of his. His grip tightened.

"No," said Rev. "You're not getting away. You're mine."

"Don't laugh at me."

"Oh, Honey, I can't laugh. It hurts too much just to breathe. But I can't chase you either, so don't get any fool notions about running away. I'll send the whole teen group after you. They seem to be pretty good at getting me what I want."

His eyelashes fanned across his cheeks. He still hadn't opened his eyes again to look at her, but Denise wiped the tears from her face and stood gazing at him. She couldn't get enough of watching him. He wasn't going to die, and they were engaged.

"You could kiss me," said Rev, suddenly. "I think a kiss has medicinal value when it's from someone you love."

She leaned over the metal rail and gently pressed her lips to those of her very own Prince Charming.

Dear Mom and Dad,

Rev is out of the hospital now. He has a smile on his stomach. It reminds me of Great-uncle Hubert's gall bladder surgery scar. I'm so glad my sisters will all be there to be my bridesmaids. Pastor Griggs' church is bringing up the whole teen group for the wedding, then afterward they are going to a Bible camp where they will work on repairing buildings and sprucing up the grounds, and then have a free week of summer camp.

Rev promises me that our honeymoon will be in a much more relaxing atmosphere than a teen camp, but he won't tell me where except to say no teens are invited.

How traditional to be a June bride! I'm thinking the old shoes tied to the back of the Harley will offset the orange blossoms and white lace.

Oh, this is fun!

I hope we have lots of girls like you do, Mom and Dad, so we can plan lots of weddings.

Mom, Dad, I hope Rev and I can have the kind of marriage you guys have. I just want to love the Lord and my husband for years and years and years.

Gushing mush,
Your sentimental baby,
Denise

P.S. Rev sends his love.

KATHLEEN PAUL

Kate has spent most of her life teaching, in fact, thirty-seven years. She's taught in public school, Christian school, home-school, Sunday school, Bible clubs, writing clubs, and by correspondence. "I think I like to teach," she says.

She is now retired and lives in Colorado Springs but still teaches. "God keeps giving me the opportunities. Why would I say no to something that brings such joy?"

She has three **Heartsong Presents** titles and several novelles to her credit. *To See His Way*, Heartsong #412 placed second in the RWA/FHL 2000 short historical fiction category.

You can visit Kate's web site at http://www.christianity.com/kathleenpaul.

City Dreams
Epilogue

by Christine Lynxwiler

O livia Delacourt leaned against the frame of her bedroom door and sighed as she watched Denise bound
down the stairs. Some things never changed.

Then again, some things changed drastically, and all at
once. The smell of turkey and homemade yeast rolls wafted up
from the kitchen, and Olivia allowed the grin she'd been hiding to blossom. She'd always been the keeper of the secrets, but
lately she was doing double duty, or rather, quadruple duty.

On days like this, it was a job she cherished, she realized as
she rummaged in her walk-in closet for a bag of items she kept
there for a specific purpose. "Never thought I'd be getting four
of you out at once," she murmured to the bag in her hand.

"Talking to yourself again?" Joseph's deep voice rumbled
behind her, and she nearly dropped her package. "Guess that's
what happens when you get to be a grandma twice."

"What about you, Grandpa?" Olivia smiled up at the father

of her four daughters, mindful of the fact that he still made her heart do flip-flops. "How do you like having the whole gaggle gathered under one roof again?"

She tucked the paper sack under one arm and gave her husband a brief hug with her free arm. "You don't have to say anything. I can see the answer in those gorgeous blue eyes."

The couple started for the stairs in unspoken agreement and paused on the landing to savor the glorious sight of their family all together. The four Delacourt girls had congregated around a small card table. Each brow furrowed with concentration as they worked to put together a jigsaw puzzle.

Their husbands relaxed on the sectional sofa, apparently entranced by the football game that blared from the big screen television. Snuggled up against Rory, three-year-old Faith napped, oblivious to the noise. Faith's cousin, Amanda, almost a year younger, had resisted Nick's attempts to convince her to follow suit. Instead, she toddled over to where Danielle's attention was on the puzzle.

Olivia bit back a giggle when Amanda's chubby hand swiped a pile of carefully sorted-out edge pieces onto the floor. The giggle erupted, though, when she saw Sabrina flash Danielle a look that said, She's adorable, but can't you stop her from doing things like that? Sharon, on the other hand, just bent over to help pick up the pieces. Olivia watched with pride as the two young mothers exchanged an understanding look.

Just as Olivia and Joseph descended the stairs and entered the room, their sons-in-law erupted with cheers as their team won in the final play of the football game. Jason got up and turned off the television, then crossed over to loop his arm affectionately around Sabrina's shoulders. She smiled up at him, and the love that flowed between them tugged at Olivia's heart.

Clearing her throat to get everyone's attention, Olivia was surprised when her eyes filled with tears. Joseph flashed her a puzzled look and wrapped his arm tightly around her waist as she opened the paper bag.

"Sometimes moms are entrusted with secrets too big to keep, so today I've asked permission to share some news with all of you and have been graciously allowed to do so." Her tears cleared, and her smile returned as several conspiratorial looks were directed her way. "As I've done twice before, I want to offer a gift," she said, turning to her oldest daughter. "To Sharon. . ." The other three girls stared in astonishment at the baby book that lay in Sharon's hands.

Before Sharon could speak, Olivia held out another book. "And to Danielle. . ."

Gasps were heard around the room. Olivia beamed at her surprised family. "And to Sabrina. . ."

Denise broke the silence with a delighted laugh. "I don't believe this."

Olivia ruffled her youngest daughter's hair and passed her a book. "And yes, to Denise."

Joseph let go of his wife and sank into an empty chair. "Four at once," he murmured into the shocked stillness, shaking his head. "Maybe they'll be boys."

As the loud laughter and group hugs that greeted his remark abated, Olivia spoke again. "As you all know, every day is Thanksgiving Day at the Delacourt house, but today it's official. Today, our cup truly runneth over."

"Amen!" the group chorused.

A Letter to Our Readers

Dear Readers:

In order that we might better contribute to your reading enjoyment, we would appreciate you taking a few minutes to respond to the following questions. When completed, please return to the following: Fiction Editor, Barbour Publishing, Inc., P.O. Box 719, Uhrichsville, OH 44683.

1. Did you enjoy reading *City Dreams?*
   ❑ Very much. I would like to see more books like this.
   ❑ Moderately—I would have enjoyed it more if _____
   _____
   _____

2. What influenced your decision to purchase this book? (Check those that apply.)
   ❑ Cover   ❑ Back cover copy   ❑ Title   ❑ Price
   ❑ Friends   ❑ Publicity   ❑ Other

3. Which story was your favorite?
   ❑ *A World of Difference*   ❑ *In the Heart of the Storm*
   ❑ *Beneath Heaven's Curtain*   ❑ *The Arrow*

4. Please check your age range:
   ❑ Under 18   ❑ 18–24   ❑ 25–34
   ❑ 35–45   ❑ 46–55   ❑ Over 55

5. How many hours per week do you read? _____

Name _____

Occupation _____

Address _____

City _____ State _____ Zip _____

If you enjoyed

City DREAMS

then read:

AUTUMN Crescendo

*Four Novellas Celebrating
the Changing Seasons of Life*

September Sonata by Andrea Boeshaar
October Waltz by DiAnn Mills
November Nocturne by Dianna Crawford
December Duet by Sally Laity

If you enjoyed

City
DREAMS

then read:

Ozarks

*The Hills Are Alive With Small Towns
and Big Hearts Revealed
in Four Complete Romances*

Hannah Alexander
Mary Louise Colln
Veda Boyd Jones
Helen Spears

If you enjoyed

City DREAMS

then read:

KANSAS

Four Prairie Romances
Dusted with Faith

Tracie Peterson
Judith McCoy Miller

If you enjoyed

City DREAMS

then read:

Romance on the Rails

*All the Enchantment of Railway Travel
in Four Short Stories*

Wanda E. Brunstetter
Birdie L. Etchison
Jane LaMunyon
Terri Reed

If you enjoyed

City DREAMS

then read:

TAILS *of* LOVE

*Pets Play Matchmakers
in Four Modern Romances*

Lauralee Bliss
Pamela Griffin
Dina Leonhardt Koehly
Gail Sattler

If you enjoyed

City
DREAMS

then read:

CALIFORNIA

From the Golden State Come
Four Modern Novels of Inspiring Love

To Truly See by Kristin Billerbeck
A Gift from Above by Dina Leonhardt Koehly
Better than Friends by Sally Laity
Golden Dreams by Kathleen Yapp

If you enjoyed

City DREAMS

then read:

FLORIDA

FOUR INSPIRING LOVE STORIES
FROM THE SUNSHINE STATE

EILEEN M. BERGER
MUNCY G. CHAPMAN
PEGGY DARTY
STEPHEN A. PAPUCHIS

If you enjoyed

City DREAMS

then read:

LOVE AFLOAT

*Drifting Hearts Find Safe Harbor
in Four Romantic Novellas*

Kimberley Comeaux
Linda Goodnight
JoAnn A. Grote
Diann Hunt

If you enjoyed

City DREAMS

then read:

the *Sewing Circle*

*One Woman's Mentoring Shapes Lives
in Four Stories of Love*

**Andrea Boeshaar
Cathy Marie Hake
Sally Laity
Pamela Kaye Tracy**